Penguin Crime Fic

Editor: Julian Sym

Let's Talk of Gra

The pseudonym of 'Robert Player' hides the identity of Robert Furneaux Jordan, the distinguished architect and architectural historian. 'Robert Player' was born in Birmingham, the son of a surgeon, and educated at King Edward's School, Birmingham, at the Birmingham College of Art and at the Architectural Association in London. After working as an architect and for the B.B.C. during the Second World War, he became Principal of the Architectural Association School. He has lectured in almost every university in the United Kingdom and has held a professorship at Leeds and at the University of Syracuse, New York.

For many years he contributed to the *Critics* Programme and was Architectural Correspondent of the *Observer*. Crime writing, he says, has been mainly the hobby of retirement. Among his publications as 'Robert Player' are *The Ingenious Mr Stone* (1945), *The Homicidal Colonel* (1970) and *Oh! Where are Bloody Mary's Earrings?* (1972). Under his own name he has also written many books, among them *The English House* (1959), *Victorian Architecture* (Penguin, 1966) and *Le Corbusier* (1972).

In retirement he and his wife live in a thatched cottage on the edge of Salisbury Plain. They both garden and paint.

Robert Player

Let's Talk of Graves, of Worms, and Epitaphs

Penguin Books

Penguin Books Ltd, Harmondsworth, Middlesex, England
Penguin Books, 625 Madison Avenue,
New York, New York 10022, U.S.A.
Penguin Books Australia Ltd, Ringwood,
Victoria, Australia
Penguin Books Canada Ltd, 2801 John Street,
Markham, Ontario, Canada, L3R 1B4
Penguin Books (N.Z.) Ltd, 182–190 Wairau Road,
Auckland 10, New Zealand

First published by Victor Gollancz 1975
Published in Penguin Books 1977

Made and printed in Great Britain by
Cox & Wyman Ltd, London, Reading and Fakenham
Set in Monotype Times

DEDICATION

TO MY WIFE

AND

to the faded memory of

HENRY EDWARD MANNING
(1807–1892)

Cardinal Archbishop of Westminster, without whom this entirely fictitious story could never have been written

'*Aut Caesar aut Nihil*'

Let's talk of graves, of worms, and epitaphs

WILLIAM SHAKESPEARE: *Richard II*

Contents

1 Testimony of Augustine

Owls would have hooted in St Peter's choir,
And foxes stunk and littered in St Paul's

THOMAS GRAY

Derravaragh, County Meath.
Feast of the Epiphany, 1920

It is not every man whose father was both a pope and a murderer. I admit that it sounds unlikely but in what follows – the story of the Barbellion Case – I shall show that it was indeed a fact.

My father's name was Barnabas Barbellion. He was an Anglican clergyman – an archdeacon, rector of a Gloucestershire parish and a married man – until he entered the Roman Catholic Church in 1855, to reign in due course, and for over twenty years, as Paschal the Fourth.

My own name is Augustine Xavier Barbellion, names given me by my father at the font in one of his fits of High Anglican enthusiasm. Fortunately my more intimate and convivial friends call me 'Gussy'. I am now seventy-nine years of age but of sound mind. I am the 26th Baron of Derravaragh in the Peerage of Ireland, having inherited my lands from an uncle on my mother's side. I am a Count of the Holy Roman Empire and a Knight of Malta. I have also been invested – for no earthly reason – with the Golden Collar of the Holy Ghost of Portugal. These honours don't bring me in a penny but I suppose they show that the Roman hierarchy is not ungenerous to even its unwanted offspring.

My sister, Maria Pia, is two years younger than me. My father had no other legitimate children. We were both born in the Cotswold rectory of Nether Molding – the house where our mother was to die so painfully. When the great débâcle came – our mother's death and our father's Conversion – we were still children but our father immediately broke up the family and never saw us again. We were packed off to an aunt – my father's sister Caroline – in Derbyshire; she sent us to Catholic schools, of Papa's choosing, but brought us up in her own fashion. It was almost half a century before my sister and I went back to Nether Molding to call at the Rectory and to walk together through the garden and the churchyard. Our mother's grave, we found, had been obliterated.

I have lived here, in my demesne at Derravaragh, ever since I inherited, on my twenty-first birthday, these ten thousand green Irish acres; I intend to die here. I was educated at Stonyhurst whence I was expelled at the end of my first term, and then at Magdalen College, Oxford, whence I was sent down after my second year. After that I enjoyed myself for a time in the University of Louvain, or at English and Irish house parties. There were also delectable holidays in Naples, at the Palazzo Barbellion alla Chiaja. My father had been born in that painted rococo house, while it was in its orange groves that I learnt to sing and to play the fiddle. There was also a Barbellion house in Rome, in the Via Tritone, where a little fountain bubbled all day long in the cortile. We often spent Christmas there until, in later years, my father needed it for one of his mistresses. Maria Pia and I were there together in 1899; we sat all night waiting for a message from the Vatican, that our father was dead.

My uncle, the 25th Baron of Derravaragh, when he left me his lands, must have expected me to lead the life of a country squire – God knows why – slaughtering all the grouse, pheasants, salmon, otters, hares and foxes in Ireland. Had he lived, poor man, he would have been bitterly disappointed. I have never hurt a fly. I prefer Derravaragh to the Latin seductions of Naples or Rome almost solely because of the pale dream-like beauty of my Palladian mansion with its surrounding hills and rushy lakes. On summer evenings it is possessed of an almost excessive beauty that pains the heart. So far from dabbling in bucolic things – as my uncle would have wished – I contemplate the landscape in all its lovely moods. I enjoy my Impressionist paintings – I have just refused a cool million for the lot – and I cherish my *incunabula* and my fine cellar.

In the intervals of this harmless life I enjoy the company of Irish *literati*, painters, actors and courtesans, spending much of my time in the bars of Dublin or upon the boulevards of Paris. When in France I visit my favourite son who – so intolerant are the English police – finds it convenient to live in Dieppe. I have never married but my happy relationship with the sweet colleens of

County Meath has enriched the world with several glorious boys and girls. I myself have a pale skin but no Barbellion was ever undistinguished. I have also inherited some Irish good looks – black curls and green eyes. In other words, I have never needed to use my *droit-de-seigneur* – the dear colleens just seem to come to my arms . . . it's as simple as that. In matters *de sexu*, therefore, although not in any other way, I must surely take after my father – a great libertine as well as a great prelate.

My days upon earth – once an unhappy childhood was behind me – have been amusing and serene. The world's changes and disasters have passed me by. In 1918 I felt some sadness at the fall of the Austrian Empire but otherwise the World War left me quite untouched. And even here, in Ireland, at the time of the Easter Rising in 1916, when so many of my neighbours' mansions were gutted by an enraged peasantry, I was left in peace. The dear Irish, after all, would not lightly attack the Pope's son.

Neither my sister nor I have ever married, nor were we troubled overmuch by parental control . . . not at any rate after our father had left us. The Roman Catholic Faith never troubled us much either. In spite of Aunt Caroline and the Jesuits of Stonyhurst – or perhaps because of them – I have always lived as a happy atheist, while Maria Pia's religious observances have never been strict. My uncle – a mere whoring and hunting animal – providentially burst a blood vessel while I was still at Oxford . . . God's Will be done. He left me these Irish lands, a house in Merrion Square and another in Belgravia. This also was providential, my father's own fortune being destined, inevitably, for the bottomless coffers of the Church of Rome.

My sister, Maria Pia, was a sophisticated and precocious child. She became a woman of independent mind – so much so that marriage was out of the question. It would have merely served to drive two people mad. She loved Derravaragh and I have always said it was her home as well as mine. However when the Pope's London solicitors told her that she could make what use she liked of the little Palazzo Barbellion alla Chiaja, she divided her time between Naples and her own pretty apartment in the Faubourg St Germain. She also travelled a great deal, in the most outlandish countries and often in male disguise. She was fond of camels and –

for unfathomable reasons – the Mohammedans always received the Pope's daughter with the highest honours. She accepted these honours as her right.

It was not until the World War put a stop to her crazy journeys that she accepted my offer of the west wing of Derravaragh – a dozen rooms being ample for her simple needs. She filled the place with all the stuff she had brought back from Naples – although I suspect that strictly speaking it all belonged to the Pope – and the rococo cabinets, beds, overmantles and Tiepolos really looked very well in my tall Palladian rooms. In the end, of course, Time caught up with her and a year ago, on Easter Sunday, she died very quietly at the age of seventy-six. She did not ask for a priest.

Before her death Maria Pia imposed upon me a kind of sacred trust – to tell the world the whole story of Paschal the Fourth. My own feeling – but then I am an easy-going sort of fellow – would have been to let sleeping dogs lie. After all, it is sixty-five years now since our mother died in the big bedroom at Nether Molding, thus liberating our father for a celibate priesthood. So long as my sister could travel or enjoy the cultivated pleasures of Naples and Paris, and so long as Paschal the Fourth reigned, she too was willing to forget the distant past. Once, however, he was in his marble tomb, by the High Altar of St Peter's, then everything was different. It was a lifetime since he had seen us but for a lifetime he had haunted us. Now he was dead. As the years passed and the arteries hardened Maria Pia would spend long days by the fire or on the Derravaragh terraces, brooding upon the past. Then it was that she produced once again, from one of those rococo cabinets, the six manuscript books in red morocco. Like so many little Victorian girls she had kept a 'journal' . . . but secretly. But now, at last, the red leather all faded, those little books, with their careful copperplate, are mine. Their secrets are mine.

In the last days of her life Maria Pia was very silent. Her mind seemed to have closed, but occasionally, of an evening, she would start talking. It was then that she would babble of many things, but almost always of our father – Barnabas Barbellion, his great crime and curious life. Yes, Barnabas Barbellion, Anglican Archdeacon of Gloucester and Rector of Nether Molding; Catholic Convert in 1855, year of his wife's death; Cardinal

Archbishop of Westminster in 1864; crowned Pope Paschal the Fourth, Pontifex Maximus, in 1878; died and entombed in the Basilica of St Peter in 1899. That, after all, was a career to stir the memory of the most senile, let alone his own daughter.

And so she would ramble on about his death – how the cardinals had let her kiss the corpse – but far more often she would talk of that bitter winter of 1855 when our mother, his 'dearest Emily', died so painfully, and of how he himself preached her funeral sermon to a crowded church; of how he buried her in a grave lined with orchids from the Windrush Court conservatories; and of how at the graveside were two little children in black clothes – little Augustine and little Maria Pia.

It all happened in the sleepy village of Nether Molding, a place nobody had ever heard of until it began to be said that a pope once lived there. It all happened in the Rectory and at Windrush Court. This was the big house over the hill, home of the Gatsbys – of Harold, the Lord Lieutenant, and of Phillippa Gatsby, my father's mistress. My father had a tiny Norman church and a huge Regency rectory. The church was full of death-watch beetles; the house was gloriously elegant and green with damp; it was full of rich and heavy Victorian furniture – all mahogany and brass and velvet; the drains smelt in summer, the bedrooms were icy in winter – all feather-beds and fleas . . . fleas which Papa killed himself with a patent arsenical flea poison. Out in the stables were ten loose-boxes and rats – rats waiting to be slaughtered with strychnine.

Papa ministered to fewer than a hundred souls but he had a curate of sorts over at Little Molding. This curate, a certain dubious Cecil Praz, was also his Confessor. I know now that he was altogether unspeakable. Papa had several such youths scattered about England. He practised pluralism and simony in a big way – enough to make the Middle Ages green with envy – drawing stipends from a dozen fat livings while putting in curates at starvation wages to take the services . . . a profitable game which he played for years. And simony, I suspect, was never very far from sodomy. He kept it all going until – freed by Emily's death – he entered upon his dizzy career as priest, cardinal and pope. Upon my father's Conversion, Cecil Praz – who had been as good as promised a mitre – was promptly unfrocked by the Bishop of Gloucester. He has not been easy to trace but a month ago I bought back the letters my father wrote to him, many of them from the Vatican. I paid fifty pounds for them, to a woman on the corner of Grafton Street.

Phillippa Gatsby, the serene and beautiful lady of Windrush, was a very notable person. She had been born a Cole-Hatt and none of the Cole-Hatts could ever have been negligible. In one sense she was just one more famous Victorian hostess, but only in her own startling and original way. Her house parties, it goes without saying, were fashionable and distinguished, but while other women filled their drawing-rooms with dukes and actors, she preferred bishops and priests – Puseyite, Tractarian, High Anglican, ritualistic and, of course, good-looking.

She had a pale, cool, phthisic and unsmiling beauty of a most seductive kind. It was said that she had inspired Rossetti to paint his Monna Vanna, and whatever the fashion might be that was how she dressed. Her intellect matched her beauty; she was no bluestocking but polemics were the breath of life to her; she could hold her own with any theologian in Europe, and in almost any language. She and Barnabas – her 'dearest Barny' – were each the evil genius of the other. They were perfectly matched, physically, sexually and . . . theologically.

That Phillippa's parents, when these two first met, should have already engaged her, in the manner of those days, to Harold, that dull millionaire squire, must have driven Phillippa and Barnabas quite frantic. That the Living of Nether Molding, in the Gift of the Gatsbys, should fall vacant in the year 1843 was an overwhelming temptation. Their own child, their pretty little bastard, was five, I was two and my sister a few weeks old. That Phillippa and Barnabas should arrange quite deliberately to live within two miles of each other was an act for which only their own Anglo-Catholic God can ever forgive them.

They had met in Eights Week. She was nineteen. He was eighteen. It was a glorious summer. There was a little dalliance and then fornication – all very romantic and elegant and absurd – on the river bank of Bablock Hythe. One can see her shawls, her cushions and her corkscrew curls; one can see his wide-awake hat, his Balliol cummerbund and his manly, rather hairy body. One can see the shy revelation of nakedness beneath the over-shadowing willows, with the rushes, the kingcups and the scudding moorhens. And then, when the child was born, they remembered the tiny flowers at the edge of the water and they called her Eirlys. She was an astonishingly beautiful little girl, and now, eighty-three years later, she is an astonishingly beautiful old lady – my 'Cousin' Eirlys . . . my half-sister really although we were brought up always to call her 'Cousin'. You see, it threw an even denser fog over her rather romantic origin.

To the end of his life – even as he lay dying with the cardinals around his bed – my father could persuade himself that that summer afternoon had been so wonderful, so magical, that in some way or other their intercourse had been not sinful but positively mystical. A future pope, after all, cannot err; sin was for all other men but not for him. And so, for them both, Eirlys was a child not only of ecstasy but of purity – a child of God. How could she not be. One has to realize that my father was really a very extraordinary man.

As for Colonel Harold Gatsby – to be cuckolded by a pale parson may have hurt his military pride . . . or so one might think. I suspect, however, that he was so soon out of love with Phillippa that perhaps he didn't care very much, not more than if one of his mares had been served by the wrong stallion. He probably consummated his marriage on the honeymoon – it was the thing to do – but after that he never entered her bed again. She remained for him a very presentable wife and a superb hostess, and that was all he asked. That they were childless could be shown to the world as their misfortune, while her religious antics were not unsuitable in the wife of a churchwarden. So he took little Eirlys into his home. He was never very kind to her and although, ultimately, she inherited everything through Phillippa, he never left her any money. However, he presented her to the world as Eirlys Cole-Hatt – Phillippa's niece. Nobody, of course, ever believed that, but appearances had been preserved.

It was lonely for little Eirlys. There were no other children at Windrush, no other children in that great house, and in those days a little girl did not play with village brats. Of course, later on, for

Eirlys there was always Micky Slate, the stableboy . . . but that was quite another matter. And so, when we were children, Eirlys would often drive over to the Rectory in her mother's carriage, and then the three of us would play together in the garden – Eirlys, Maria Pia and me. And then, three or four mornings a week, she would take lessons with us in the schoolroom. By some uncanny prescience our father decreed that we should all learn Italian, and that was how Jane Grigg, our governess, first came to Nether Molding. It was not every Victorian governess who could teach Italian . . . dear Jane Grigg, destined to mean so much to us all.

The arrangement worked well enough. It gave Eirlys a little companionship. And then as she grew up, more and more did the lonely child and the lonely governess confide in each other. A strange and even passionate affection sprang up between them so that in the end there was nothing about Windrush Court or the Rectory that they did not whisper to each other. It never seems to have occurred to Phillippa or to Barnabas that with Eirlys sleeping next to her mother at Windrush and with Miss Grigg's room at the Rectory on the same landing as my mother's and father's bedroom, the governess and the clever little girl might exchange secrets. I suppose they looked upon Eirlys as a mere child and Miss Grigg as a mere employee – as if that made any difference. For many years, long after Jane Grigg had seemed to vanish from our lives – until she died in 1910 in a Home for Distressed Gentlewomen at Tunbridge Wells – she and Cousin Eirlys wrote to each other every week. Eirlys was always on the move, a life of expensive hotels and ruinous casinos in beautiful places, but year after year those confidential letters, love letters almost, sped across Europe . . . in Italian.

I have always wondered, and I always shall, why Cousin Eirlys has never let me see Jane Grigg's letters . . . after all, it was a long time ago. Eirlys, in her old age, rambles on and on as my sister did about so many things, but never, never about dear Jane Grigg. Again and again, whenever I visit her at her suite in the Negresco in Nice, I bring her back to it but always, tight-lipped, she changes the subject. So there were these two, Eirlys and Jane Grigg, exchanging secrets through the years, and there was my sister writing it all down in her little red morocco books. And now, at last, I have the red morocco books; perhaps one day I will also have the letters.

Yes, that schoolroom arrangement – Eirlys having lessons with her two little cousins – worked well enough. She and her mother – Phillippa so grand and Eirlys so pretty – would drive over from Windrush, with Tomkins and Bowlby very erect and liveried upon the box-seat. As they drove through the villages and passed the farm gates, the mother and daughter could be seen, so to speak, to be each other's chaperone. And always, conspicuously, they would be taking flowers, hot-house fruit or other pleasant things in basins or jars, to poor, dear, frail Mrs Barbellion for whom, from the parlourmaid at the Rectory door, they would inquire so solicitously. And then sometimes Phillippa but sometimes Eirlys would take the fruit or the jars upstairs to Emily's bedroom. Really, you know, everyone thought it all so kind, so smart and so obviously *comme il faut* . . . nobody could suspect a thing.

All very convenient . . . it was found that almost always Phillippa could wait at the Rectory until, lesson time being over, she could take her little daughter home to luncheon. She would put it about that she had been sitting all morning with poor Mrs Barbellion, at the bedside, that Mrs Barbellion was very poorly or, perhaps, that she was brighter. In fact, for that hour or even two hours, she and her Barnabas, her 'dear Barny', would sit by the study fire, or in summer they might walk in the garden or the churchyard, discreetly beyond the yews – discreetly, although it was surprising what one could see from the privy window. And then it was found, too, that Phillippa's Auricular Confession and Absolution could be made very easily to fit with the Italian lessons. The servants would be in the kitchens beyond the red baize door. Out in the drive, but on the other side of the house, Tomkins would remain rigid upon the box, the whip in the gloved hand, Bowlby at the horse's head. Upstairs Emily might be dozing uneasily or lying with her eyes closed, heavy-lidded. The Bible, with its markers in, might be at her side but more often it would be Keble's *Christian Year* that was open on her lap . . . as if she was choosing hymns for her own funeral. They would give her the flowers, the fruit or one of the delicious concoctions from the Windrush Court kitchen.

'How kind, how kind . . .' she would murmur, and then close her eyes again. On the same landing, but safe behind mahogany doors, would be Jane Grigg and her three little charges – their heads over their books.

It must surely have been at the Rectory, on one of those school-room mornings, rather than at Windrush Court, that Phillippa Gatsby, sixteen years after the birth of Eirlys, conceived another child . . . a child destined, as it happened, to be born dead in Holloway Prison. It was surprising, really, that it had not occurred years ago. That Eights Week, that 'mystical' summer afternoon at Bablock Hythe, had been quite cataclysmic for them both. They had conceived Eirlys, the child of God. And now, through the years, every week, the Lover and the Mistress had met as Priest and Penitent. Opportunities had been manifold, respectability secure. It had been bound to happen.

They had no scruples. Phillippa had always loathed the country-gentleman to whom she had been almost forcibly married. She had been the most beautiful debutante of the year; there had been a wedding at St George's, Hanover Square, and then the hunting field and all that. It had been utterly ghastly. Barnabas, too, the moment he and Emily left the altar, realized that she was really a poor, commonplace little thing – soft-spoken, ineffective, loving her children, rather pious, but not by a million miles fit to be his wife. But of course, in fairness to Emily, it must be remembered that nobody less than Cleopatra, Helen of Troy or, just possibly, Phillippa Gatsby, could ever have been fit to marry Barnabas Barbellion.

My mother, Emily Leapingwell, was the daughter of an enormously rich Irish landowner of the Protestant Ascendancy – hence my inheritance, here at Derravaragh. It may also have seemed to my father that she might make a good wife for a village parson. But, and this was the decisive thing, he had one night been taken by a friend – a sprig of nobility and a gentleman commoner of Balliol, – to a ball at Blenheim. And there, that night, in that vain-glorious palace, he had danced with her. He had walked with her in the gardens. Now whether it was Blenheim or the Vatican, my father was always utterly bemused by the occasion, by the glamour of time or place. Poor, plain Emily, whether by moonlit fountains or valsing beneath a thousand wax candles, took unto herself that night a quite spurious splendour . . . it was her undoing. He lost his head. He made love just as if he really was in love . . . perhaps he believed it himself. There was an absurdly romantic wedding in County Meath and then, in Naples, a honeymoon of complete disillusionment.

He once said that he married Emily for the purity of her mind, the piety of her soul and the passion of her heart. He could hardly have added the prettiness of her face. Anyway it was all a lie. He had wooed her romantically in the Italian Garden at Blenheim and then married her for her father's money. He begat two children upon her, of whom I was one, and then destroyed her. In any case, after the birth of Maria Pia – a cruel and prolonged confinement with a gin-sodden village midwife – Emily took to her bed, her Bible and her solitaire. So far as the village was concerned, 'the Rector's wife' simply became 'Mrs Barbellion – poor thing' and was hardly seen again. So far as my father was concerned, his marriage was over – he had had two nights of sex and was done with her. So far as Phillippa Gatsby was concerned, Emily was simply an obstacle to her happiness and would be so as long as she lived. So far as Emily was concerned, Papa had told her that it was the Will of God that women should suffer in travail; so she faced her lot with Christian fortitude, in other words with stunned fatalism and the terrifying thought that having been joined to Barnabas at the altar, she would have to share Eternity with him. He had made that quite clear.

Of course all the outward forms were carefully preserved. The mere existence of two Barbellion children was something. And then the great lady from Windrush Court, with her pretty little 'niece', paid such regular and kindly visits to the Rectory, reporting afterwards upon poor, dear Mrs Barbellion's health – usually so wretched. The big four-poster – in spite of a bed in the dressing-room – was still used, otherwise there was no knowing what the servants and the governess might have said, but for over ten years between the Rector's study and his wife's bedroom there was an icy gulf . . . a gulf that could be ended only by death.

Emily Barbellion, after years of ill-health, died in the end after a few weeks of diarrhoea, vomiting and sweating. She died at

Christmas, that cold Christmas of 1854. She died within a few days of my father's return from Rome, where, although still an Anglican Archdeacon, he had had his first audience with Pius the Ninth. Maria Pia, therefore, was about twelve and I was fourteen when – dressed in what the parlourmaid called our 'garb of woe' – we stood by our mother's open grave, a few snowflakes falling quietly on the coffin while our father – to the amazement of the mourners – chanted the Catholic Offices of the Dead, in Latin. Almost immediately after the funeral he wrote to Monsignor John Talbot, the Papal Chamberlain, to tell him that Emily was buried ... and that he should tell the Pope.

Harold Gatsby, after some palpitations of the heart, had died very suddenly the previous August. He had collapsed on the lawn at Windrush Court – it was a very hot day – and had had to be carried into the house. Indubitably, therefore, and within six months of each other, there were two unnatural deaths in Nether Molding that year – the summer death of Harold Gatsby when they were playing croquet and eating strawberries and cream in the shade of the deodars, and the winter death of Emily Barbellion when the children were playing in the snow and sliding on the Rectory pool. The wreaths for Harold Gatsby were all roses and carnations, those for Emily were all holly and fir-cones.

My father's sensational Conversion – and it was Gladstone who remarked that it was a blow under which the nation staggered like a drunken man – followed within a few days. He immediately dismissed our Jane Grigg, his four servants, his coachman and the knife-boy. He would have no Anglican under his roof. He then left home himself, to be received into the Holy Catholic Church by the Oblates of St Charles in Bayswater. Maria Pia and I were escorted to London the next day, by Cecil Praz, there to be freshly baptized by Cardinal Wiseman in his private chapel at York Place. We were then packed off to Derbyshire, to school, and to live with our Aunt Caroline. Our father never saw us again.

I have said that my father, Barnabas Barbellion, was bemused and bewitched by the sheer glamour of an occasion or a place; never more so than when Barnabas Barbellion, the eternal actor, was at the centre of the stage. This was obvious when, as Cardinal of England, he would sweep through London drawing-rooms or down the Great Hall at Arundel, for kneeling ladies to kiss his ring, or when, as an old man, he was carried through St Peter's on the Gestatorial – the Te Deum echoing in the great vault. It was all part and parcel of him. Even at Harrow he had been a most stylish boy, bullied for his dandaical clothes and his affected airs.

At Oxford he cut a great figure, not only with his champagne breakfasts after Communion – which were usual enough – but for the spanking way he would drive his four-in-hand up the Henley Road, or gallop his chestnut mare along the Broad – tassels to his Hessian boots and a miraculous cravat devised to force the chin high.

In his own little Norman church at Nether Molding he had the stage to himself . . . he made the most of it. With his eternal-torment-body-and-blood-of-Jesus kind of sermons, he packed the place morning and evening – golden vestments, black in Lent, paid for out of his own pocket, candles blazing on every altar, clouds of incense hanging in the air. A few staunch Evangelicals went over to Guiting each Sunday – to take the sacraments from Barnabas Barbellion was more than they could bear. That didn't matter – carriages, gigs and governess-carts came from all the country round. The whole thing was an astonishing drama, a kind of ecclesiastical *succès de scandale*, earning more than one rebuke from the Bishop . . . as if that mattered. The sermons, of course, as Barnabas Barbellion's eyes flashed, as his beautiful hands were deployed in an actor's gestures, as his fine voice reverberated through the tiny church, were not really sermons at all; they were declamations in the grand manner. The Eucharist was more a ballet than a rite, more Byzantine than Roman, let alone Anglican, with chalice held aloft, sanctus bell ringing and Barbellion and Praz continually bowing to the monstrance and to each other. Even the gentry, let alone the little choirboys, hardly knew whether they were on their heads or their heels. They cringed as his tongue lashed them, but not for worlds would they have missed it.

If my father was bemused by the occasion, how much more so by his own divinity, his own Apostolic Succession, his own powers to bind and to loose. If Barnabas Barbellion really murdered his wife, then his sole motive was not sex but ambition . . . but ambition for what? As he looked down upon her wasted little body, as he sprinkled Holy Water upon her, as he made his children kiss her forehead, he was aware of one thing above all – he must have been – an obstacle had been removed, an obstacle to something infinitely good in the eyes of God – his own Catholic priesthood. His wife was dead, his children could be sent away. At last he could be a priest, a real priest, as was Melchisedec – 'without father, without mother, without descent, having neither beginning of days nor end of life, but made like unto the Son of God . . . a priest forever . . . holy, harmless, undefiled, separate from sinners, and made higher than the heavens'. Again and again he had read Hebrews, chapter seven. And what was murder compared with that? For nearly two thousand years, after all, the Church had been soaked in adultery, slaughter and rapine . . . and in the highest places. And now Emily was dead; if he played his cards with cunning – and who could do so better than Barbellion? – there was nothing between him and a Cardinal's Hat or even – why not? – the Triple Tiara.

On that winter evening of 1855, standing by his wife's corpse, he must have been quite dizzy with ambition – the Papacy in this world, bliss and eternal life in the next, with a place close to the Heavenly Throne. As for Phillippa . . . well, with Harold Gatsby dead, then his dearest Phillippa was also free – free at last in the very highest Borgia tradition, to become a papal mistress; the Vatican, he believed, had several charming little villas at its disposal, both in Rome and out in the Alban Hills. Yes, he had done well. He arranged the shroud over Emily's shrunken white face . . . this, surely, was the work of the Holy Ghost.

He might be a murderer. He was an adulterer. He was a priest. He was ruthless but, oddly enough, I don't think he was a hypocrite. It was simply that the divine nature of priesthood, his power to bind and to loose, justified all things. As I write these words in 1920 I find that very few people now understand the Early-Victorian religion of my father and of his Oxford contemporaries. Their religion was – how shall I put it? – so tense, so absolute. To that generation Virtue was one thing, Religion was another. Virtue meant honesty, chastity, charity, being pleasant and, above all, not being found out – respectability. That was Virtue. Religion meant belief, theology, superstition, the colour of a stole, the nature of a sacrament, church attendance and the observance of fasts and feasts, prayer, reading the Bible and the Collects, Confession, having doubts – or not having doubts – about the Trinity or, say, the Socinian Heresy, what you did on Good Friday – not how you lived – all that was Religion. My father was not a hypocrite. He simply accepted the ethos of his generation as he accepted the air he breathed. He was exceptional only in taking the whole thing to its terrible logical conclusion. Logical conclusions are usually terrible; they were Barnabas Barbellion's great luxury.

No, he did not mean to be wicked. He lived in a world where crime hardly came into the scheme of things–not into that scheme of things which revolved around an Oxford college, a cathedral close, a rectory or a country house. Crime was something never mentioned, something vaguely associated with manacled convicts in Dartmoor quarries, or with the gallows. Wickedness, on the other hand, was all round one. It lay in playing cards on Sunday, in gambling, eating too much in Lent, in swearing, in lustful thoughts or disrespect for one's betters. Barbellion knew, of course, that murder, like stealing, was a crime . . . but for others, not for him. Quite honestly, I don't think he ever saw the destruction of my mother as being a great sin in the eyes of Almighty God . . . it served such a glorious purpose, giving one more priest to Christ, so many thousand souls saved from perdition.

No, he did not mean to be wicked. It was quite simply that he, Barnabas Barbellion, was about to submit eternally to the Holy Catholic Church founded by Christ upon the Rock of Peter, and not – as with the Anglicanism he was discarding – to a wholly heretical, protestant and infidel Parliament with, as it happened, a Jewish Prime Minister, and a Privy Council that could – and had – changed the sacred doctrines of the Church. Henceforth he would live in strict obedience to his Creator and his Saviour – not to the Home Secretary. As a High Priest he could indeed thank God that he was not as other men.

He never doubted his own Divine Nature conferred on him by Apostolic Descent. Even in his Anglican days, as a simple country rector, he gave orders that at dinner he should be served before his guests; they were shocked; he told them that it was homage to his divinity ... something he did not deserve as a man, only as a priest.

I have recently talked to Edward Marshall Hall, the greatest counsel of the criminal courts. He said that had my father been arraigned for murder he would have immediately entered a plea of insanity – religious mania. Barnabas Barbellion would never have allowed it. He would have preferred the rope ... he had so often said that the Church needed a martyr. The English Tudors, he would recall, disembowelled their heretics or burnt them alive, for Jesus' sake. And even that, he would add, was nothing compared with the Day of Judgement. When they built the Martyrs' Memorial in Oxford they asked him for a subscription; he retorted that he knew nothing good of the saintly Cranmer except that he burnt well ...

As the Middle Ages had believed in Divine Kingship, so the Victorians, in their odd way, believed in Divine Priesthood – Roman, Lutheran, Anglican, Presbyterian – the Priest as God Incarnate ... the fingers raised in benediction, the chalice kissed, the hands laid on the head, the Holy Water on the forehead ... and behold there was magic. My father believed every scrap of it. His ambition was to be God, to be Infallible, so that in the end it was all too wonderful, too marvellous, just to be himself ... striding down the marble corridors of the Vatican beneath the Raphaels, or prostrate in adoration beneath the great dome ... poor little Emily, deep in her coffin at Nether Molding, could then so easily be forgotten.

An enormity of megalomania, of course, but there was another facet of his ambition – simple vanity. As Pope he never looked grander than on the white mule or washing the beggars' feet. As at Balliol, as in the pulpit at Nether Molding or as Cardinal of England, he looked splendid. Always, with calculated panache, he played the part and looked it. In his austere, almost emaciated way he was an extremely handsome man – all the Barbellions are – and he also had to perfection the *physique du rôle*, to the last flicker of an eyelid, to the last snap of the fingers, to the final curl of the lip.

He died peacefully on a pale winter morning, just as the sun was rising behind the Capitoline. He managed to utter the Pontifical

Benediction of the City and the World, *Urbi et Orbi* . . . for even in his last moments he would keep the act going. He whispered the dying words of Alexander the Second: 'I am sweeping through the Gates washed in the Blood of the Lamb'. Death then had to have its own ritual. He received Extreme Unction and the Viaticum. Cardinal McClocky, in his tremulous and comic Irish–Latin, intoned the Commendation of a Christian: 'Saints of God advance to meet him, receiving his Soul, offering it in the sight of the Most High.' And then they lifted him to his feet to symbolize the Passage of that Soul from Purgatory to the Brightness of Heaven. The golden hammer had to be struck upon his forehead while his own Confessor called the name his mother had given him in baptism – 'Barnabas, Barnabas!' There was no reply and only then was Peter truly dead in the arms of Caesar . . . Vicar of Christ, Pontifex Maximus, Servant of the Servants of God, Ruler of the World.

And so, at last, Cardinal Cavalle could beckon the women to the bed chamber. My sister and the German nuns – those good women who do the Pope's cooking – were waiting and praying in the next room. Yes, they allowed my sister, Maria Pia, to see him. With a nun on either side she kissed him on the brow as forty-three years before he had made her kiss the cold corpse of her own mother. Now she was in the Vatican, kissing a dead pope, surrounded by vermilion cardinals – a strange moment for any woman, and yet, as she has so often told me, all she could think of was that Cotswold night when the Rectory chamber-pots were frozen and Jane Grigg had lit the log fire in the night-nursery.

They embalmed him very beautifully according to a recipe of the Coptic Church. And then they entombed him very gorgeously – a little to the north of the High Altar, in the shadow of Bernini's huge baldacchino. He lies next to his spiritual master, Pius the Ninth, and not too far from Christ's First Apostle. '*Capax imperii nini imperasset*.'

He departed this world – or so all those vermilion cardinals told my sister – in the odour of sanctity. His Confessor, a haggard and aged Hieronymite monk – Brother Justin – was never seen in public, but within the Vatican was my father's shadow, padding after him down vaulted and painted corridors. Brother Justin always swore that His Holiness had confessed and repented of all his sins a few minutes before his death . . . and then silence, the Seal of the Confessional. Well, we shall see, we shall see.

My own view is that whatever his Confessor might say my father should have been arrested in January 1855, brought to trial at Gloucester Assize, taken thence to the County Gaol, there to be hanged by the neck until he was dead. In view of his own implacable belief in Hell Fire – the Lake of Fire and Brimstone that burneth forever – I cannot speculate as to whether his own God will have mercy on his soul. What I do know is that just as Barnabas Barbellion fooled everyone in this world, from the simple peasantry of Nether Molding to the whole College of Cardinals, so in the next world at the Day of Judgement he will assuredly pull the wool over the eyes of Almighty God . . . Once again he will, as they say, 'get away with it'.

In actual fact, even while the sod lay freshly upon Emily's grave and he should have been languishing in the Condemned Cell, contemplating the Last Things, he was cruising happily among warm Aegean islands in the Admiralty yacht, *Enchantress* – Lord and Lady Granville, the Duke and Duchess of Norfolk, Lord Acton Dalberg, Cardinal Wiseman and the young Prince of Wales being of the company.

If, in this matter of Emily Barbellion's death, the lovely Phillippa Gatsby, my father's mistress, was an accessory after the fact, well and good. If she also poisoned her own husband, Colonel Harold Gatsby, then she paid the price, dying in Holloway Prison after giving birth to her still-born child. She certainly never confessed to the Prison Governor, as she might have done on her deathbed. Nor did she ever give the name of the child's father. She said it was her husband's conceived two months before he died. What she said to the priest whom they allowed her is now known only to God. He thought her innocent. The fact remains that Phillippa Gatsby was convicted while my father went scot-free . . . to die gorgeously, more than forty years later, in that great bedroom of the Vatican Palace.

For me, therefore, the murder will always be that of my own mother – the unsolved killing of the mother whom, in my childish way, I had loved. It is my father's life, therefore, that I must now examine, his acts and his character . . . 'the priest who was the slayer and shall himself be slain'. What a theme! Ambition before all, but hard on the heels of ambition came cruelty, vanity, lust, great scholarship and – oddly enough – a very real piety. Or perhaps not oddly enough since, after all, every man in his own life creates his own God in his own image. The God of Barnabas was never a loving Father; he was an Old Testament God, a tyrannical Jehovah, enthroned in Wrath and Glory – the God whom Barnabas saw in his dressing-room mirror every morning of his life.

I have no wish, in the quiet days that remain to me, to be pestered either by newspapermen or by inquisitive strangers, spoiling my serene existence here at Derravaragh . . . I have already had to set the dog on one or two of them. I have, therefore, given my Executors instructions that this true and definitive story of the Barbellion Case is on no account to be published until ten years after my death. Those instructions may be overridden only if an innocent person should be brought to trial. Meanwhile this document will rest in a steel box at the office of my solicitors, Messrs Healey, Healey, Macnamara and Spillane, of Plunkett Street, Mullingar, in the County of Meath, of which firm the only sober and, indeed, the only surviving partner is named Wilkins.

Signed: Augustine Xavier Barbellion
26th Baron of Derravaragh in the Peerage of Ireland.

Witnessed: Eirlys Magdalen Cole-Hatt, Spinster.
Sean O' Suilleabhain, Solicitor's Clerk.
15th Day of March, 1920.

2 Tractarian Croquet

Their tears, their little triumphs o'er,
Their human passions now no more

THOMAS GRAY

We may, I think, take our first and most revealing look at my father, not in his own rectory at Nether Molding but rather in the gardens of Windrush Court, the great Gatsby house over in the next valley. For one thing, he was always so much more at home there than in his own village.

His own church and his own rectory were not really important to him. They served – the church as a stage for the priest, the rectory as a base from which to plan battles . . . that was all. Of course he would say – he was always saying – that the pulpit and the altar were everything in the world to him. And so they were, not for the sacrament or the sermon, but because it was there that he could display his priesthood and preen himself, acting out his own drama – the rolling eye, the catch in the voice, the calculated gesture and the tight mouth breaking into the sweetest smile imaginable. And it was there in his study – a Regency room with tall windows and calf-bound books – that he planned everything. That was the centre of the spider's web. It was from there that the letters – dozens a day – went out to the great ones of the Earth . . . everywhere. It was there that the articles and reviews were written – so shocking, so brilliant and so readable, intended to take his name to every breakfast table. His methods were meticulous – every letter was acknowledged but none was ever written in kindness. He wrote only to raise himself in the eyes of the world or to destroy his rivals – gross flattery or biting irony.

The only other letters he ever wrote, those to 'darling Phillippa', written every night whether they had met that day or not, were reminiscent in their wilder flights of the Song of Solomon. Either those letters are evidence of madness or they are among the great love letters of the world. They are now in the secret drawer of my bureau.

Nether Molding was a tiny village, buried in a hollow of the Cotswold Hills. It was just what he wanted. The parochial duties, apart from the Eucharist which he celebrated to his own glory, hardly existed. Cecil Praz, that dubious youth, did what had to be done, evicting sabbath-breakers from their cottages, and so on. The 'parson's freehold' was invaluable and my father used it as his conscience bid. Having been meant by God to be a cataclysmic figure, not a parochial one, Nether Molding, as a home, was as good as anywhere, supplemented of course by his chambers in Albany. He took the Sunday services with tremendous *éclat* but the men and women in the pews meant nothing to him – mere *canaille*. To Barbellion it was only Barbellion that mattered . . . Barbellion and Phillippa. Twice every Sunday in the panelled Gatsby pew, in tremendous style – with the carriage waiting at the Lych Gate – sat Harold, Phillippa and Eirlys . . . Harold sometimes dozing a little, Phillippa with her head proud and erect – her gaze never off her priest – while Eirlys's eyes, big and grey, were downcast in piety. It was for the Gatsby pew, every week, that my father performed his sublime act.

Barnabas Barbellion was an Early Victorian but by no stretch of imagination could he be seen as the old-style country parson – neither the sporting nor the scholarly nor the saintly. He had a good seat in the hunting field, he was the most learned theologian of his day and his religious observances were, to say the least, strict, but for his fellow clergy he had no use whatever – only contempt.

All those gentle English graduates of Oxford . . . one can see them in their tense and callow youth, so black in cap and gown, crowding the High on a summer afternoon or walking out to Littlemore, the dreaming spires seen across cornfields; or one can see them on a winter evening in the gas-lit aisles of St Mary's, hanging breathless and enchanted upon the lips of the preacher – a Pusey or a Newman. And then, a little later, one sees them again, each on the coach-top going down to the country, to some parsonage hidden deep in English shires, to baptize, marry and bury until they too could rest beneath the graveyard's tall grasses. 'Along the cool sequestered vale of life, they kept the noiseless tenor of their way' . . . the poet's vision hardly applied to Barnabas Barbellion; from *his* sequestered vale he set out only to trample upon the world – this world and the next – to conquer both.

He was a materialist intent upon the satisfaction of his appetites, but for the 'three-bottle men' coursing hares by day and carousing at night, he had only contempt . . . had he not heard that they administered the Sacrament with their top-boots under their surplices! As for the boast of the Establishment that at least it put a gentleman and a scholar in every parish he could offer nothing but a sneer. He had no use for the Parson Woodfordes of the Church, while even a man like Keble, quietly – through the long years at Hursley – composing the facile rhythms of *The Christian Year*, Barbellion had no word of praise . . . the fellow was so pale and ineffective. As for the more famous author of 'Lead Kindly Light', he was little better . . . for all his sycophantic disciples and the agonizing drama of his Conversion, he was still so Oxfordian, so damned Anglican. And then there was that man Hurrell Froude, in his vicarage above the Dart, always analysing his own 'vile thoughts' or pulling his own soul to bits to see how it was getting on.

These gentle saints may have been necessary to that awakening of the English Church – necessary to Tractarianism or High Anglicanism – but really Barnabas Barbellion had no patience with them. Their fasting, he suspected, showed only a poor appetite, their virginal lives a poor virility – or something worse. No, it was in the glamour of worship, the exotic beauty of the Eucharist, that the Anglican Church could be saved from itself, if indeed it really was the True Fold of Christ . . . something that seemed more doubtful every moment.

And all that, oddly enough, was why on this particular day of August in the year 1854, the croquet mallets clicked and the balls rolled noiselessly across the turf. In the background were the gables of Windrush Court, all golden stone losing itself in a patina of mullions and leaded lights, of wistaria and clematis and carved beasts. The house basked through the long afternoon, the yew trees, so old and dark and fantastically shaped, huddled around it. Everything shimmered in a haze of heat. The wide lawns, so perfect and so emerald, set between the yew garden at one end and the shade of the deodars at the other, was now a stage for the slow-moving ballet of the croquet players.

This was one of those gatherings known to the initiated as a Gatsby Tractarian Party, to others simply as a Reading Party. Outwardly it was just a house party of sombre creatures worried about their own salvation; it was also a very smart affair – if it had not been for all the dark clothing one might even say 'glittering' – certainly the smartest affair of the ecclesiastical calendar . . . the elegant reply of the High Church to the revivalist meetings of Methodism. Outwardly, that is; in reality these parties were staged by Phillippa – Harold loathed them – almost solely for the glorification of my father, that she might display his brilliance in front of several 'useful' bishops. There were peacocks on the terrace; he was another, a clerical peacock with his tail up.

Each morning, after prayers, in the Great Hall of Windrush, there were tense discussions – theological and exegetical – broken off only at the Canonical Hours when, with a twirling of parasols and with black crinolines brushing the grass, they would all walk over to the Gatsby chapel – that last carved and gilded Pugin masterpiece, built by Phillippa with Harold's money. These were annual parties, timed for the Oxford vacation, but the croquet was this year an innovation. It had been a concession to youth but already it had been decided that it must never happen again. It was too worldly; it might not be sinful but it was certainly lax. The word 'lax' was much in use. Among the spectators, beneath the deodars, there were pursed lips, tightly closed eyes and fingers twisted in rosaries. Yes, indeed, croquet was lax.

The sounds of the game, the gentle voices, the rare touch of colour in dress or bonnet, these were the only positive notes in this scene of English peace . . . and English security. These and, of course, the two little girls – all sprigged muslin and large shady hats – threading their way among the guests, the tea-tables and the gilt chairs, as they played together. There – and I can see it all so clearly – there was Maria Pia, my sister, playing with our 'Cousin' Eirlys, the child who bore the name of Cole-Hatt, the darling Eirlys. She must, that summer, have been, I suppose, about fifteen; I was some three years younger and Maria Pia only eleven. We had been brought over from Nether Molding that afternoon by our dear Miss Grigg. And now in the deep shade Jane Grigg sat alone, except for me, little Augustine, as I stood at her knee drawing pictures. I remember it well. Maria Pia and Eirlys might play among the 'grown-ups' but I was different. I was always a very shy boy and – specially for the Gatsby party – I had been dressed in cream velvet with buckled shoes . . . I did not like at all my very Fauntleroy look.

That Miss Grigg should sit apart was only seemly – the status of a governess being above that of the housekeeper's room, below that of the drawing-room. It was known that Miss Grigg was well educated – was she not teaching us two languages – and that she was the daughter of a Judge. That made no difference – it would have been inappropriate for a governess to play croquet with a bishop. It wouldn't do and therefore it wasn't done. Miss Grigg – with her own room and the schoolroom on the same landing as the big bedroom where my mother died – it was Miss Grigg, with her quiet tongue, sharp ears and watchful eyes, who knew so much and, in the end, might have told so much.

The figures on the lawn moved slowly in the heat of the afternoon, each following his own croquet ball as his adversary sent it spitefully into the azaleas. They moved slowly . . . but very graciously. If they spoke, and to speak was a frivolity, they were answered by a masculine bow or by lowered feminine eyelids. A gentleman, scoring a point, would bow all over again, apologetically, to his opponent, deferentially to his partner, slightly raising his hat. A gentleman would hold a lady's parasol while she wielded the mallet, again raising his hat as he returned it to her . . . the revolving ballet of the Windrush lawns.

Those hats, those gentlemen's hats – they were mainly of the shovel kind, or bishops' toppers with rigging, although one episcopal spark had sported the fashionable boater – a speckled boater displaying his college ribbon. The only laymen in all Windrush – Harold Gatsby and Lord Halifax – wore *café-au-lait* toppers, gleaming in the sun. It set them very nicely apart.

To the spectators under the trees the game of croquet seemed endless. They could not be said to be following it; they watched it listlessly, sometimes sleepily, disapprovingly. At that moment Phillippa Gatsby and Archdeacon Wilberforce were well matched against my father and a nun – a nun with a black habit and a white parasol . . . very chic.

Within a few months Robert Wilberforce, so beloved in his Yorkshire parish, would have followed my father into the Roman Church. The famous Wilberforce–Barbellion correspondence is one of my main sources of evidence, especially for my father's days in Rome. It was known at Windrush Court that dear Wilberforce was already in agonies of doubt, already on his 'Anglican Deathbed', ready to 'go over'. And yet . . . here he was actually playing croquet! Miss Mozley closed her copy of Law's *Serious Call to the Devout Life* upon its purple marker and turned to her neighbour in the next *chaise longue*. She, in her turn, closed her Paley's *Evidences*. They agreed that the whole thing jarred terribly . . . what was Mrs Gatsby thinking of? There could be only one explanation – Archdeacon Wilberforce's agony was over – he had 'crossed the bridge' and was now within the One Fold. It had indeed been whispered only that morning that his trousers were grey, not black, and that he could no longer, therefore, regard himself as within Anglican Orders. And yet, that would not do either . . . only a few hours ago he had received Anglican Sacraments in the Gatsbys' Pugin Chapel. It was inexplicable . . . and such a good man, so truly dogmatic and gloomy. And yet here he was, his whole salvation hanging by a thread, thousands waiting for the signal, and he was playing croquet! One did not comment – eyes could only look into eyes in shocked bewilderment.

At last the game seemed to be coming to an end; they were playing through the last hoop. But also, somehow, the game no longer seemed to matter. There were other things afoot. Some thirty guests, mostly pale, solemn and learned, were gathered in the deep shade . . . really, it all looked like a fashionable funeral. At last they were free to talk and the croquet had become irrelevant.

The older ladies, all in black, if not actually in crêpe, did not in any case play games. That would never do; so many were in perpetual mourning, if not for their own departed, then certainly for the crucified Jesus. Some of the more youthful also wore black, even if touched with white or purple. Three or four among them, including Flo Nightingale, wore curious hoods, insignia of an

Anglican sisterhood. But if many were sombre others wore marvellous dresses, huge sweeping crinolines below tight bodices – all in lavender or white. The clergy moved among them like so many thin black lines threading their way through fleecy summer clouds.

Barnabas Barbellion, even though he could see these glorious creatures only across the wide lawns, and they were in the shade and he was in the sunlight, quivered with excitement. He could hardly wait for the end of the game . . . why was that nun so slow, why was Wilberforce so precise? My father adored lovely girls in tight bodices; he would do so until that day he died . . . probably thinking of them as he looked out across Tiber to the Palatine. So, on that afternoon at Windrush Court, so long ago, he could really hardly contain himself. In a few moments now he would move under the deodars, then he too would be quite close to those tiny waists and those rounded breasts. In a few moments he too would be passing them the cucumber sandwiches or strawberries, perhaps even pouring out their cream. He almost choked with excitement. In such charming pleasures he saw no sin. He had long since done his duty by Emily and more than his duty. His love for Phillippa was on an altogether different plane – sacred, sanctified in the eyes of the Lord. No, all these pretty bosoms, breasts and waists were a peccadillo – not even that . . . God had surely made them, as he had made those roses and azaleas, to be looked at, to give joy.

And now the game was really over; the players strolled from the sunshine into the shade. Down one side of the lawn afternoon tea was being borne in procession. Four footmen, in the black and buff Gatsby livery, followed by parlourmaids, were carrying their trays in single file – all marshalled under the eye of Featherston, the Gatsby butler . . . he at least would live on and on to tell the tale of that afternoon. The great *repoussé* tea-kettles flashed in the sunlight above their spirit lamps, only to vanish into the cool shadows. And there under the trees that college ribbon on the boater, those occasional dresses of white or violet, or a feather in a bonnet, might have been the only sign of colour . . . might have been . . . in actual fact, there, in the centre of everything, was a single great splash of vermilion. There, enthroned in honour in a basket chair set upon a carpet, was His Eminence Cardinal Patrick Nicholas Wiseman, that oily but amiable prelate – as Greville called him – almost the only Roman fish in this Windrush shoal of High Anglicans. Cardinal Wiseman was drowsily letting his thoughts run on ... how very useful, for instance, all these very rich people might be to him or, as he would prefer to put it, how truly God-sent were all these saintly folk, how helpful they might be in his great mission – a mission blessed by the Holy Father – the Conversion of England. Yes, convert the rich and the others would soon follow. He knew that he was being criticized for going too much with wealthy heretics, that he loved society. He suffered in silence, knowing very well that he was doing God's work. Every week, indeed, he would write to the Vatican to report how well God's work was getting on. Newman, undoubtedly, had been his first big catch, but now, here at these Gatsby parties, were a score of others ready to go over to Rome ... not least this brilliant and very handsome Archdeacon of Gloucester, Rector, so Wiseman understood, of the neighbouring village of Nether Molding.

It was known – indeed it was almost a scandal – that Archdeacon Barbellion had many penitents, lady penitents, and none knew better than His Eminence what marvels could be done through the Confession Box. The priest would work upon the lady, then the lady would work upon her husband in bed ... and thus would God's Kingdom be brought about on Earth.

Archdeacon Barbellion ... yes, he must make much of him, cultivate him, tactfully and suavely of course, until he too was a ripe plum ready to fall into the Roman basket. Yes, mused the Cardinal, these Gatsby parties, how invaluable they were, what opportunities they offered. Barbellion – there he was, over there, almost lost among a posse of admiring young women, lost in a fine flurry of muslin, chiffon and pretty faces. The man, damn him, could not help his good looks, but what a triumph his Conversion would be ... so many would follow him, a triumph for the Church, for God and – although this was quite incidental – a triumph for Cardinal Wiseman.

His Eminence was now almost asleep. He roused himself with a start. He had his duties as a guest. He swallowed his fourth sandwich before turning to Lady Halifax, fanning herself at his side.

'The mercies of Providence,' he told her, 'are very great; are they not, dear Lady Halifax?'

'Certainly, Your Eminence, but why particularly . . .'

'Oh, well, just think for instance, dear Lady, how truly Providential it is that the strawberry season should never fall in Lent . . . most mysterious but surely most merciful.'

'Yes, indeed, Your Eminence.' Lady Halifax lowered her eyes but her mouth twitched. 'Yes, indeed – one of the delights of an English summer.'

Her companion waved her fork in disapproval. God must not be mocked. She decided that she did not like this fat priest. Perhaps, after all, the dear old Church of England was the safest place . . . it was all very disturbing.

His Eminence fell silent. His thoughts still ran upon Providence but this time they were unspoken. Really, there was no end to the goodness of the Almighty. How Providential, for instance, was the crinoline. What a beautiful thing it was, thought the Cardinal, a smile playing on his thick lips. True, the crinoline, when it first came in, had been a rather clumsy affair, radiating from the shoulders so that every woman was a walking tea-cosy. Now, however, it was different; its new piquancy lay in the subtle contrast at the waist, just where the full skirt met the tightly tailored bodice – huge panniers below, little rounded breasts above, point counter point . . . all very lovely. Very Providential, too, for another reason; while not actually disguising the bust it miraculously allowed a young mother to play croquet into the seventh or even the eighth month unsuspected, except of course by the Cardinal's expert eye. Yes, indeed, most Providential . . . Adam and Eve, he reflected, had had only fig leaves; the Almighty, in His infinite wisdom, must surely have been keeping the crinoline up his sleeve, so to speak, ever since the Fall, in readiness for Victorian house-parties. How true, he muttered – grinning – how true that the ways of God passeth all understanding.

The hum of voices disturbed these pleasant thoughts. He looked around; what a scintillating scene, all these fashionable people moving together in the shade with just a little dappled sunlight filtering through the foliage. These wealthy English . . .

how luxuriously he absorbed it all. Then, rather startled, he sat bolt upright and put on his spectacles.

A few yards away a footman was serving sandwiches to the Bishop of Exeter and to a very beautiful girl – a suspiciously beautiful girl. She was a brunette and His Eminence had always preferred brunettes. She was so sylph-like that he could not take his eyes off her, and yet – surely he must be mistaken – no, he was not mistaken, definitely she was *enceinte*. He purred with pleasure. At that most crucial point, just where crinoline curved inwards and bodice curved outwards, the sylph-like silhouette was marred. How expert he was!

There was nothing wrong with pregnancy of course – in fact he could see a ring of some sort on the finger that lay against the edge of the saucer – but that the girl should be here at all, mixing with strangers of both sexes . . . that was brazen. Motherhood was nothing to be ashamed of, on the contrary it was sacred, but this was no longer the Regency . . . things had been different when Wiseman was a boy; now we were in the reign of Victoria, and decorum was all.

As to crinolines, of course he had only been joking with himself just now. To appear in public like this was to take advantage of an absurd fashion. What on earth was the girl's husband thinking of . . . presuming she had one. Well, well, it only showed. One never knew where one was with these rich people. One was positively surrounded by sin. His duty was clear: one by one he began to examine with care, through his spectacles, the waist of every young woman within range – a most painful task. He was thoroughly enjoying it when, suddenly and crudely, a loud voice disturbed the whole party.

'Harold, do look after your guests! And don't let me have to speak to you again. Really, Harold!'

Phillippa's voice was not usually unpleasant; indeed it was much admired. But this – this breaking in upon the Cardinal's happy task and upon everyone's enjoyment – was not only crude, it was worse – it was embarrassing. Colonel Gatsby might be stupid and unattractive. He was both. In this company he was also . . . lax. Phillippa, however, was unpardonable. In the months to come, at the time of the trial, this episode in the gardens of Windrush Court would be talked of again and again. It would be talked of – if in more hushed tones – later that afternoon.

'Harold, did you hear me? I said, do look after your guests. You can't expect the servants to do everything.'

Ladies turned their backs upon her. The Vicar of Saint Monica's, Mount Street – so young and handsome and with a whiff of incense still hanging in his cassock – walked over to Harold and made himself pleasant – in an obvious way.

Even we children knew that something was wrong. Poor little Maria Pia ran to Miss Grigg, to bury her head in a kindly shoulder. Eirlys stood where she was, alongside her mother; in her big grey saucer eyes, shaded by the big Leghorn hat, the tears welled up to run slowly down her cheeks. To day, in her senility, she remembers it well. As for me, decked out in my cream velvet suit – and I too remember it well – I howled.

'Really, Harold, what will people think?'

'I'm sorry, Phillippa, but I'm feeling this heat. If I'm no use to you here I'd better go indoors . . . cooler in the Library you know.'

'Nonsense, Harold, the heat is the same for us all. There's Miss Nightingale over there, talking to dear Mr Froude. They seem to have no tea. Pray see that they are served.'

Phillippa Gatsby now turned towards my father – her Rector, her Confessor, her lover and her 'dearest Barny'. He had been long enough with that posse of lovely girls; he must be detached and passed on to some 'useful' bishop or other, or introduced to His Eminence. But, as Phillippa turned, His Eminence saw her full-length, silhouetted against the sunlight – the brilliant light, beyond the trees. Good God! Was he going mad? He could hardly believe his eyes, but there was no doubt about it, no doubt whatever. Of course it might be dropsy – how sad if it was – but really that was not very likely – Phillippa was such a healthy woman. It was still early days – he could see that – perhaps only the second or third month, but His Eminence had a good eye for these things. He was a man of experience who had so often and so carefully studied the penitents as they came to Confession. Yes, he had a good eye. But really, it was too extraordinary . . . no sooner had he indulged in a few innocent thoughts about babies and crinolines and he was positively surrounded by pregnant women. And – and – dear Mrs Gatsby of all people! Why, surely, she must be nearly forty. In any case – forty or not – the world knew that the Gatsby marriage had never been anything but a fiction, a device – a device doubtless pleasing to Almighty God – but only a device for pouring Gatsby money into the Church while providing Harold, as Lord of the Manor and Lord Lieutenant of Gloucestershire, with a beautiful hostess.

It had worked, and for ten years the Gatsbys had kept the act going. And now this! It was incredible. And dear Phillippa Gatsby of all people – so pious, so chaste, so truly devout. Harold could hardly have recovered either his love or his virility at the age of sixty odd. But of course – and the Cardinal suddenly remembered – yes, he was almost sure . . . that dear little girl over there, in the big shady hat – what was her name, Eirlys Cole-Hatt. Yes, of course, this pretty little thing was spoken of as Mrs Gatsby's 'niece' but – it had been whispered to him – she was really all the evidence he needed – evidence that however barren the Gatsby marriage might be, it was certain that Phillippa could conceive a child all right . . . if asked.

Cardinal Wiseman shrugged his shoulders. He was a man of the world and he knew that in the highest and the lowest circles such things must happen. Well, well, at least it made the party more spicy. How fascinating life could be . . . and quite suddenly in the middle of a glorious summer afternoon. All this . . . and strawberries too! There, over there, were Phillippa Gatsby and Archdeacon Barbellion – he must watch them. He must pretend to snooze. With his eyes shut he would be able to savour his delicious thoughts unsuspected. He shut his eyes. That was no good; he opened them immediately for just one more look. She was half-hidden now by the trunk of a deodar, but not the half that mattered. All her guests had been served and were at last neatly paired off with the right people. She was free to talk to her Barny.

They had found a table for two. Featherston himself was serving them with tea, while the tallest footman was setting out the sandwiches and the *petits-fours*. Now, the Cardinal asked himself, when a glamorous hostess and a handsome Archdeacon put their heads together, surrounded by some of the most respectable people in England – how can one tell whether or not they are infatuated?

Cardinal Patrick Nicholas Wiseman found no difficulty at all. He knew all the signs . . . the sort of eyes such people make at each other, their smiles and gestures. This was a clear case. He beamed all over his round red face. Sweating with excitement he again donned his spectacles – tiny silver ones – the better to see with. He must watch carefully this sophisticated billing and cooing. He did so with the eye of the happy connoisseur, with all the practised expertise of the celibate *voyeur*.

He gave them ten delicious minutes together. Then he acted. He had not come to Windrush Court merely to titillate his senses with vicarious flirtations. There was God's work to be done. He knew why he was there. He had to bring Barnabas Barbellion, so gently but so finally, into the ever-open arms of the Roman Church. Cardinal Wiseman, to the end of his life, always said that it was the Holy Ghost who had guided him that afternoon, who told him that the decisive hour had come.

On that summer day the Holy Ghost certainly did well by his own. Wiseman was right – this was indeed a decisive hour. When, years later, he lay dying in the great bedroom at York Place, he recalled that afternoon, knowing that in all probability my father would succeed him as Cardinal of England. It was always a grief to my father that old Wiseman should not live to see his apotheosis, to see Barnabas Barbellion upon the Pontifical Throne. And when, a few months later, Phillippa died in Holloway, it may have consoled her just a little to know that it was she who had brought the two men together . . . to the greater Glory of Christ.

Wiseman knew perfectly well that the only reason he had been invited to Windrush Court – a Roman cuckoo in this Anglican nest – was to meet my father. They had to meet . . . it was written in the stars. So, why not now . . . His Eminence swallowed another gateau, wiped his fingers on his watered-silk cassock, heaved his elephantine bulk from the basket chair and bowed to Lady Halifax. Then he shambled across the grass bent upon his prey.

'Pardon this interruption, dearest lady, but Archdeacon Barbellion and I . . . we have not met, I think.'

There was a flurry and a fuss, a thousand pardons, elaborate introductions, a curtseying and a kissing of the ring, even a perfunctory benediction . . . and then the alert Featherston arrived with another chair, more tea, more *petits-fours*, more strawberries.

A beam of sunlight had found its way through the trees to shine momentarily upon the scarlet and the black. The whole thing – nobody quite knew why – was touched with drama. The Bishop of Ely told his wife to remember what she had seen, that this might be an historic moment, that he prayed that it might be to the greater glory of God, but that he trembled to think . . . that one could only pray, watch and pray. Of course they all knew that this meeting between the Cardinal Archbishop and the Archdeacon, Rector of Nether Molding was, this year, the real reason for the whole Gatsby party. They all knew that this meeting might portend nothing less than 'another Newman' and that the history of the Church was being changed under their eyes. And, you know, remembering the tomb of Paschal the Fourth, close by the High Altar of St Peter's, I would not say that these English ladies and gentlemen were altogether wrong.

A number of things now seemed to happen all at once. Cardinal Wiseman and my father were far too absorbed in themselves to notice anyone else. And yet the things going on within a few yards of them, trivial as they may have seemed at the time, may have changed the history of the world.

First, then, the two little girls, Maria Pia and Eirlys, had dried their tears and had now left the warm comfort of Jane Grigg to stand shyly, solemnly, but with enormous curiosity, alongside their elders. Perhaps they had been drawn there by the sight of the fat man in vermilion, or perhaps it was the footmen with the strawberries who had, in their usual way, been neglecting a mere governess and her charges. Anyway, my sister – Miss Grigg having tied the hat ribbons in a big bow under the chin – now watched the 'grown-ups' avidly, listening with her pretty head on one side – alert. Eirlys, holding her hat by its ribbons so that it touched the grass, edged a little closer until both of them, seen but not heard, listened and watched, retaining it all in their young but precocious memories . . . Maria Pia to write it all down that night in her 'journal', Eirlys to engrave it forever on her mind.

The second thing that happened was that at the back of the crowd, in even deeper shade, Harold Gatsby collapsed, panting, with closed eyes. His skin, in these last days of his life, was always copper-hued, but now all colour, save for purple blotches, was drained from his plump face. Father Martin, Vicar of Saint Monica's, Mount Street, held his hand. Featherston plied him with iced lemonade, while a pretty nun – helpless, useless, hovering angel – dabbed his brow with a wet napkin.

Wiseman and Barbellion talked on, oblivious, unaware that all they said was being stored up in those two little girls' heads, unaware that the collapse of Harold Gatsby was the first act of a great tragedy. They talked on and on under Phillippa's adoring eyes.

'This is a very great honour, Your Eminence, for a humble village priest.'

'The honour is mine, Archdeacon. I am so glad to be able to congratulate you, personally I mean, on your article in *Blackwoods* last month . . . so truly ecumenical. It could hardly offend your own flock, yet it certainly delighted mine . . . truly ecumenical and yet, at the same time, so Roman.'

'Roman, Your Eminence?'

'Of course, my dear Barbellion. There was nothing to offend *us*, much to please us in fact. Your dissertation upon Galatians v. 15, was quite masterly. Nay, I would go further; I would dare to say that the whole thing charted a course towards reunion . . . oh, yes, I am sure of that.'

'And to think that I am nobody, a mere presbyter, like a thousand others . . . I am overcome.'

'Not at all. I mean it. And let me tell you that only last week I dropped a line to dear Monsignor Talbot – the Papal Chamberlain, you know, and how fortunate we are to have an Englishman at the Papal Court – dropped him a line and also a copy of *Blackwoods*. By now, therefore, your article will assuredly be on the Holy Father's desk . . . His Holiness is always interested in Anglican talent . . . one never knows . . .'

'I can hardly speak, Your Eminence.'

'Say nothing. I only did my duty. If one sees a man doing the work of God, then one makes sure that his light is not hidden under a bushel. The Holy Father, dear Barbellion, has a most remarkable memory. Your name will now be stamped upon his mind. It is as well, anything may happen.'

'Anything may happen? In what way, Your Eminence?'

'Anything – to you or to me. In a month's time, in six months' time – only God can decide – your position may be very different from what it is now. It is changing all the time, is it not? Today you call yourself an Anglican priest . . .'

'A staunch Anglican.'

'Oh, quite, quite. I would not for worlds suggest otherwise. But your brain is alive, and your soul. The world moves, God moves and you move with him. You are staunch. Tomorrow you may find your own sacraments unacceptable – as Newman did – and your Church in schism. I only say that you may. Then, suddenly, in a moment, you may desperately need the Holy Father. And, you know, he may need you. *We* would not waste your talents, dear Barbellion. Pius the Ninth is a compassionate man . . . when the time comes he will offer you all the love of Christ. We shall see, we shall see.'

The two men crossed themselves. Joined with them, if only in fascinated silence, was their hostess – Wiseman's hostess, Barbellion's mistress. At this precise moment a footman offered his salver of strawberries . . . they seemed to be crossing themselves to the scarlet fruit and to the jugs of yellow cream. The footman took back an astonishing story to the Servants' Hall.

'Your Eminence will be ever in my prayers. What else can I say?'

There was a necessary pause while Cardinal Wiseman carefully but lavishly poured his cream.

'Tomorrow, dear Archdeacon, I shall say three Masses for you. By the way, have you ever actually been to Rome?'

'Only as a boy, with my parents. We travelled with the Ruskins; John, I remember, was just my age.'

'Ah, yes, I have just read his new book – *Stones of Venice* – an eccentric and unbalanced work, such artistic sensitivity, such rabid Protestantism. Most extraordinary. But we were speaking, were we not, of Rome, not of Venice. Now Rome . . .'

The Cardinal was again interrupted. It was really very trying, talking in the middle of this garden-party – all this chatter round one. This time it was Featherston, *sotto voce* to his mistress.

'Excuse me, ma'am.'

'Not now, Featherston. All you have to do is to look after the guests. See that they are served and accommodated in every way but do not disturb me – there is no need. That will do, Featherston, thank you.'

'Excuse me, ma'am, but I must speak. The master has been taken ill.'

'How very trying, and today of all days. Not his palpitations, I trust.'

'I fear so, ma'am. Oh, yes, ma'am, the palpitations, definitely the palpitations . . . sweating and trembling.'

'Very well. We needn't go into details. You know what to do, Featherston. You had no need to trouble me. The master must be taken to his room and told to lie down. Kindly see to it.'

But now another figure was behind the butler, Father Martin, the Vicar of Saint Monica's, Mount Street.

'I am sorry about all this, Mrs Gatsby – and in the middle of your party – but your husband is quite prostrate. It is more serious than you seem to think.'

'Oh dear! But how very trying of Harold to choose today – so like him. Fortunately these palpitations, although distressing at the time, soon pass. Thank you all the same, Father Martin. Most kind.'

'But he is ill, Mrs Gatsby.'

'Yes, of course, Father Martin, but you really must not trouble yourself with our affairs. Featherston can quite well assist Harold to the house, and his valet will be there to help him to bed. There is no cause for alarm.'

'But Sister Jessica – she belongs to a Nursing Order – as well as Featherston here, who knows his master well, share my alarm. He is barely conscious.'

'How thoughtful you are, dear Father Martin, but really Featherston can so easily deal with this. You know what to do, Featherston – get your master to bed.'

'Yes, ma'am, but in this heat we shall have to carry him across the lawns.'

'Of course. One of the footmen can help. Don't make difficulties. Oh, yes, and one other thing, Featherston.'

'Yes, ma'am.'

'In the little corner cupboard in *my* bedroom, *not* in the master's bedroom – he will overdose himself so – there is a bottle of white medicine, prescribed by Doctor Clayton for just these occasions. It has a heavy sediment and needs shaking. See that the proper dose is given; it is on the label. And if you think he could take a little brandy – well, the key of the tantalus is on your master's key chain. Thank you, Featherston, that is all. You may go. Yes, Father Martin?'

'Mrs Gatsby, please let me go with your husband and, surely, we should summon the doctor . . .'

'Totally unnecessary, I assure you, but if you must, you must. No harm can be done, I suppose, by sending a groom into Stow-on-the-Wold, with a note for Doctor Clayton. And thank you again for your kindness . . . and now that is that. Your Eminence was speaking of Rome, I think, when we were interrupted. Please go on.'

'Ah, yes, so I was . . . speaking of Rome. So, Archdeacon, except as a boy, you have never been to our beloved Rome, our Eternal City.'

'Alas, no, Your Eminence. After Oxford I was only a poor curate, and since then the demands of this large rural parish as well as my – er – more polemical activities . . . well, they have been all-absorbing.'

'Well then, we are agreed – a visit is overdue.'

Once again it was becoming hard to concentrate. The Cardinal, my father and Mrs Gatsby were pretending not to see what everyone else was staring at – the ridiculous spectacle of a stout Featherston and a skinny footman bearing the master across the wide spaces of the Windrush lawns. Featherston had him beneath the knees, the footman beneath the armpits – an awkward posture causing them to stagger. Father Martin and Sister Jessica fussed on either side.

'. . . as I was saying, dear Barbellion, a visit to Rome is overdue. Only last year I was in the Holy Land where, of course, every inch of ground is sacred, but somehow, you know, it was nothing, nothing at all compared with Rome.'

'I can understand that – I must go to Rome before I die.'

'Don't leave it too long. Rome – Rome Pagan and Rome Christian – she winds herself into the heart, you know. She first enchants and then she captures . . . there is magic in the air. It is not just St Peter's, I can assure you of that. There are the catacombs, memories of the noble army of martyrs; the Colosseum is deeply moving – I was there with the Gladstones – and then all the relics and miracles – all truly marvellous. And for you, Archdeacon, there will of course be a special welcome at our English College. Go, and go soon.'

'Yes, indeed. I have dreamt of it, but somehow when it comes to the point, Your Eminence, I always think of those swarms of Yankee globe-trotters, with their twang and their Baedekers . . . the vulgarity of it all, the desecration of the Holy See.'

'Oh, my dear fellow, I will look after all that. You shall visit Rome as a privileged person – I promise you – almost as a guest of the Curia. Why, I know a house, a pretty little *palazzo* in the Via Tritone, fashionable but modest. Rent it, dear Barbellion, rent it for the Season and then – take my advice – hire a good cook and entertain all those who may be useful to you – useful in God's work of course. To entertain, in any case, is expected of you in Rome, and when in Rome you know . . .'

'Your Eminence is kindness itself.'

'This coming Advent then. That will be the time. Christmas in Rome is always joyful, but this year above all years . . .'

'This year particularly?'

'Oh, yes. You mean to say that you don't know – really, you Protestants do live in darkness, don't you. My dear fellow, it is this Advent, the Advent of 1854, which will see the Definition, the proclamation of the glorious Dogma of the Immaculate Conception. All Rome will be *en fête*. The Holy Father will proclaim the Dogma in the Sistine Chapel, to the Kings and Princes of the Earth – five emperors will be there. Oh, I can assure you that there will be a chance to meet all the best people . . . such useful people. Surely, Archdeacon, you must move among them . . . it would be most opportune.'

Cardinal Wiseman paused. He smacked his lips. Things were going well. He rubbed his hands together. He beamed upon Mrs Gatsby whose eyes were glowing with the fires of ambition for her lover. The Cardinal beamed upon the Rector of Nether Molding, the Archdeacon of Gloucester . . . who beamed back.

'But tell me, Your Eminence, how can all these fine people – the aristocracy of Europe, I take it – how can they possibly be useful to me? I am nobody and I know nobody.'

'Pooh! That is easily put right. A line from me to Monsignor Talbot – a reminder that you are the author of so many brilliant articles, of so many remarkable sermons, and all doors will be open to you. Your name will be bandied about Rome – fashionable Rome, that is. We may even get a dispensation for you to preach – to the English colony of course . . . San Carlo in the Corso is, I think, the usual church. Rome wants you, dear Archdeacon, it wants your brilliance and your talents. The Church at the moment is filled with mediocrities – saints and scholars perhaps, but it badly needs a genius. The Holy Father feels it strongly. He will welcome you with open arms. Go to Rome, dear sir, go to Rome and kneel at the Pontifical footstool. Rome will look after you.'

'Your Eminence, I am overcome.'

'Say no more – leave all to me. The word of the Cardinal of England means something, you know . . .'

At this critical moment – critical perhaps in the history of the Christian Church – there was a stir among the guests, a rustle and a murmur. All eyes, once more, were turned towards the empty sunlit croquet lawn. Featherston was literally running towards them. His stoutness hindered him. Myopically – since butlers on duty do not wear spectacles – he fell over a croquet hoop. He arrived panting, sweating, gasping. At all times he was a sweaty and breathless man.

'I want the Rector – the Archdeacon. Oh, sir. Thank God you are there. Oh, sir, I must have a word with you . . . a private word with the Rector, Mrs Gatsby, if you please, ma'am.'

'Nonsense, Featherston. Anything you may have to say to the Rector you can say to both of us. Now compose yourself, and then speak up.'

'I'm sorry, ma'am, I'm sure, ma'am. But that there Father Martin said that as we were in the Rector's parish I should speak to him first, and then he would break it to you, ma'am.'

'Break it to me? What rubbish! This may be the Rector's parish but we are all his parishioners. Now what is it, Featherston, for Heaven's sake?'

'Oh, ma'am, it is the master, ma'am. Mr Gatsby, ma'am. He's gone, I fear.'

'Gone! What on earth do you mean – gone where?'

'Oh, gone, ma'am, gone! Passed away!'

'I see. What you mean, what you are trying to say is that your master is dead. Thank you for telling me, Featherston. That will do for now.'

She was very beautiful. She was quite colourless – grey eyes in an ashen face. She was quite unmoved. She was like ice. My father touched her hand and she did not even notice. Cardinal Wiseman muttered something, probably the prayers for the dying, but again she did not notice. She sank to her knees at the tea-table and he gave her his blessing. There was complete silence among all the guests.

'Take me to him, Barny.' She declined his arm. She put up her parasol and together they walked through the heat of the afternoon towards the old house.

Jane Grigg, in her wisdom, immediately took my sister and me to the stableyard. I can see it all as if it were yesterday. She harnessed the piebald pony herself and then drove the governess cart back to the Rectory. She had offered to take Eirlys to stay with us for a few days, an offer firmly declined.

Our father did not come with us. It was only hours later, as the light was falling over the Cotswolds, that the Rector of Nether Molding, tight-lipped and blind to the beauty of the evening, was driven home. His hooded barouche, which through the years had travelled so many miles through Gloucestershire lanes, was a familiar sight in the villages.

He did not leave Windrush Court until Phillippa had gone to bed and seemed likely to sleep, not until everything was in good order and fuss and panic had died down. In the Library there had been an unseemly scramble – bishops and nuns all trying to get hold of Bradshaw, or filch telegram forms from Harold's bureau. There was a battle for grooms and footmen, to send them scurrying off to the post-office or to hire carriages. Featherston produced some kind of cold collation and then, whether from heat, shock or excitement, went quietly mad. He was eventually found in his room, delirious. I have known him since in his dotage, as butler to Eirlys Cole-Hatt in her little house in Montpelier Square. He was never the same again but she was always kind to him. He would always be rambling on about that hot afternoon at Windrush Court . . . he gave me some surprising information.

Doctor Clayton had not hurried over from Stow-on-the-Wold. He had known those palpitations for so many years and was quite unconcerned. He arrived nearly two hours after Harold Gatsby was dead. He was shocked to find a corpse awaiting him but in view of the general state of the heart, of Harold's well-known predilection for the whisky bottle, and the great heat, he gave a certificate without a moment's hesitation, almost without looking. It was only as he was leaving the bedroom that he turned to Featherston – it was an impulse.

'When you brought your master in from the garden, Featherston, what happened? What did you do?'

'Oh, please, sir, just what the mistress had told me. We got him to bed, partly undressed. I sent Beaver – that's the valet, sir – for the brandy and we got a little between his teeth although the jaw seemed locked.'

'Quite. And then he regained consciousness?'

'Yes, Doctor Clayton. Then I was able to do as the mistress had said. It was the white medicine from her own cupboard, sir. Beaver held the mouth open and I managed to pour the correct dose down his throat – his tongue was in a terrible condition – yes, sir, the correct dose – one teaspoonful.'

'Really! Did you say one teaspoonful?'

'Yes, sir, according to the label. And then, sir, it was all terrible, just awful. I have never seen such vomiting. I wouldn't have thought it possible, sir. I thought it would never stop. Then there was a struggle, an arching of the back, sir, and a trembling of the limbs . . . and my poor master died. Father Martin was saying his prayers all the time, sir, and crossing himself and all that . . . and that there nun, sir, was kneeling over there by the chest of drawers. Beaver was very cut up, sir; he had been Colonel Gatsby's gentleman's gentleman for many years, sir.'

'Yes, yes, of course. You all did your best and you did just what Mrs Gatsby had told you to do, Featherston. You have nothing to reproach yourself with. Now the vomit – I suppose you got rid of it – you have a water-closet in the house?'

'Oh, yes, sir – every convenience. I have cleaned up everything myself, sir.'

'You have, Featherston – almost too well. But you are a good fellow. And this is the bottle of medicine. Yes, I see – it's on the label, one teaspoonful. Well, I will keep this.'

Doctor Clayton slipped the bottle into the pocket of his tailcoat. Then he asked for Phillippa. Featherston said she was with the Rector and must not be disturbed. Doctor Clayton could take a hint. He also knew that his own dinner would be waiting for him. Moreover, there was no hurry – he had the bottle.

A temporary coffin – to be inserted later into a more gorgeous affair – had been brought over from Stow-on-the-Wold. By nightfall the late Harold Garlick Gatsby, K.C.B., lay in state before the altar of Pugin's newly gilded chapel. It was all extremely odd. The Churchwarden of Nether Molding was now sprinkled with Holy Water by the Cardinal Archbishop of Westminster, and was laid to rest fortified by the Offices of a Church to which he had never belonged . . . but such was Windrush Court. Phillippa could sleep peacefully. Never in her life had she taken a sedative. There was no reason to do so now. As a woman she had hated her husband and had been his wife only in name – now she was free. As a great hostess she was presenting the right picture to the world – there had been a show of grief and now Harold, high on his catafalque, was covered with the Gatsby pall of martlets sable and volant diapered on a field argent. He was also flanked by six huge candles burning in six huge sconces of gold. Only once did Phillippa wake. She got out of bed and went to the little corner cupboard; the bottle was gone . . . but of course – how stupid of her – Featherston would have left it in Harold's room. It didn't matter. She slept again, without qualms or dreams.

Back in his own Rectory, buried in its wooded valley, Barnabas Barbellion lit his candle in the hall and then went straight up to his bedroom. All was quiet and dark on the landing – Miss Grigg and the children must have been asleep. He was very tired. Standing by the big four-poster, he looked down upon his wife. Emily was such a poor little thing, quite lost and buried among the pillows and bedclothes. As usual she tossed in her sleep . . . the only living thing now between him and everything in the world that he desired.

He knelt at the *prie-dieu*. His prayers, tired though he was, took longer than usual – half an hour or more. One might have thought of Cromwell's phrase – 'wrestling in prayer' – or of Newman in his room at Oriel, his prayers audible all across the quad. As Barbellion climbed into bed he realized that his anguished cries to God had woken Emily from her disturbed sleep.

'You're late, Barnabas, the children were back hours ago.'

'Yes, Emily, I was kept at Windrush Court.'

'You often are . . .'

'I have my duties as a priest. You know that, my dear. I had to give what comfort I could to a poor bereaved parishioner – to Mrs Gatsby in fact. Harold Gatsby died very suddenly this afternoon – he had had a bad heart, you know, and it has been a terribly hot day.'

'Harold Gatsby dead! Oh, dear me, how very sad. Poor dear Mrs Gatsby. I shall pray for her. She was often so kind to me.'

'Kind to you, Emily . . .'

'Oh, yes, she would bring me things – fruits and flowers, and things in jars, you know – soups and jellies and savouries. The Gatsbys have a wonderful chef . . . only last week it was a delicious goulash. And when I was very poorly and could hardly sit up in bed, she would actually feed me herself with a spoon.'

'Really, Emily, I am amazed you never told me this.'

'Oh, yes, and if she was downstairs in the study talking to you about religion and all that, she would send up Eirlys to see me – such a sweet child. Well, and so now her Harold has gone. Dear me, dear me! I suppose we shall have to send a wreath.'

'Yes, Emily, we must send a wreath . . . or a cross, perhaps, as a symbol of suffering.'

'Oh, yes. And at this time of year, Barnabas, there are the roses. They are lovely just now.'

'Yes, dear, red roses will do very nicely . . . blood red.'

'Oh, Barnabas, what a thing to say . . . but red roses, I think, always look so lovely on a coffin.'

3 The Dream of Power

. . . to wade through slaughter to a throne
and shut the gates of mercy on mankind

THOMAS GRAY

And so my father went to Rome. His first visit to the city, as he had told Cardinal Wiseman that afternoon at Windrush Court, had been as a boy. That visit would take us back to the far-off days of Pius the Seventh who had crowned Napoleon in Notre Dame. It would take us back to the time when the Emperor's mother was in the Palazzo Venezia and his sister, his little 'Paulette', was a Roman princess in the Villa Borghese.

Even as a boy Barnabas Barbellion seems to have been bewitched by the 'goings on' inside those churches where he was taken by his Evangelical parents as, so assiduously and as English tourists, they 'did' the sights. The magic of the city, even then, would seem to have entered into his soul. As a boy he already adored every relic, every miracle. He did so to the end of his life. He came to Rome in his father's travelling carriage. With its postilion and courier this luxurious affair had dragged them over the Alps and so in the end across the Campagna, to enter Rome through the Flaminian Gate. And there – his first glimpse of it all – he saw the pines and the walnut trees, and the church built by Paschal the Second . . . whose name, sixty years after, he took unto himself upon the Pontifical Throne.

That had been the planting of the seed. Then came the years at Harrow and Balliol – years of eccentric behaviour, dandaical display and coruscating scholarship – followed by ordination, by the winning of golden opinions, by the preaching of flashy sermons, a useful marriage – £15,000 per annum – the Living at Nether Molding – £7,000 per annum; and then the reorganization of the Diocese of Gloucester rewarded by an Archdeaconry – £3,000 per annum . . . and then after that Windsor, Belgravia and the great country houses . . . and Phillippa Gatsby. Good going, even while still within the Anglican Fold.

And so he came back to Rome. He came, as Wiseman had suggested, in the winter of 1854. He came at the season of Advent – the Advent of 1854 when Pius the Ninth was to proclaim the Dogma of the Immaculate Conception – the dogma that not only was the Mother of Jesus a Virgin 'unspotted by sin' but so also, in her turn, was her mother, the blessed St Anne . . . and so, one must presume, unspotted virgins all the way back to Eve . . . and he who disbelieves it let him be anathema. This rather surprising event, to be saluted by bells, gunfire, balloons and fireworks, was the ostensible reason for Barbellion's journey. He took a lease of that fashionable little house in the Via Tritone – recommended to him by Wiseman – it is still in my family – and there he dined and wined such princesses, eminences and monsignori as could be bothered with him. It must have been hard going – after all he was a nobody in Rome – but in the end it was his ineffable charm, cunning and flattery that triumphed. Nevertheless it was only on the last morning that he found himself actually inside the Vatican. He kissed the Papal toe just in time to catch his train and be home for Christmas.

As to what really happened that Advent, as to his deepest feelings, I have a great deal of evidence. For facts, dates, events, my father's letters to his Emily are enough; they were kept by my sister and I have them now in my Library. They were curt and dry – to write at all was his bare marital duty. By 1854, except as an obstacle, Emily meant nothing to him, but his letters to her are just a little better than nothing.

My richest source, of course, is the famous Barbellion–Wilberforce Correspondence; these are the letters he exchanged with Robert Wilberforce, his croquet partner and his 'dear brother in Christ', the last of the Wilberforces to follow him into the Roman Church. These uninhibited pages were endorsed by both of them as being 'under the seal' but their eventual publication let loose upon the world some of the floodwaters of Barbellion's mind.

There are also revealing remarks – mixed up with admissions of petty failings – 'I hurried my prayers this morning' – in the letters to his Curate-Confessor, Cecil Praz. For these letters, as I have said, I had to pay cash. They had descended to some derelict associate of Praz whom I tracked down with difficulty. It was worth it for a single sentence: 'I have just been told, my dear Cecil, that the Holy Father may not like my marriage; it cannot be permitted that Emily's frail life should frustrate the Will of God ... my own destiny is written in the stars.' And then, of course, there were the letters to Phillippa ...

My father's thoughts during that Roman winter are the key to everything. It was almost certainly in 1854, at the time of the Dogma of the Immaculate Conception and after his Audience with Pius the Ninth, that he made two irrevocable decisions – to join the Roman Church and to murder his wife. That, at least, will always be my own opinion. Naturally it was convenient and only decent, after his return to Nether Molding, that there should be an interval. For a few days he still administered the Anglican sacraments and even, at least in the presence of others, displayed an unwonted affection for Emily. Yet, it must have been during those days, brooding in the Rectory study all through Christmas, when the ponds were frozen and the ground too hard for the grave-diggers, that he planned his great crime ... either then or perhaps a little sooner, as he lay in the sleeping car of the Express as it wound its way from Rome to Paris. But in any case, once the decision had been taken, he would have added, 'And may the Lord have Mercy on her Soul.'

An Advent morning, then, in 1854 ... the Pincian Hill and the Gardens of the Villa Borghese in the December sunshine. All Rome – the fashionable Rome of Pius the Ninth, and indeed the fashionable Rome of all Europe, of the Czar Nicholas, of the Second Empire in France, of the Kingdom of Savoy and of the States of the Church – it was all there under the ilex trees ... glossy mustachios and ringlets, glossy toppers, glossy carriages and horses. There was frost in that luminous air. There was the distant sound of an Austrian band. There were the cries of children at play. There was the gentle music of fountains beyond the cypresses, mingling with the voices and the laughter, with the jingle of harness and the crackle of wheels on watered gravel.

It was all very vivacious, very scintillating. Barnabas Barbellion, however, stood by the balustrade of the Pincian, with his back turned upon it all. He faced the view, not the crowd. He was alone and, with all the world at his back, quite apart. He gazed out over the City – a famous panorama – and now and again raising his binoculars, would identify the buildings and great monuments, all so clear in the winter sunshine. For an hour he had stood like this, utterly alone with his thoughts. He was becoming conspicuous in his isolation. In his curious and emphatically clerical and Anglican way he had seldom looked so impressive – so severe and aloof, so poised and self-conscious . . . in fact, so noticeable.

Roman society, drawn for this very special Advent from the palaces of Europe, from Madrid to Petersburg, stirred behind him – elegant, decadent, seductive and, every now and again, grotesque. They stirred and they talked. Barbellion neither stirred nor talked. He was rigid, as rigid as a column of black basalt. Only his ice-blue eyes moved, sliding to the right, to the left, absorbing all Rome, from the Leonine Hill to the Palatine.

He had always seen himself, even at Harrow, as the hero of some cosmic drama. So now, although only a country parson among cardinals and princes, he had, from sheer habit, to cast himself in some rôle or other, to be the central figure in one of his own perpetual daydreams . . . eternal hero of the World of Barbellion. And upon this occasion he was in no doubt as to what that rôle should be – starry-eyed advance guard of High Anglicanism in the City of the Popes. Barbellion, and Barbellion alone – not that fellow Wiseman – could convert England, leading her back into the arms of the only true Church – a modern Saint Augustine realizing the dreams that Gregory had dreamt a thousand years ago. Barbellion was here in Rome proudly to offer, not humbly to receive.

And yet, somehow, something had gone wrong. He was wondering whether he would even be welcome in this city. His self-consciousness, as always, was boundless; he was aware – and how could he not be – of the fine figure he cut – so tall, so severe, so distinguished, so well-tailored, so forbidding. In the drawing-rooms of London or Gloucestershire, most of all in his own pulpit, his own appearance had always given him immense satisfaction. But now, upon this joyful and very special Advent day, he felt rather less self-satisfied than usual – much less. It was inexplicable. He not only felt out of place but also, which was odd, unduly conscious of himself and of his clothes . . . and in the wrong way. He always dressed with care – a cold bath and an hour in his dressing-room every morning, even in Lent. His garb, of course, was always black – even his gloves – but it was immaculate and correct, his crucifix his only jewel. And yet, somehow, he seemed to be so different, from those priests over there, for instance, strolling so nonchalantly by the grotto; he felt so Anglican rather than Roman, so pastoral rather than sacerdotal, so gaitered rather than cassocked. Why, even that 'crocodile' of seminarists, youthful and smooth-faced in their soutanes and soup-plate hats, seemed nearer to Christ than did the Gloucestershire Rector.

This was terrible. His carefully cultivated, if rather funereal austerity, seemed – here in Rome – to shame him, to set him apart. He usually loved to feel set apart – after all he was not as other men – but now he felt set apart to his own detriment. Incredibly he felt himself to be, if not a freak, at least an oddity. It was inescapable – his very clothes had become a humiliation.

This feeling of humiliation was to him as a nagging tooth. He put it from his mind. It came back. It was not only unbearable, it was impossible. Why should he, of all people, he, Barnabas Barbellion, feel odd? This must be something far deeper than his appearance, something perhaps upon which his very salvation might depend. Who was he? What was he, not in the eyes of this worldly crowd in the Borghese Garden, but in the eyes of his Creator? Was not he, too, like those nonchalant figures by the grotto, also a priest of God? But was he? His Apostolic Descent, surely, was beyond doubt, no less certain than theirs – but was it? For years, ever since his ordination, it had been the very centre of his being. Barnabas Barbellion, he told himself every morning when he woke up, was a priest, a priest by the laying-on of hands, all the way back to Peter and to Jesus – a priest by Apostolic Succession. It could never be otherwise, whether in this world or the next – 'a priest forever'. That is what he had always believed and yet, somehow, suddenly, here in Rome, it seemed that just possibly it might not be so.

Was it perhaps that some strange Roman spell was beginning to work upon him? He knew that it had happened to others but he, surely, was different. He brushed the thought aside. It came back. True, his ordination had been within the Anglican Fold, but then surely that Fold, reformed though it may have been by King Henry, was still part of Christ's one and only Catholic Church . . . or was it? As he stood there on the Pincian Hill, with all Rome below him, Anglicanism, Oxford, Canterbury, Westminster, the Royal Supremacy, even the Diocese of Gloucester, all seemed so very far away . . . they all seemed so much less certain and, yes, so terribly provincial. Doubt, that winter morning, was raising her ugly head.

At Oxford, years ago, he had known, naturally, all about Tractarianism and the great Anglican Revival. Those were the years when all Oxford was thick with sanctity. He had been part of it. He had known Keble and Pusey and Hurrell Froude; he had been stirred by Newman's dramatic Conversion, and by all those young men who had followed Newman into the Roman Church . . . all so pure, so pale and intense, so concerned with their own 'high, severe ideal of chastity', and with the state of their own souls. All that, he told himself, had been part of his life and yet, somehow, at the time he had been immune to it. He had known that for him chastity was just not possible – already there was Phillippa – and so here he was . . . an Anglican priest from an English village. And yet, thanks to Oxford, he had exorcized the ghosts of his Evangelical childhood – the ghost of Rome as the 'Scarlet Woman', the ghosts of the wicked Jesuits and the Inquisition . . . he stood today, on the Pincian, both an English rector and a man who adored Rome. He adored ritual; every day of his life he invoked the Saints and Our Lady; he would talk of the Eucharist; he absolved sins and upon his altar he kept the sacramental elements within a pyx of gold and chrysoprase. But nevertheless he was still, so far, an Anglican. His priesthood was real and must, therefore, be within the true Church . . . but where, oh where, was that Church to be found? He could hardly believe that he would ever have to ask such a question, but now, within sight of the Vatican, it was beating upon his brain.

He was a priest, with the power to bind and to loose; nothing else was conceivable. And yet . . . over there, across Tiber, on the

Leonine Hill, he wondered whether he would be a priest at all. He had come to Rome to be received, honoured and welcomed – Wiseman had assured him of that. He felt sure that he would be invited to preach in some really fashionable church. But now that he was actually here, it was all so different. The most impossible things suddenly seemed possible. Could it be that through the years he had lived in schism, in sin, that even *his* salvation was in doubt? Here in Rome it seemed perfectly possible. Here in Rome he might be nothing more, it would seem, than a Methodist preacher or a Salvation Army lass.

And yet, only a year ago, in white and gold and purple, he had preached the Christmas morning sermon in Westminster Abbey. After the service Mr Gladstone had said that no power on Earth could keep him from a mitre. That had lifted him to the very Seventh Heaven of Delight. But now he seemed to be nobody, just one of the small fry of this rich, cosmopolitan and crowded city. Even a mitre, a mere English mitre, suddenly seemed so dull. Here, in the Borghese Gardens, in the winter sunlight, it was the round scarlet hat, with its fifteen pendant tassels, that shimmered in the air before him.

This was the Agony in the Garden. The ice-blue eyes closed. The lips moved as he murmured a 'Hail Mary' and then the mouth tightened. The fists at his side were clenched. He winced. He was being crucified. He could hear all the sounds of the throng behind him – the voices, the fountains, the laughter, the children, the horses and the distant band. He could even smell the gentlemen's cigars. He could feel, or he imagined that he could feel, a thousand eyes boring into his back – stares of curiosity or of contempt. Worse still, perhaps they were not even bothering to stare.

Then, quite suddenly, such was his resilience, he found an explanation. He was alone . . . it was the immense loneliness of the Northern heretic in the Catholic South. He was a spiritual alien. He was alone in the most ancient and sophisticated of all cultures – the old, old world of the Mediterranean – the world not only of the Madonna and of the Saints, but the even older world of 'wine dark seas', of marble temples upon headlands, of Zeus and Artemisia, of the Legions and of Constantine. He was out of his depth.

There were all these fabulous creatures behind him in the Borghese Gardens – creatures who belonged to this world of the South. They were Romans or they were guests of Rome – guests of the Vicar of Christ – whereas Barbellion was only a tourist . . . with a couple of letters of introduction in his bag. These creatures, all bowing and chattering, were the élite of the Earth and he could not even share a chalice with them. He looked over the City. Michelangelo's dome glittered in the frosty air. The Rectory at Nether Molding – with Cecil Praz reading Matins, the children playing in the garden, and Emily so pale and prayerful . . . it was all more infinitely distant than the farthest stars.

This, he told himself, just would not do. Only twenty-four hours ago, as the night-express pulled into Rome, he had been trembling with excitement, the excitement of ambition and high purpose. When he entered his little house in the Via Tritone he had been almost sick with excitement. And now this! It was absurd. His 'mission' had hardly begun. He must pull himself together. Only two hours ahead was his luncheon with Monsignor Talbot, the Papal Chamberlain; that might change everything, for him and for mankind. One could not put it too high.

So . . . he might be a trifle homesick but he had nothing to fear. He was still what he had always been – the Lord's Anointed. He stiffened his shoulders. He raised the binoculars. Below him, far down in the pine-scented bowl, he could see the cavalry coming from the Corso into the Piazza del Popolo. The Zouaves were fanning out to take their places around the obelisk, wheeling their white horses as if in some equine ballet. Even from here, high on the Pincian Mount, Barnabas can see the swords flash. It is almost noon – the crucial hour of this Immaculate Conception Day. At dawn he had heard the minute guns firing from the Janiculum and from the Quirinale – a preliminary rumble. In a few minutes now all the cannon of the Catholic World will fire their salutes and then a great hush will descend upon Rome . . . to be broken in the end by the bells from three hundred and sixty churches.

His heart seemed to miss a beat. He again focused the glasses upon St Peter's dome. Later, its curves would be traced in the blue evanescent evening by a thousand tiny Bengal lights. Even now, at midday, he could see the black cluster of figures around the cupola, with hundreds more on the leaded roofs. He was fascinated. He was the rabbit and St Peter's was the snake. His eyes moved to behold the mass of the Vatican Palace. The hard mouth twitched and the whites of the eyes showed all around the ice-blue iris. He had never seen the Dalai Lama's palace at Lhasa, nor the Forbidden City of Pekin. It would have made no difference; that long windowless wall screening the Court of the Belvedere would always be to him the shrine of the God-King. He thought of Lambeth and sneered.

That palace over there across the river – could it ever be his home . . . Ruler of the World, Source of all Salvation. He pushed the thought aside. It came back. It was so delicious. But of course it was absurd. Why was it absurd? He was not yet forty. It was not too late. All those desperate, virginal young men from the Oriel Common Room – they had found peace within the arms of the Holy Roman Church; they had all been welcomed as the first swallows of a great summer – the Conversion of England. Why had he never been among them? Suddenly he knew. Their Conversion, for all the stir it had caused, had in fact been a humdrum affair, mere theological hair-splitting. His would be glorious. He had been kept back by God for this moment. They, it is true, had wrestled with their souls in prayer before saying farewell forever to their Anglican friends, but while Newman's Conversion may have shaken England, Barbellion's would be celebrated on High. It would be an apotheosis, like that of Saul on the road to Damascus. He would pass, as it were, trailing clouds of glory, from Gloucestershire to Rome; there would be Hosannas in Heaven and a leading article in *The Times*.

He turned his binoculars downwards, glimpsing the Piazza del Popolo between the dark foliage of the stone pines. The cavalry was now drawn up in meticulous ranks. The cannon had been wheeled into position. The hour of the Virgin had almost struck.

He turned to take one more look over Rome. He recalled how Edward Gibbon – it must have been eighty years ago – had pondered upon the barefooted friars chanting in a near-by church, contrasting them with the ruined marbles of the Caesars and the Empire lying all around . . . and had then written his history. Barbellion thought also of a saying of Hobbes's that 'the papacy is not other than the ghost of the deceased Roman Empire sitting upon the grave thereof'. Yes, surely it was so. He thought of the legionaries outside the walls of York, raising Constantine upon their shields, to become the first Christian Emperor of the world . . . an event second only to the Resurrection and, moreover, an English event. And if Constantine, then why not Barbellion?

So his confused mind ran on seeking balm for his bruised vanity. In the World of Barbellion he had only to think of Caesar and, behold, he was Caesar. So now, on this stage that he was conjuring out of the Roman air, he had to play a leading rôle . . . Caesar or Pope, what did it matter, they were all Pontifex Maximus, Divine Kings. And then he came back to earth.

Down there among the streets of Rome, city of steps and fountains, he could pick out the line of the Corso, also in the clear air the bulk of the Capitol and of the Palazzo Farnese. Far off, beyond the slums of the Trastevere, was the dark foliage of the Gardens of the Villa Pamphilia Doria. And then he found what he was really looking for.

The great dome of the Pantheon, for all its breadth, was low and inconspicuous. He remembered that a thousand years ago it had been covered with golden tiles to make of it a golden sphere to reflect the sun. Hadrian had built it as a sky temple – all symbolic of sun, moon and stars. Barbellion pondered upon Hadrian, that restless Spaniard, marching his armies across Europe and across it, from Solway to Babylon. He thought of him building his great cavernous temple – appeasing the Heavens until Christ came to soothe all fears . . . and it was Hadrian, not Christ, to whom at that moment Barbellion was offering his prayers.

Swinging round his binoculars he now discovered Trajan's Column, triumphal banner of a thousand victories. He remembered how Trajan, with a flotilla of purple sails, had gone down the Euphrates and out on to the Persian Gulf – Roman ships upon Arabian seas. And how, lying there with Antinous, naked upon the sun-baked decks, he had dreamt of a Roman India. India – and Barbellion's mind habitually took these great leaps – was British now. Why, therefore, should it not be Christian . . . not the insipid Christianity of the Missionary Society, but a whole continent of baptized Rajahs. Then, one day, as Cardinal of England, he would lay this vast province at the Pope's feet . . . how many million souls saved from perdition? Barbellion was almost choking with excitement. A puff of smoke rose from one of the Seven Hills, then from the others. The cannon were booming out their salute to the Immaculate Conception. It was noon.

He turned his back upon the panorama of Rome, to face the crowd in the Gardens. The occasional strident laugh, a coachman's command to his horses, the slamming of a carriage door, the yapping of a poodle, the chatter of a Punchinello, children at play – he had been close to these things all morning and only momentarily had they interrupted his dark and exotic thoughts. He had been far away with his dreams but now, now, he found himself deeply envious of all this smart and heraldic elegance, all these personable men attendant upon all these seductive women . . . they had so much self-confidence, so much sophistication, such an air.

But then, really, he was looking upon an astonishing sight, and a beautiful one . . . if only Manet or Boudin had been born in time to paint it for us. The undulating turf, the little dells and groves and, here and there, the white flash of an old marble bust or a lichened god . . . the Gardens stretched for nearly a mile, from the Pincian Mount to the Villa Borghese where governesses and children were at the windows. The grass, after autumn rains, was emerald, while the foliage of ilex, cypress, pine and laurel was black – the magnolias tall and glossy. Jets and cascades tumbled and sparkled among the shadows. It was all an echo of Respighi's symphonic poem . . . one remembered that Velasquez had walked this way.

And now, as the cannon boomed, it all quivered with life. There were, perhaps, two or three thousand people, so much confetti spilt upon the green carpet. But this confetti moved, all coloured fragments revolving as in a toy kaleidoscope . . . or like tropical birds in a gigantic aviary. They fluttered and bowed and talked without cessation, each speck of colour, to the last lemon-tinted glove, to the last osprey, clear-cut in the cold air.

This was the year '54. As Cardinal Wiseman had observed only a few months ago, at the Windrush Court croquet party, the year of the largest crinolines God ever made – coloured, embroidered and tapestried beneath vast panniers of satin. Thrown over them, this winter day, were mantles twinkling with diamanté or jet, mantles of black lamb or ermine, large Spanish shawls. There were darker notes of bottle-green, chocolate and deep blue – the gentlemen's swallow-tails, dark above the white and beige of nankeen trousers, trousers strapped ever so tightly. And over there, on the sunny side, little girls in pantalettes bowled their hoops while little boys in sailor suits flew their Chinese kites.

The nursemaids gossiped around their bassinettes – each bassinette beribboned in honour of the Virgin. In such a polychromatic scene it is always the blacks that matter – the priests were enough, so many crows among the Birds of Paradise. Under the trees a few *carrozzi* plied for hire – all jingling bells – but were outnumbered by all the elegant carriages. Some of these had been driven on to the grass where footmen were unpacking luncheon hampers . . . really it might have been Longchamp or Ascot.

And now, at this moment, there arrived a most gilded and rococo coach. Four black Barbary horses had lugged it up the hill from the Vatican to the Borghese. A cardinal – an aged cardinal – having sat like a painted mummy to be drawn through the streets, a scarlet flamingo draped in galloon lace, was now offering his ring to rosebud lips and to the seminary boys. Barbellion glowered. He should have been that cardinal; he would have done it all so well, so much better, with such an air.

Moreover – and this was what wounded his conceit – he knew nothing of this High European society. All the Almanach de Gotha was there and he did not even know the names of these Polish counts, Spanish princesses and Bavarian barons, let alone which was currently committing adultery with which. In spite of himself he was vastly impressed by it all – and this annoyed him. This was the Catholic laity. It had to be captured. His lip curled, his eyes closed, his shoulders were hunched. His contempt for them all was equalled only by his envy. One moment he told himself that they were probably all whores and libertines; the next he desperately craved their company. They are rotten, he muttered to himself, absolutely rotten. Then something else, something outside himself – the Holy Ghost perhaps – told him that one day they would grovel to him, that one day he would deal out his benedictions to them, his anathemas, dispensations and excommunications, as if they were no more to him than the old women in the cottages at Nether Molding.

But now the last salute had been fired – the smoke was clearing – and upon the Borghese there descended a great stillness. Barbellion knew exactly what was happening all around the world. Down there in the Corso they were throwing flowers and wearing comic masks. Everywhere statues were being hauled on to pillars and pedestals. At that moment, in the Piazza di Spagna, a starry-crowned Virgin was being winched slowly on to her Corinthian column; there was another in Munich and one in Lisbon. In the streets of Naples they would have put out iron baskets on poles so that with the night the smoky flames would rise into the sky. All the gondolas of Venice, pennants flying, would at this moment be in procession down the Grand Canal, while tonight the rockets would scream over the Lagoon. The Puerta del Sol in Madrid was carpeted with lilies. At the other end of Europe, at St Basil's by the Kremlin, the peasants were coming in from the snow to watch the lighting of a thousand blue lamps hung from gold mosaic – blue for virginity. Cardinal Wiseman would be saying a special Mass at Moorfields – a catena of Masses – and Father Faber would be doing the same in Brompton. In the dark small hours of a Chicago night candlelit churches would be packed to the doors. In the grey wet dawn of Limerick they knelt as the banners went by.

The Papal flag rose over the Castel St Angelo . . . a signal *urbi et orbi.* In the Sistine Chapel, the Pope, 'Father of Princes and Kings', before a congregation of princes and kings, was declaring the Virgin Mary as being of immaculate descent through all time. The great stillness in the Borghese Gardens now gave way to a flurry of devotion. The little girls had stopped bowling their hoops. The little boys had pulled down their kites. The footmen had stopped unpacking hampers to stare respectfully into the scarlet linings of cockaded hats. Close to Barbellion a dozen Thuringian nuns on a marble bench had turned round and knelt, thus converting the bench into a *prie-dieu.*

They were throwing out carriage cushions on to the turf that gentlemen might kneel without soiling those nankeen trousers. The priests, more ascetic, knelt on gravel – gravel now thawing to dampness – doffing birettas proudly to display tonsures. The seminarists were torturing their knees upon the cobbles, casting perplexed eyes to Heaven, the Immaculate Conception being far too sexy to explain to adolescents.

Again Barbellion felt conspicuous. Laying his handkerchief upon a marble slab he too knelt, but to kneel is not to pray. He was all eyes, knowing and alert, studying these beautiful degenerates so carefully. With his Evangelical childhood he might have been shocked; he was not shocked; he was fascinated – fascinated by these children of Satan whom he was destined to rule, whose souls he was destined to save.

This was a society that could, very nearly, recall the First Empire, those great days when 'Genoa and Lucca were family estates of the Buonapartes'. That old roué over there, for instance, lounging back in his carriage, puffing his cigar, was he not the Hyppolyte Charles, the Empress Josephine's first lover, once famous on the boulevards for the 'beauty of his hips'? This was a society born in the Vienna of Metternich . . . the Congress that Danced was the source of all its proud legitimacy. Barbellion quite suddenly realized, with a pang, that the strict morality and marital bliss of Balmoral and Windsor had never crossed the Channel . . . was undreamt of here. England suddenly seemed dowdy.

He looked carefully at those nearest to him. There might, he thought, be one or two whom he had met in London drawing-rooms – the drawing-rooms of the old Catholic squires, Wardours, Jerninghams, Talbots and the rest . . . they, surely, should be here for the Immaculate Conception or, on second thoughts, perhaps not – not in the hunting season. There might be a few others – kings or queens – whom he would know from their portraits or their fame.

Yes, sure enough, over there, with his ugly snout, was 'Bomba', the sadistic King of the Two Sicilies, and of Naples. He was kneeling by his own carriage – a yellow Berlin – while sharing a breviary with his Yorkshire jockey. But then the Borghese, that sunny morning, was sprinkled with various jockeys, prize-fighters and card-sharpers – 'personal gentlemen without credentials'. There were other oddities – splendours and miseries of humanity.

Quite near to him, for instance, buried in the pillows of a huge bath-chair, was a hag so old, so dim, toothless and tremulous, that she might well be a hundred. Later he asked about her. She had, it seemed, as midwife and wet-nurse to Pius the Eighth, been mildly ennobled. But now she could burble only of Byron – Byron in Rome – and of her own eleven children: seven sons all colonels in the crack cavalry regiments of seven countries, four daughters all Sisters of St Vincent de Paul . . . seven sons with corsets, four daughters without. The old woman was deaf and blind – a white film was on her eyes. She waved a lorgnette to make people think she could see – a lorgnette in one hand, a crucifix in the other.

And now, there under the vine *treillage*, was the grandest of all the carriages, its cream panels blazing with two-headed eagles and high Slavonic crowns. The footmen were powdered, the outrider had his sword drawn. There should have been an escort of the Preobajensky Guard. The Czar Nicholas the First, however, with his Guard outside the doors, was kneeling in the Sistine, kneeling between Spain and Austria; and so, for his Czaritsa and Czarevich a single outrider must suffice. Barbellion merely noted that this former Lutheran princess was rather handsome in a florid and Germanic way – too *en bon point* for his taste. His virility remained unstirred. The Czarevich, upright at her side, was another matter – waxen, pale, delicate, heavy-lidded, the quintessence of etiolated decadence.

And now, over there, at last, was a woman he actually knew, or knew by sight. Undoubtedly this was the Princess Bourbon-Parma. He could see that her eyes were closed, long lashes lying piously and also deliciously upon velvet cheeks. He thought he must be looking upon the most beautiful woman in the world; he often thought this but for once he may have been right. Two years ago, when the English royals were at Badminton – and a few Gloucestershire clergy were invited – he had seen her dance the *polonaise* with Albert . . . memories came rushing back so that the binoculars trembled in his hands.

It was hard to tear himself away from long lashes on velvet cheeks, but once more he began his hunt for some acquaintance. He found none; but there – twenty yards away – was a carriage no less grand than that of the Czaritsa – the postilions, indeed, were the only ones in Rome outside the Vatican. The whole equipage was very *distingué*, carrying with it an air of the Palais Royal so that even the cardinal's lumbering coach was made to seem shabby. Barbellion studied the canted heraldry – an hortensia, an eagle and the Napoleonic bee. This, then, must be the young and lovely Eugénie, Empress of the French, and so new to the throne. The young man, one arm resting nonchalantly on the carriage door – he must be the Prince Imperial, so unaware that somewhere in the world an assegai was waiting for him. Eugénie meant nothing to Barbellion, nor did her son, nor did her syphilitic Emperor at that moment watching the clouds of Sistine incense around the yellow tapers. They none of them meant anything to him – not really – except that having been born in sin they might one day be his penitents, on the floor at his footstool . . . and so once again his thoughts were away and away . . . in dreams of power.

And now the Borghese ceremony – although one could hardly call it that – was over. The cardinal, from some kind of wooden pulpit, was showering blessings and short-sightedly sprinkling holy water on the grass. Near by the Archbishop of Paris, Darboy, destined to be slaughtered in his own cathedral, choking in his own blood, had set up a rival shop; standing upright in his carriage he was flinging benedictions promiscuously around him.

But it was over. The Papal banner had been hauled down. The chatter had begun again. The band had started to play and the Punch and Judy show to chirp. The footmen unpacked the hampers for those who would brave the December sun. For the rest the horses' heads were turned and away they went to exotic luncheons in the Hotel Bristol or in palaces of yellow stucco . . . and then, after that, the siesta. Wistfully Barbellion watched the coaches, the postilions, the priests and the bassinettes until they had all gone. Then, utterly alone, he walked across the grass and hired a *carrozza*.

They had all gone off to their own devices. Later they would fill St Peter's for a great Te Deum. Barbellion would be there too, kneeling with them on the marble pavement . . . they could hardly deny him that. And then, that night, they would all be there again in the Villa Pamphilia Doria – fireworks in the sky and both banks of the Tiber blazing with light – the Ball of the Five Emperors. He might have danced with the Princess Parma-Bourbon . . . it would have been the valse, in his view the most intimate and most pleasant of dances. He might . . . but in fact he would not. He had not been invited.

It was not until within a few days of Christmas that he found himself in the presence of Pius the Ninth, kissing the toe and being offered a crimson chair. Rome had been packed, every ambassador demanding an Audience for his royal master. There was always somebody's carriage waiting at the bronze doors of the Scala Regia. Even the Swiss Guards, those arch-snobs of Europe, had become blasé, while a mere English clergyman had to take his turn . . . and his turn came last.

Those days of waiting were not all loss, neither were they easy. Cardinal Wiseman – so amiable and so persuasive as they ate their strawberries under the deodars that afternoon at Windrush – had promised so much. But now my father, I think, although he never said so, felt that Wiseman had let him down. True, there was the letter to Monsignor Talbot – the starting point – and there was also a letter to the English College. True also that the little *palazzo* in the Via Tritone had materialized in all its charm. Wiseman, however, had never warned him that the rent would be exorbitant nor that the landlord, upon Barbellion's arrival, would clap on an Immaculate Conception Surcharge of some thousand lira a week. Wiseman had fixed no date for an Audience – he left Barbellion to play his own cards with Monsignor Talbot as best he could. The English College gave him a cool welcome. He had hoped to say a few words to the boys – possibly on some ecumenical theme with an analogy drawn from cricket. He was politely received, had to listen to much praise of dear Father Newman, was given coffee, and as politely dismissed.

However, there was no doubt about the charm of his little house. Its *sala* had marble floors, it had a painted ceiling and a few lovely Della Robbias on the walls. At the back, through glass doors, the fountain tinkled in a tiny orange garden. It was all very chic and very pretty. He had to exploit it as best he could. On the second day he hired a smart carriage and a good cook. For all that, these weeks of social climbing, of flattering, of leaving cards and of being snubbed, were exhausting. These weeks of dining and wining as many princes and monsignori as would submit – they too took their toll. There were times when he yearned for the warm familiar comforts of the Rectory study, his slippers by the fire, the *Diocesan Journal* and a French novel. He also yearned for Phillippa.

The letter from Wiseman to Monsignor Talbot worked rather better – John Talbot, the fat Camerlingo, Chamberlain to the Papal Court, the *éminence grise* who, so dramatically, would change Barbellion's life. It was on the evening of 18 December – and Barbellion remembered it ever afterwards in his prayers – that Talbot brought with him to the Via Tritone the young Cardinal-Deacon, Francesco Cavalle, and also Niask, Cardinal Bishop of the Sacred College.

For these priests, so near the Throne, to dine with this unknown heretic was indeed a feather in Barbellion's shovel hat. They were given a very good dinner. They talked late over their coffee, their cigars and their liqueurs. By the time they kissed their farewells the room was thick with smoke, with theology, malice and intrigue. Moreover, thanks no doubt to the Holy Ghost, millions of souls had been saved. It had been a good evening.

Cavalle and Niask parted in the moonlit shadows of the Colonnades.

'These Protestants, Your Eminence, I shall never understand them. They are all the same. They think God is an Englishman.'

Cavalle laughed.

'True, my Lord Cardinal, but don't you see that that is their strength. Do not underestimate them.'

'And this man Barbellion – he will come over to us, like Newman and his gang, another fish to our net?'

'Of course, otherwise he would not be here. Wiseman would not put us to all this trouble for nothing. No, mark my words, my Lord Cardinal, this is not just one more Conversion. The Church has not heard the last of this Barbellion, this – er – this Archdeacon as he is called in the Anglican Heresy. Remember – we shall hear of him again. Well, it is late and I have an early Mass tomorrow, so good-night to you, dear Cavalle.'

'Good-night, Your Eminence.'

The friendship with Talbot ripened very quickly. A later generation was to see it as an historic friendship. Talbot and Barbellion found that they could be of use to each other and that was all that mattered. They would write to each other with great regularity. Newman, Faber, Wiseman, Palmerston, Gladstone, Acton, the Fenians, the Queen – not one of them would be able to lift a finger, whether in London, Oxford or Dublin, but that it would be known in the Vatican by the next mail. And on the other side . . . well, every morning of his life Talbot had the ear of the Supreme Pontiff. That was enough. Between Talbot and Barbellion there arose a solemn pact.

'Do not worry, dear Barbellion. Do not push yourself. One must never push oneself in Rome. I will speak for you, suavely and blandly. Your name will always be upon my master's table – as if by chance. It is very strange but I have always noticed that what I wish comes to pass. Come over to us, dear Barbellion, come over to us. We will look after you . . . but always of course it will be for our Dear Saviour's sake, for the sake of His Church . . .'

'Of course, my dear Talbot. One would not have it otherwise. Advancement, authority – what are these but dust and ashes, useful only because of what one may do with them. And we together could surely do so much, as you say, for His Church . . .' And he crossed himself.

'Of course, of course. All the cards are in our hands. We have only to play them as the Holy Ghost may direct.'

That Talbot certainly, and Barbellion, were already as mad as hatters – should have been obvious in 1854. It seems likely that in that week before Christmas both men, in their own minds, were already setting out to rule the world. One cannot but think so. Barbellion, as it happened, never entered an asylum; Talbot died in one – a very expensive one at Passy. That was the difference between the two men.

A Papal audience for Barbellion was now certain and in the days of waiting he and Talbot were exceedingly close to each other. When it was cold and the *tramontane* whistled down from the Apennines these two Englishmen would sit before a very English fire of cedar logs, drinking punch. When the sun shone they would walk in the Vatican Gardens, in the soundless grass-grown lanes of the Trastevere or by crumbling aqueducts – their heads together. Then, when one could almost smell the Roman spring, they would drive out to Castel Gondolfo and to the Alban Hills to walk in wooded paths above the Lake of Nemi – that magical lake, so round and deep and dark. Perhaps it was there, by Diana's ruined temple, remembering her sinister and Pagan rites – torches flickering in midsummer woods, and the priest, sword in hand, prowling around his shrine, 'the priest who was the slayer and shall himself be slain' . . . perhaps it was there, thinking upon the nature of that other priesthood, infinitely older than Christ, that these two men went off their heads.

It was one frosty evening, driving back into Rome, that Monsignor Talbot broke the news.

'Be ready tomorrow at ten o'clock, dear Barbellion. I will call for you in one of *our* carriages . . . correct archidiaconal attire of course, with, I think – yes, definitely *with* your pectoral cross. His Holiness has an hour to spare.'

The obeisance being over, Pius the Ninth offered him a chair, which was more than his own Queen would have done. It was a baroque chair, designed by Fontana in 1589 for Sixtus the Fifth – gold and scarlet. The Vatican is like that.

'And so, my dear Archdeacon, this is your first visit to the Eternal City as we like to call it, those of us who live here.'

'The first since I was a boy, nearly thirty years ago. How much has happened since then, Your Holiness, both in your Church and in mine.'

Pius the Ninth ignored the opening thus offered him. Why come to the point so quickly – how English! He would do it, but in his own way.

'And to what, Archdeacon, do we owe the pleasure of your visit? Monsignor Talbot told me that you wished to come to me, and so here you are. But I am at a loss, pray enlighten me.'

'The real occasion of my visit to Rome, Your Holiness, was the blessed and marvellous Dogma of the Immaculate Conception.'

'Quite, quite, but that, surely, is not an Anglican doctrine – not yet. Am I not right?'

'Alas, yes, Your Holiness, but, as I was saying, things are changing in England. So much so that I myself – if I may speak humbly and personally – cannot remain much longer within our Anglican

Communion – a few weeks more perhaps. I can no longer partake of the Anglican sacraments.'

Once again the Pontifical eyebrows were raised, but Barbellion was allowed to continue.

'The last few years, Your Holiness, have indeed been a time of most blessed and Divine intervention – the Catholic Emancipation Act, Roman dioceses set up in England, the Oxford Movement, Newman's Conversion, Cardinal Wiseman's great mission to convert the English . . .'

'I am aware of the facts, Archdeacon. My staff keep me in touch with events, even in the smallest heretical countries. But what is *your* mission to me? Please come to the point.'

The Pope glanced at the big ormolu clock.

'In a nutshell then, Your Holiness, it is to ask upon what terms – if I may use so crude a word – upon what terms our two Churches, with God's blessing, may enter into communion one with the other. It is a weighty question but I know, Your Holiness, I know that the Holy Ghost has guided me into asking it.'

Pius the Ninth never hesitated.

'The lost sheep, Archdeacon, will always be welcomed back into the Fold. There is more joy in Heaven over one sinner that repenteth . . .'

'Oh, quite, Your Holiness, but upon what terms?'

'The Doctrines of the Council of Trent are clear. What more do you want?'

'Alas! Your Holiness, for so many of my brethren they are also unbridgeable.'

'Alas! Archdeacon, they are also irreformable. You must know that.'

It was a dusty answer. Barbellion changed the subject.

'Rome, Your Holiness, is a great feast of beautiful and glorious churches. Had my stay here been long enough I would have wished to preach – on some ecumenical subject perhaps. I speak Italian.'

'Ah, yes, Archdeacon. There is, I understand, an Anglican church, without the walls of course. You would surely be most welcome there.'

It was another dusty answer. Barbellion tried again.

'At least, Your Holiness, my own mind is made up. A little time to put my affairs in order and then – it is all arranged – Father Dominic the Passionist who received our dear Newman into Christ's Church, he will do the same service for me.'

'That is indeed a blessed thing. Your fame as a theologian and as a preacher has reached us here in Rome. We have a place for you. Come over to us, dear Barbellion, we will look after you.'

'The decision is already taken, Your Holiness. It is irrevocable.'

'Praise be to God! Come, my son, kneel here in front of me.'

Barbellion knelt, folding his hands on his breast.

'And now, Barnabas – *Benedicat te, Omnipotens Deus, Pater, et Filius ✠ et Spiritus Sanctus. Amen.*'

The hand was held out. As Barbellion leaned forward to put his lips to the ring he could see the tiny fisherman's barque engraved upon the amethyst. He was raised up and kissed.

'And now, my son, go in peace.'

The Audience was over. Talbot was at his elbow to conduct him through the great marble corridors, back to the world. The Pope came to the door of the room.

'And so, Archdeacon, you will be with us for Christmas – the great midnight Mass . . .'

'Alas! No, Your Holiness. I take the Paris Express this afternoon. An English Christmas is, I fear, a very domestic festival; I must get back to my wife and little ones.'

It was a disastrous utterance, the most disastrous of his life. The silence was thunderous. He could have bitten off his tongue. For days he had hardly given a thought to Emily or to home . . . and now it had slipped out like this. The three men stood immobile, silent and shocked. It was Talbot who first found his own voice.

'Married! Married! Oh! And you never told me . . .'

'I never thought . . .'

'If only you had . . . oh, if only he had, Holy Father, I would never have troubled you. What was dear Wiseman thinking of. . . ?'

'I met Wiseman only at a garden party. My wife was not there – she is an invalid. I am deeply sorry, but . . .

The Pope raised his hands to silence them.

'It does not really matter, Talbot. His soul has been saved. His academic qualifications are sound. You went to Balliol, I think, Archdeacon. Well then, in a seminary – yes, even the Jesuits allow it – a Catholic layman can teach Latin, Greek and Hebrew to the boys. Yes, yes, dear sir, we will give you a job as a schoolmaster.'

'But, Your Holiness.' I am already a priest . . . a priest forever according to the Order of Melchiztdek.'

'Do not kick against the pricks, sir. You know – you must know – that from the moment Father Dominic receives you into the Church you cease to be a priest. Doubtless, in normal circumstances your ordination could soon follow, quite quickly. But the circumstances are not normal. You are not celibate.'

'But, Holy Father, if a man is *already* a priest . . .'

'Pooh! An Anglican and married at that.'

'But I shall be chaste. Ever since I was at Oxford I have understood the high, severe Catholic ideal of celibacy. Ever since my daughter was born twelve years ago I have been continent. And now – why now, I will "put my wife away privily".'

'Really, sir, you would compare yourself to the Blessed Saint Joseph.'

'Not that, Your Holiness, not that of course . . . but something surely . . . something can be arranged. Your own Pontifical powers . . .'

'. . . have no effect in English Law, in the sight of which you are a married man.'

'I see that, Your Holiness, but what matters now, surely, is my status in the Catholic Church. Your own powers . . . there are precedents – our own Henry the Eighth, Napoleon . . . hundreds of others.'

'You, if I may say so, Archdeacon, are not in that category. You are married and "whom God hath joined together . . ." but there, I need not quote your own Prayer Book to you. You have had my blessing. Now go, Barnabas Barbellion, back to connubial bliss and your Anglican altar.'

Spring comes early in Rome and before Monsignor Talbot had heard from Barbellion again, the City was filled with the scent of thyme and rosemary as well as dung. Once Epiphany was past the Pope had gone out to Castel Gondolfo, where he worked a little, played bridge and sipped wine, all to the music of cicadas and cascades.

Monsignor Talbot had remained in Rome. He had business to do – he always had business to do – and was working that morning in his room next to the Private Apartments. It was warm. The Papal Chamberlain wore long combinations beneath his serge cassock. His big body was gently sweating. He was a fat and sweaty man.

He sorted his letters. From England, as always, there was Cardinal Wiseman's diplomatic bag. There were bags from almost every country in the world – Catholic, Protestant and Heathen. There was also a single letter from England. John Talbot was still English enough to know that the post mark, Stow-on-the-Wold, was the postal town for Nether Molding. He had expected this for days but as he slit the envelope he was conscious of a quiver of excitement. His plump hands flattened the paper upon the table.

The Rectory,
Nether Molding,
Gloucestershire.
Septuagesima, 1855.

My dear Monsignor Talbot,

Every day I remember you in my prayers. Since my return from Rome I have said ten masses for you. I remember as if it were yesterday our wonderful talks as we strolled in the Alban woods and by the Lake of Nemi. How could I forget them when they were so unforgettable?

It is a truism to say that God works in a mysterious way. Our sorest afflictions may prove to be our greatest blessings. That is why we must always say 'His Will be Done'. It has pleased Almighty God, in His Infinite Wisdom, to take unto Himself His servant Emily, my beloved wife. She suffered much. Pray for me.

On Tuesday last, at the little Mayfair church in Farm Street, Father Dominic the Passionist received me into the one true Fold of the Holy Catholic Church. *Laus Deo*. And so – I am, in the same moment, crushed with grief and lifted up with joy.

I now need rest and recuperation. My worldly affairs have to be put in order. By chance, however, my good friends Lord and Lady Granville have been lent the Admiralty yacht, *Enchantress*, and have invited me to join them on a cruise to warm Aegean islands. Cardinal Wiseman will be of the company so we may have many fruitful talks. On my return I shall immediately set out for Rome. I rejoice to think I shall be with you again, certainly before Eastertide. I presume that the canonical intervals between my being made a Deacon, taking Minor Orders and full Ordination can be very brief – almost formal. Praise be to God – the clouds have lifted. You will, I know, drop a word in the Holy Father's ear. I need say no more – we still understand one another.

I leave this house tomorrow – forever. My address, meanwhile, is 18 Albany, Piccadilly, whence letters will be forwarded.

I am, dearest Monsignor Talbot, your brother in Christ,

✠ BARNABAS BARBELLION

4 Carriage Lamps under the Trees

Alas, regardless of their doom,
The little victims play!
No sense have they of ills to come,
Nor care beyond today

THOMAS GRAY

Strange things happened at the Rectory that week, by day and by night – I mean that week at the end of 1854 when my father came back from Rome . . . strange things almost every day. But it was by night, a few days before Christmas, that the lanterns moved among the trees in the churchyard, terrorizing two little children. I remember it all so clearly, how Maria Pia and I stood by the window in our nightdresses until we were driven back to bed by the cold, to bury ourselves in the blankets, hiding ourselves from that kind of fear that only children can know.

Yes, I remember every moment of it. After all I was fourteen. My little sister, Maria Pia, was only twelve but was already keeping her secret 'journal' in those red morocco books. Eirlys Cole-Hatt, so often with us in the schoolroom, was older than either of us . . . more than sixteen years now since that summer afternoon by the river at Bablock Hythe. Eirlys, therefore, should have remembered it all more clearly than either Maria Pia or me . . . had she been there. Of course she was never there at night, and not once, you know, while Papa was in Rome did Phillippa and Eirlys ever drive over from Windrush Court in the carriage. For three weeks they never came near, never came to Nether Molding at all. And, oddly enough, it was during those three weeks, with Papa in Rome and Phillippa at Windrush, that Mama seemed so much better. Even we children noticed it. She even played card games with us on her bed quilt.

But still it was strange. All that time Phillippa and Eirlys, mother and daughter, must have been at Windrush Court, quite alone, with the snow outside but with servants and good food and great log fires indoors . . . but alone, Phillippa at one end of the huge dining-table and Eirlys at the other end – a footman behind each chair and Featherston at the sideboard. Poor, pretty little Eirlys, with Phillippa always petting her and showing her off in public, and always so unkind when there was no one to hear, or only the servants – who didn't count.

For three whole weeks then – those weeks when Papa was giving dinner parties in the Via Tritone or strolling with Monsignor Talbot by the Lake of Nemi – Eirlys missed her lessons with Miss Grigg, while Phillippa – incredibly – was depriving herself of the Sacraments and allowing her manifold sins to go unabsolved. The Body and Blood of Christ from the hands of Cecil Praz, Papa's curate, did not seem to interest her, while as a Confessor he must have appealed to her even less than as a Celebrant.

Remembering Cecil Praz as I do, and his malign influence upon Papa, I can hardly blame her. As children, however, we never could understand why the 'grown-ups' so disliked the man. He was, or so it seemed to us, so gay, so good-looking and always so fond of children. When Papa was away, preaching in cathedrals or visiting grand people, Mr Praz took all the services, and took them very beautifully . . . or so at least we children thought. He was always very kind to us and indeed made a great fuss of us. He used to ask the choir-boys to tea at his cottage, one by one. Then came the day when he asked me. Papa just shrugged his shoulders but Miss Grigg was furious and forbade it with a vehemence that was quite beyond our understanding. It must have been a few days before Christmas that we asked him about the lanterns in the churchyard. His gay manner disappeared. He became very silent and brushed our question aside, saying, as Miss Grigg would do, that it was all a dream. But that, of course, was nonsense. I said so, but he just ran his hand through my black curls and walked off up the lane towards his own cottage at Little Molding. He had also given me a kiss. What a nice man, I thought.

Those lanterns – it had only been a day or two before Papa's return from Rome that Maria Pia had woken me in the middle of the night, shaking me by the shoulder. I sat up, rubbing my eyes.

'Augustine! Augustine! Wake up! There are men in the churchyard, with lanterns. I can hear them. They are all among the trees. Wake up, Gussy! I am so frightened.'

And so we stood together by the window of Maria Pia's room – the night-nursery as we still called it. It was a hard winter and we stood there, looking across the moonlit lawn towards the church, until we were quite blue with cold, not even thinking to pull a blanket around us. The lanterns were flitting between the trees and now and again we could hear a sound as of spades, as of hammers, as of men whispering.

When morning came, and it was a long time coming, we told Miss Grigg all about it. It was, I remember, when she was dressing Maria Pia. She said immediately that we must have been dreaming. We knew better than that, and so did she. At breakfast time, with the fire burning brightly in the schoolroom grate and Holman Hunt's *Massacre of the Innocents* over the mantelpiece, she was very quiet and very pale. Her hand trembled as she poured out the coffee. We both noticed it and Maria looked at me, as if telling me to speak out. So I did.

'Miss Grigg, you know, it wasn't a dream. Oh, no, Griggy, it was real. I saw the lanterns and I heard those men, truly I did. The lanterns were like fireflies among the yews.'

'No, you dreamt it, Gussy. You must have done. It just couldn't happen, dear boy. Now tell me, how could it?'

'But, Griggy, it did happen, you know. We heard the spades and we saw the lights, didn't we, Maria? Didn't we?'

'Oh, yes, we did. We stood by the window until we were, oh, so cold. And I was so frightened.'

'Yes, dear, but you know brothers and sisters often have the same dreams. So just forget about it, both of you. It just couldn't happen, you know. Not a thing like that.'

'But it did happen, Griggy, it did. I dropped my rag doll by the window. Why, she must be there still. Go and look, Griggy.'

'Hush, dear! That is enough. It is time now for you both to go and kiss Mama "Good morning". Off to her room.'

And then as soon as we had gone, Miss Grigg went into the night-nursery. She picked up the rag doll lying by the window.

We went to Mama as we always did. Bridget, the schoolroom parlourmaid, was sitting there but she left us all alone together. The winter sun had been bright in the schoolroom but Mama's room was always dark, the serge curtains always pulled. And there in the dark, with her tiny white face, Mama seemed almost lost in the big pillows. But then in my whole story Mama is no more than a wisp, a shadow. The only light was the little red lamp in front of the Spanish Madonna, that and a pencil of daylight creeping between the curtains to catch the white page on the *prie-dieu*. There was the heavy scent of half-dead hot-house flowers that Phillippa had left there nearly three weeks ago. There were the stale and unmentionable smells of a sick-room – of Mama's room – dark and airless. Our own windows looked out on to the garden and across to the churchyard – sunny rooms. Mama's room – Mama's and Papa's that is – looked on to the drive with its big dank elms and shrubs – a sunless room.

We poured out our story to her. She always got tired so quickly, but that morning she listened to us, and was kind. No, she had seen nothing but, yes, certainly she had heard a carriage in the night, wheels and hooves on gravel. She thought it might be Papa – back from Rome on the mail train from London. But it had all come to nothing and she had gone to sleep again. She tried to soothe us. She reminded us that it was Christmas time and that perhaps someone going home from a party had come to the wrong house, and hunted around with one of the carriage lamps. That was clever of Mama – better than Miss Grigg's silly idea of a dream – but of course we didn't believe either of them. You see, we knew. Mama blessed us and then, as always, sank back against the pillows with her eyes closed. That was three days before she died.

We went back to the schoolroom. Miss Grigg had not put out the lesson books. She had a treat for us. We could go out into the garden to play, snowballing and sliding on the little pond in the orchard, until luncheon time. Wouldn't that be lovely . . . Well, yes, we supposed it would.

'But remember,' she added, 'the churchyard is sacred ground. You must not play there; Papa would not like it. You must play only in the garden and the orchard. Now on your honour, children, promise.'

This was something new. We had always played in the churchyard, but of course we promised.

Listlessly we made a slide on the weed-grown pond, because we had been told to. We threw two or three snowballs, wetting the gloves Mama had knitted for us. And then, without actually breaking our promise, we stood by the wall between the garden and the churchyard, looking at the gravestones with all their Christmas wreaths. Old Riddle, the gravedigger, was at work. We liked old Riddle and could usually chat with him. But that morning even he was silent. He kept his back to us for a long time and when he turned it was only to tell us to be off.

'I be busy now. Be off with ye, to ye play.'

'What's wrong, Mr Riddle?'

'Nowt's wrong, as I know of. Be off, I be busy. They do want this grass quick.'

He was putting down fresh turf – fresh turf in that hard frost if you please – on Harold Gatsby's grave. Four months now since Harold Gatsby had died at the croquet party, and yet still no tombstone, only a grassy mound. We had thought this odd, and even sad, until 'Aunt' Phillippa had told us of the lovely coloured marbles coming from Italy, and of a clever man in London who was carving angels and cherubs and a beautiful Jesus. All this, she said, would take time – Harold would understand – and hence the grassy mound.

It was the next afternoon, I remembered, just when Miss Grigg was setting the table for tea, that Papa returned from Rome. At the sound of the barouche we ran to the window . . . carriage lamps among the trees, always carriage lamps . . . we caught our breath. At the sound of the wheels most children would have run downstairs to welcome their father with kisses; most fathers would have embraced their children, bringing them gay Italian toys. But life at Nether Molding, you know, was just not like that.

Already, even in this world, even with his own infallibility a quarter of a century over the horizon, Papa was a Messiah, somewhere half way between us and God. We never really talked to him; we were summoned to his presence. Perhaps this was because he had never wanted us to be born – children of duty rather than children of love. It was Eirlys who was the child of love but also, as he would tell her, the child of sin. And so every day of our lives we children – Eirlys too if she was with us – would take our meals upstairs with Miss Grigg. Every day of his life – often with

Phillippa – Papa's four-course luncheon or eight-course dinner would be served on the mahogany, with the Crown Derby and the Venetian glass. Occasionally he would entertain bishops, statesmen, editors, the High Anglican or Catholic laity. But sometimes he would dine alone and then, only when he had said grace aloud to an empty room, did he ring for the footmen to carry in the tureen.

It was a surprise, therefore, that winter afternoon, when an order came that we were to take China tea and plum cake in the study. It was a greater surprise, when we reached the study, that we should first of all have to kneel and thank Almighty God that, in His Infinite Wisdom, he had brought Papa back to us across the perils of the Deep. It seems to me now, looking back, to have been an odd way to speak of the Dover Packet, but we were very young and I suppose that we thought only of Papa in some raging tempest.

'My dearest children, eat up your cake. I have something to say to you – something important – important for the eternal salvations of us all.'

'Yes, Papa.'

'Do not interrupt. You know from your scripture lessons – or you should know – that hundreds of years ago Our Lord Jesus Christ ...' we all crossed ourselves '... founded His Church upon Earth and that His dear friend, Saint Peter, took that Church to Rome whence it has spread to all the world, that those who believe in it might have Eternal Life.'

'Yes, Papa, but ...'

'Pray do not interrupt, Augustine. The Church of England, to which at the moment we all of us here belong, has for some three hundred years been a kind of inferior branch of that Church – the one founded by Saint Peter. Now I have to tell you – and I do so with tears of joy – that when in Rome a few days ago I visited Our Holy Father, the Pope ...'

'The Pope! Oh, Papa! Had he got on his golden hat?'

'Maria Pia, I must ask you not to interrupt. Yes, the Pope, direct successor of Jesus himself. He blessed me and then he kissed me; it was all too wonderful for words. I promised him that I, too, would join that One and Only Church, the Fold of Christ. In other words, my darling ones, your Papa will no longer be the Rector of Nether Molding. We are all to become what people in England call Roman Catholics . . . there, is not that marvellous!'

'Yes, Papa. You mean that we shall leave Nether Molding to live somewhere else.'

'Yes, Augustine.'

'How exciting . . .'

'Yes, but it is nothing at all, Augustine, compared with the fact that we may now be sure of our own salvation. Moreover, I may tell you that our dear friend Mrs Gatsby – your "Aunt" Phillippa as you call her – will follow my example, with her niece. So, you see that your playmate, Eirlys Cole-Hatt, although born in sin may yet be saved.'

'How nice for her, Papa. May we tell her?'

'No, you may not. I will do that. And now, dear children, it is Christmas time when we all remember the Birth of Our Lord Jesus at Bethlehem and, for some strange reason, give each other presents. I have brought you each a present from Rome. I also have one for Eirlys. They will be the finest presents you have ever had.'

'Oo! Whatever can they be?'

'A moment's patience, Maria Pia. They are your new prayer books.'

He now produced two books, each bound in fine white vellum, each with a gold cross upon the cover and scarlet markers of fringed silk.

'These, my darling ones, are your new prayer books, or as we call them in the Catholic Church, breviaries. Many of the prayers are just like the ones you know but there are others which you may find a little strange at first. We Catholics, for instance, think as lovingly of the dear Mother of Jesus as we do of Jesus himself. But the strangest thing for you will be to find everything in Latin – the glorious and ancient language of the Church. The English version you will find at the bottom of each page. You must learn both versions very diligently. You will incur my displeasure if you do not.'

'Yes, Papa. Thank you. What lovely books!'

'In any case, you, Augustine – and this is something else I have to tell you – will be learning Latin immediately after Christmas. You will be going to school.'

'To school!'

'Do not echo my words, Augustine. Listen. I say that you will be going to school. It is high time. After all you are fourteen and, as I have noticed, much given to indolence – a dangerous fault tending to the Deadly Sin of Sloth – a sin deserving of Hellfire. Your high-pitched laugh suggests also a tendency to Frivolity. I am arranging, therefore, that you shall go to Stonyhurst – the best school in the world. The good Jesuit priests will teach you excellent Latin and will root out both Sloth and Frivolity. You are indeed a most fortunate boy.'

'Oh, yes, Papa. Thank you. Thank you very much. And Griggy – I mean Miss Grigg – what is to become of her?'

'You are, I know, very fond of your governess – one most undesirable result of being saddled with an invalid mother. Miss Grigg has been a loyal servant, but only a servant. I cannot force her to change her religion and of course I can now have no Protestant under my roof.'

Maria Pia now began to sob.

'Maria Pia, you are a most ungrateful child. I bring you back gifts and tidings of great joy from Rome – an assurance of everlasting bliss – and you cry like a baby. But I have other good news for you, so dry your tears, and listen.'

'Yes – er, yes, Papa.'

'You must realize that in our new life I shall be a very busy man – active in God's work – travelling between London and Rome and elsewhere – possibly even America – preaching and lecturing. You may see very little of me. That, I know, will be a terrible grief to you, one of those great afflictions that we all have to bear with fortitude, but God's Will be done. Do not weep my children. It will all be for the sake of Our Lord. Do not weep.'

'No, Papa.'

'Now, I must tell you that I have already arranged with your Aunt Caroline – a devout and pious lady who has already "crossed the bridge" before us into Christ's Church – that you should live with her in Derby.'

'Aunt Caroline!'

'You, Augustine, will board at Stonyhurst – I understand that the fare is wholesome – and you, Maria Pia, will be going to a very wonderful school, a Convent of the Sisters of St Charles Borromeo. This Convent is some miles from Aunt Caroline's but she will be able to visit you each term, as permitted by the rules. You and Augustine will meet at Aunt Caroline's home in the holidays. It may appeal to the feminine in you, Maria Pia, that all the girls at the Convent wear a most becoming uniform – black cloaks.'

'Yes – er, yes, Papa. Oh, yes, Papa. Thank you very much.'

'Now you must not cry. You must rejoice. And when you say your prayers tonight you must thank the Lord God for having given you such a kind and thoughtful father.'

'Yes, Papa, we will.'

'You must say an extra prayer for Mama. She is worse.'

'Oh, is she very ill, Papa?'

'Very ill indeed. We must all be glad that it is now God's Will that she will soon be with Him in her Heavenly Home. Pray for her.'

'Yes, Papa. We thought she was better . . .'

'No, not now. That is enough. Go to the schoolroom and tell Miss Grigg that I wish to see her immediately.'

'Yes, Papa, but . . .'

'No more. Do as I say. Now go.'

'Yes, Papa.'

Poor, poor Miss Grigg. That night we all cried ourselves to sleep. She had been given a week's notice.

That was Christmas Eve. Plum cake and tea in Papa's study had made it a red-letter day. The rule that we should take all our meals in the schoolroom brooked no exception – not even on birthdays or at Christmas. Christmas at the Rectory, therefore, had always been somewhat bizarre; that year it was macabre. In the morning we had been into Mama as usual, giving her our little gifts – a cross-stitch pin-cushion from Maria, and from me a button-box upon which I had glued coloured pebbles. We sang our carol for her, 'Silent Night', and then left her to fall into an uneasy sleep. Yes, she was worse. She had been sick many times in the night and was almost too feeble to thank us for the presents. Her dry lips just moved.

We had our new breviaries from Papa and so we did not go to the study . . . we would never have dared to offer him a present. On Christmas Day, that year as all years, we saw him only in the pulpit and at the altar, at his most splendid – an apotheosis. Eucharist, Matins, Vespers were all indescribable . . . a Patriarch of Old Byzantium could not have done it better. While 'Aunt' Phillippa, upright in the Windrush Court pew, wept tears of emotion, Eirlys sat goggle-eyed, bewitched by the antics of Papa and Cecil Praz as they gave each other the Kiss of Peace. The smell of incense had even crept across into the garden.

After Matins we all walked back to the house. Five months ago, at the Windrush croquet party, Cardinal Wiseman had chuckled to himself. His perception and experience had not betrayed him. 'Aunt' Phillippa, in her widow's weeds – her veil thrown back from her face – was big with child.

She had kissed us all in the church porch. Then we four, the schoolroom party, Miss Grigg, Eirlys, Maria Pia and I, had walked sedately across the white lawn, sedately but bent upon our Christmas dinner. Papa followed with 'Aunt' Phillippa. The widow, carrying her baby in her womb and walking so slowly on the Rector's arm, was probably intended to bring tears to the eyes, a calculated act, a parade of pathos. If so, then, among those simple folk pouring out of church, it was a failure. They were shocked. Even the Gatsby carriage servants, Tomkins and Bowlby, as we passed them in the drive, averted their gaze, tight-lipped. And so, too, in the schoolroom, as Bridget slammed down the heavily laden tray, she was scarlet with indignation . . . 'they've begun their dinner, those two – champagne, and the missus dying, poor love . . .' and then, with a great sniff, she banged the door behind her.

It was my turn to say grace. There was a little holly and some trails of ivy on the damask cloth. Mistletoe was forbidden – a Pagan symbol. Only after dinner were we allowed to display our presents. 'Aunt' Phillippa had matched Papa; as 'a start to your new and glorious life in Christ's Church' she had given us each a rosary, expensive rosaries with settings by Cartier. They were pretty things and, not knowing what to do with them, we hung them up as part of the decorations. Our dear Miss Grigg produced a new Ludo set and had even smuggled in a few crackers.

Papa may have told the Pope that Christmas in England was a very domestic affair, but at Nether Molding it was more like some peculiar Sunday – an amalgam of gloom in the house and of exotic glory in the church. After dinner we should have practised our carols for the Evening Service, but Mama must not be disturbed. Very quietly, therefore, we played games – paper games and Ludo. Never have children's minds been further from their play. We played with the dark shadow of Aunt Caroline, of Stonyhurst, of the Convent and of Life without Griggy hanging over us . . . and Mama dying in the next room. And there, playing with us at the schoolroom table, was our Eirlys. Her Christmas, too, had been spoilt by 'Aunt' Phillippa's perpetual taunts. Three weeks alone with Phillippa at Windrush Court had left their mark on Eirlys forever . . . she had suddenly grown up.

It must have been about half past two on the afternoon of 25 December 1854, between a game of Consequences and one of Ludo, that I visited the lavatory – that familiar flowered porcelain affair in its mahogany pedestal – another ghost from my childhood. The lavatory was a sunny little room and I sat quite a time enjoying the view of the church tower, but also wondering about those priests at Stonyhurst. I knew that they had a thing called a tawse. Well – as they say these days – I would give them a run for their money. I came out on to the landing again. It was lit only from an odd kind of Regency cupola and after the sunny lavatory it seemed dark. The heavy panelled doors could be seen only because of the glint on the brass knobs . . . a heavy and carpeted silence . . . no sound at all.

Suddenly there was a click. It was Mama's door being opened. Behind me there was a sharp catch of the breath, almost a little cry of surprise at finding me there at all – or was it, perhaps, a cry of alarm.

'Augustine! Augustine, dear boy, I thought you were all still at dinner.'

In the gloom, with all her crêpe and bombasine, I could hardly see anything except the white face – eyes like big black smudges –

and the silver spoon in a bowl, the white bowl with the forget-me-not pattern from which, as a small boy, I had taken my gruel.

'No, we have finished dinner, "Aunt" Phillippa. We don't have as much as you and Papa, you know.'

'Oh, Augustine, what a thing to say!'

'Well, we don't, do we? Thank you very much for those lovely rosaries. They are so pretty, are they not?'

'Use them all your lives, dear.'

'Yes, we will. So you have just been to see Mama.'

'Yes, Augustine, you and Maria Pia must pray for her. I have been feeding her – a morsel at a time. Your Papa had a little minced goose prepared for her – appetizing and sustaining – but really she had only a mouthful. She is very ill, Augustine.'

'I know that. She could hardly speak to us this morning, when we sang our carol for her, you know. She was better a few days ago, but is worse now – ever since Papa came back from Rome.'

'It is a sad Christmas for your Papa, for us all. I do so love your darling mother. Of course your Papa is a tower of strength as well as being a saint . . . in the pulpit this morning . . . marvellous . . . who could have known that he had this great sorrow on his mind. Now I must get back to comfort him. Tell the others to play quietly. Mama may sleep a little. Bridget is with her but later your Papa will try to give her a nice cool drink. Her mouth is so parched.'

'Bridget is all very well, but should there not be a proper nurse, "Aunt" Phillippa . . . a real nurse?'

'Yes. Mrs Williams has been sent for.'

'Pooh! She is only the midwife. She nearly killed Mama when Maria Pia was born . . .'

'Hush! Hush! You cannot know anything about things like that. Just fancy – at your age.'

'And she's always tipsy.'

'Hush, Augustine! You must not speak like that. Your Papa knows best. Mrs Williams is a good woman. Papa has sent for her and that should be enough for you.'

'And a doctor, "Aunt" Phillippa. Not old Doctor Potts, I hope. He's nearly blind and very deaf and no use at all. He thought my nettle-rash was chicken-pox . . . silly old fool!'

'Really, Augustine, you must not speak like that. You are upset about your dear Mama – of course you are – otherwise, you know, I should have to tell Papa about you that you might be punished. It is very wicked to say things like that. A midwife is a very good kind of nurse. Doctor Potts may be old but it is experience that matters. Besides you must know that everything your Papa does is always for the best. He is one of the best men who ever lived, and he does love your Mama so much . . . he would do anything for her.'

'Very well, "Aunt" Phillippa, but I don't care what you say, I know.'

'Hush! You really must not speak to me like that. I forbid it. Your Papa has great faith in Doctor Potts and that means that he must be a very good doctor. Papa knows best. That is enough.'

'All right . . . but I don't have to shut up, you know, just because you tell me to. You are nobody in this house – nobody at all, although we all know why you are here. So there!'

Looking back, you know, down the years, I suppose I hardly realized what I was saying. But I'm glad – I'm still glad – that I said it. Of course I could expect the worst from Papa – a caning and bread and water – but that didn't matter a scrap. Quite suddenly – like Eirlys – I had grown up. I could defy everyone. For a little longer I must pretend to be the submissive child – 'yes, Papa', 'no, Papa' – but not for much longer. From now on I would say what I liked to everyone – to 'Aunt' Phillippa, to the priests at Stonyhurst, even to Papa. It was a marvellous feeling. The Lord of Derravaragh was being born.

'Aunt' Phillippa went a little whiter – if that was possible. She blinked as if she had been hit. She did not say a word. When she spoke again it was as if nothing had happened.

'Now, you must none of you make any noise this afternoon. And you, Augustine, do not laugh so loudly when you are playing. We all hope that Mama will sleep. I shall see you at Vespers.'

Very slowly, trembling, she went down the stairs, clutching the balustrade all the way.

It was not until tea-time that I peered out once more on to the landing. I had heard the clink of glasses. It was Papa, his clerical collar and crucifix gleaming in the darkness and – once again – that silver spoon. Carrying the 'nice cool drink' – a glass jug with a silver lid – he disappeared into Mama's room, the heavy door closing behind him.

It must have been an hour later, almost Vespers time, when Bridget burst into the schoolroom. The woman was transformed by hysteria. Her dear mistress had been violently sick five times – Bridget just didn't know that our poor human bodies could hold so much. The sickness, the diarrhoea, the sweating and the cramp – dear God – had been too terrible! She cried out that it was all beyond her now. Mrs Williams had been sent for and Mrs Williams, drunk or sober, must deal with it now. Where was she? Why hadn't she come? Bridget almost shrieked at us that she could do no more. God was so cruel, just like the master . . . downstairs with that woman . . . while poor, dear Mrs Barbellion died by inches. Oh, God, her agony!

'That will do, Bridget. You may go.'

'Aunt' Phillippa was in the room. She had come in very quietly and somehow I knew that she had been listening at the door.

'Eirlys, my love.'

'Well, what is it?'

'Don't speak to me like that, dear. It's not ladylike. I came to tell you that you need not come to Vespers. We are all going over to the church now but we will excuse you. Here is your poor "Aunt" Emily's medicine. Put the correct dose – it gives it on the bottle – in some warm milk – warm, remember, not hot – and try to get a few drops between her teeth. She may take it from you. She seems fond of you – I can't imagine why . . .'

'Very well.'

'If she knows you – that is. She hardly knows anyone now.'

I shall always believe that my mother died on St Stephen's Day, in the small hours. Children sleep soundly but I woke four times that night – once to hear a door bang, once to hear the flushing of a closet; the third time was on account of a fleabite, some flea that had escaped Papa's patent killer. The fourth time it was carriage wheels. In my bare feet I crossed the landing to where I could look on to the drive. I trembled, not with cold but with fear. Carriage wheels, carriage lamps, carriage lamps, always lamps among the trees. Papa came out of the front door to help Doctor Potts from his carriage – so decrepit that he seemed almost dead himself. Death, and always those lamps among the trees. And now, two black-coated figures in the shadow, one evil and one senile. And then the dark and silent landing as I groped my way back to bed.

Perhaps Mama, at that hour, was already a corpse. We were told nothing the next day until after tea when, for the second time in a week, we were summoned to the study. While we were dressing we heard the Windrush Court carriage arriving . . . so, they were back already, before we had had breakfast. Phillippa vanished into the study. Eirlys, tears welling up in her big grey eyes, sat by the table holding Griggy's hand. Last night her mother had been unkind – reproaching her as never before with her 'base birth' – the 'little bastard' and the 'child of sin' – and telling her how grateful she should be to have a home at all . . . soon it might be a Convent school.

Again that day there were to be no lessons, and no games either. Once more it was to be a peculiar kind of mid-week Sunday. We must not play, we must not shout or laugh; we could read only our Sunday books – Dante's *Inferno* for me with Doré's pictures of the damned which I adored, but for poor Maria Pia only her *Pilgrim's Progress* which she knew by heart. The only game allowed was the Noah's Ark, a biblical game. So, we were sent for a sharp walk. In our woolly hats, gaiters and mufflers we set off – two disconsolate children with nothing to do except to crack the ice on the puddles.

Astonishingly, Eirlys stayed behind to chat with Miss Grigg by the schoolroom fire – two 'grown-ups' by the fire while the children went for a walk. Suddenly our Eirlys seemed much older – Griggy's friend all of a sudden rather than ours. To us it was incomprehensible but it was the beginning of a friendship. It was a passionate friendship that would last for years – far into the next century. And always, to the end, they wrote each other those mysterious letters which, even now, I have never seen.

Of course we came back from our walk far too soon. It must have been barely midday when from the shrubbery we saw 'Aunt' Phillippa. She was walking slowly and alone across the lawn, and so through the churchyard to the West Door. Another hour passed. What was happening? We went from the garden to the churchyard. We passed the newly laid turf on Harold Gatsby's grave – laid since the snow fell, it was a green square. Somehow, we were sick with fear. We were also devoured by curiosity. It was Maria Pia, her little mouth grimly set, who resolved to finish the matter.

The West Door, beneath its heavy Norman arch, had always creaked. We need not have worried. Papa had locked it on the inside. Then Maria Pia remembered that almost always the tiny door to the vestry was never locked; it was left ajar for the choir-boys and the bell-ringers. She signalled me to go away while she tiptoed round the church. She was hidden from the house.

The vestry, as she told me afterwards, smelt of candlewax, old books, dust and rats. It was very dark. To Maria Pia, coming in from the sunlit snow, it was black. When, carefully and quietly, she had closed the door behind her, she could see nothing, nothing but tiny sparks of light on the bottles of Eucharistic wine.

She found the inner door and opened it inch by inch. At first the church seemed as dark as the vestry. It was a very small church, all its light coming from four narrow lancets, their stained-glass dimmed by the dust of centuries. She squeezed through the door into the nave where she hid behind a stone pillar. She sniffed. The smells, redolent in the darkness, were different from those in the vestry – the smell of the death-watch beetle, of old hassocks, of damp and of incense . . . also, faint but delicious, the smell of perfume hanging in the heavy air. Maria Pia thought it must be violets.

Far away in the chancel two candles were burning on the altar. Maria Pia opened her mouth in astonishment. She almost choked as she held her breath. There was a big chair in front of the altar. Papa sat very upright, holding his book to the candlelight. He wore his surplice, his scarlet hood – the Oxfordian hood – and also those pretty gold bands, from his neck to his feet, which the Anglican nuns had embroidered with the thorn and the vine.

And there, kneeling on the altar steps, bowed to the floor at Papa's feet, her muff, reticule and gloves all thrown aside on the Minton tiles, was Phillippa. Maria Pia did not understand. She did not know how or why, but she did know that this was part of the evil that, for so long, had haunted the house and our lives. From the altar came the murmur of voices. Maria Pia could not hear what 'Aunt' Phillippa was saying but Papa spoke in his 'churchy' voice. His intoning rose and fell.

'Renew in her, most loving Father, whatsoever hath been decayed by the fraud and malice of the devil, or by her own carnal will and frailty.'

Then he started to give the Blessing.

'In the name of the Father, of the Son and of the Holy Ghost . . .'

Maria knew that this signalled the end. Papa had turned to face the Sacrament, crossing himself and bowing. He laid his book upon the altar and bowed again to kiss it. Phillippa came down the steps to wait for him in the nave.

Maria Pia fled. What would Papa say if he caught her there, prying. She tumbled through the darkness of the vestry. She knocked over a stool. She went out into the sunshine and the vestry door slammed behind her.

I was waiting for her on the lawn. She signalled to me to go away, to go back to the house. Then, crouching behind a huge eighteenth-century tomb, she waited. Papa had had to unrobe himself but at last those two – Papa in his long black coat and his shovel hat, and 'Aunt' Phillippa in all her crêpe – came out of the West Door. They hesitated, looked round – Maria Pia held her breath – and then half hid themselves behind a buttress, trails of ivy on the stone gleaming in the sun. For many minutes – to Maria Pia it seemed like hours – they were ecstatically lost in each other.

Maria Pia could hear only a little of what they said; sometimes they whispered, sometimes they seemed angry. The child could not understand what it was all about but – with that amazing memory of hers – she got it into her 'journal' within the hour. The red morocco book is by me now, so many years after, with the brown ink and the careful copperplate abandoned for the hurried pencil scrawl . . . getting it down at all costs. I think it must have been from that moment that her 'journal' became secret.

'But, Barny dearest, after all that has happened, all the wonderful years since Bablock Hythe . . . and now Harold gone and Emily gone . . . and all for nothing. Oh, Barny, Barny!'

'Not for nothing, dearest one – for everything. I adore you, I worship you, as I have always done, only now, somehow, a thousand times more than I ever did. You are really mine, now, in this world and the next, for ever and ever, in the eyes of God.'

'But, Barny, I just don't understand – we are in sin – a celibate priest.'

'No. The world, my darling one, has always allowed something to a celibate, you know, as it has to kings . . . not that I care about the world . . . I am a priest but God did not make me to be chaste. He gave me you. Our marriage is a mystical marriage, made by God years ago on a summer afternoon. What is a sin for others, my dearest, is for us a glorification of the Lord . . . in itself a sort of Hosanna. After all marriage is a sacrament, and God has made me a giver of his sacraments. Don't you see, my beloved, don't you see that we are different?'

'I see, or I try to see, my love. But, oh, Barny, not to be my husband after all – after all that we have done.'

'Husband and wife – it is a thousand times more marvellous than that. You, my Phillippa, must know – surely you must know – that you could never be just the wife of a mere village parson. What are you thinking of? That would, you know, be the real sin – self-betrayal. You and I, my darling, were not made for that. We are among the great lovers of the world . . . and, also, I am a priest. Our joy must be absolute – surely, surely.'

'But, Barny, what is to happen to me?'

'You will never be far from me – wherever my work may take me. Always some lovely little house near by. Whatever the world may think of that it will be a glorious thing in the eyes of God. You will be the mother of my children, as you are now. I shall be your priest, your Confessor and your lover – to all eternity.'

And then they went across the garden and into the house. Maria Pia gave them ten minutes. And then, sobbing and bewildered, she followed them. Her whole instinct was to get back to Griggy, to me and to all the warm familiarity of the schoolroom. She did not understand what she had seen and heard, she only knew that she did not like it. She was not even sure, now, whether Mama was dead. As she crossed the hall the voices – rather angry now – were coming from the study where the door was ajar. The little girl started to climb the stairs. Half way up, her ear to the balusters, was Eirlys, finger on her lips. Maria tiptoed past. They understood one another.

Somehow, in some vague way, Maria Pia knew that this thing concerned Mama. Yes, she would tell Mama – if Mama was even alive – and ask Mama what it was all about. She turned the brass knob. Mama's door was locked. She rapped on the panel. There was no reply, only a silence like that of the grave, and on the dark and airless landing a smell like that of violets.

And now at last the time had come. We had heard the carriage wheels as Eirlys and Phillippa started on their drive back to Windrush in the fading light. Years later, sitting under the pleached limes at Derravaragh, Eirlys would tell me every word, every episode of that cataclysmic drive with her mother through the Gloucestershire lanes. While she and Phillippa were talking in the carriage we were with Papa in his study . . . for the last time in our lives.

We had schoolroom tea in deathly silence. The summons came. We followed Miss Grigg past Mama's door. Miss Grigg, suddenly rather formal, ushered us into the study, a hand on each shoulder. Her mouth was tight. After all, she was a servant under notice.

It was a large room. Some people would have called it the library. It had three tall Regency windows opening on to the lawn, their red blinds now lowered to the floor. In one corner was a little altar with candles – now lit – a crucifix and a tabernacle. Over the mantelpiece was a bad copy of Gerard's *Deposition from the Cross*. All the rest was books – mainly huge vellum-bound editions of the Early Fathers – a St Chrysostom even now lay open on the table beneath the green lamp.

Barnabas Barbellion drew himself up to his full archidiaconal height. The ice-blue eyes were piercing. The iris was entirely surrounded by white. The thin-lipped, clean-shaven mouth was like a rat-trap, a straight line of monstrous cruelty. He remained at the far end of the room, forcing us, shy and tremulous, to walk its whole length. He then addressed us by our full names – those he had bestowed upon us at the font.

'Augustine Xavier and Maria Pia . . .'

We stood open-mouthed, too terrified to giggle. Miss Grigg's mouth twitched ever so little.

'Cross yourselves. Do you not know that the Lord Jesus Christ is within this room . . . ?' and he made a gesture towards the tabernacle on the altar.

'Now kneel down.'

We knelt on the Turkey carpet. Papa bowed his head over his clasped hands.

'Now, carefully and reverently, repeat after me the prayer which you say night and morning – the "Our Father". "Our Father which art in Heaven . . ."'

He now intoned as strongly as if he had been in Gloucester Cathedral. This enhanced his vanity. It also, each Sunday, sent a little sexual tremor through the ladies of the congregation. It did not impress his children; we had lived with it too long.

As Papa prayed I peeped between my fingers. I have always peeped and always shall. It was only then that I noticed a tray on a table in one of the tall windows. There was that bowl with the forget-me-not pattern, with a little minced goose still showing above the rim. There, too, was the glass jug with the silver lid, and the beaker with the silver spoon; there too was Mama's medicine bottle – the one that 'Aunt' Phillippa had given to Eirlys the previous night, just as we were all going over to Vespers . . . all these things on a tray in Papa's study, unwashed. And there too was the old jam pot in which Papa had always kept his patent flea killer. That flea killer was called 'Hartley's Bug Specific', but I know now that it was simply a mixture of arsenic and soft soap. Anyway, there it was with the other things on the tray.

'. . . the Power and the Glory for ever and ever, Amen.'

'Amen, Papa.'

'Now stand up.'

He put a hand upon each head. Our faces must have been drained of blood, as white as the papers beneath the lamp.

'My dearest children, I have something to tell you. I thank God that since the hour of your birth I have dedicated you to your Saviour, Jesus Christ. That should help you to bear this crushing blow.'

The tears were now welling up in our eyes although we were still not sure what he was talking about.

'This, my darlings, is a tragic day for us all. It is also a blessed day. It has pleased Almighty God, in His infinite wisdom, to take from us His servant Emily – my beloved wife and your dear mother. Liberated from all pain she is with Christ her King, in Glory.'

Maria Pia could bear it no longer. She dared to interrupt.

'Papa, do you mean that Mama is dead and that we shall never see her again?'

'Yes. She is with Jesus. You have to bear your grief for just a little while, until the Resurrection Morn when we shall all be gathered before the Judgement Seat. You need not fear for your dear mother. In her last hours she sinned. In her agony she craved medicine to lessen her pain. I could not allow that. Suffering is our lot in this world, part of God's plan. What were her sufferings compared with those of Jesus upon the Cross? But God is very merciful; He will forgive her. Moreover, in the very hour of death I myself absolved her of all her sins. As I administered Extreme Unction she gave a sign that she accepted the teachings of Christ's One Church. We may, in our prayers tonight, thank Almighty God that she died a Catholic.'

Even now our tears did not flow freely. He had frightened us. He had bewildered us and puzzled us. We had not understood half of what he said, but he had not finished.

'This, dear children, is now a house of mourning. The blinds of all the windows – let this be clearly understood – must remain drawn until your dear mother is buried in the cold earth. Miss Grigg, you will tell the servants that. And you, my dear ones, will for many months wear black clothes if only to remind you, each morning, of your unutterable grief. The clothes have been prepared, Miss Grigg?'

'Yes, sir.'

Only now – it was at the thought of the black clothes – did Maria Pia begin to howl. Miss Grigg tried to comfort her, wiping her eyes. I stared blankly at my little sister, still uncomprehending.

'And now, children, we will go upstairs to the death chamber. There you may both kiss your mother farewell. It is for only a little time, till the shadows flee away.'

In obedience and, except for Maria Pia's sniffling, in silence, we followed him across the hall and up to the landing. He unlocked the bedroom door.

There was a fire in the grate but it had been necessary to open a window. The cold air of the winter afternoon moved the curtains so that a beam of sunlight would, now and again, fall upon the white sheet. Almost all else was dark. The red light, as always, twinkled before the Madonna. On the *prei-dieu* lay a book, a few of its pages marked with lace-fringed pictures. These things – and the white bed – stood out in the shadows. Then, on two stools at the foot of the bed, we saw the empty coffin. It did not frighten us; we merely thought it a pretty thing with its mauve satin quilting. Papa lit the candles.

Mama – poor, pathetic little Emily Barbellion – had been laid in the centre of the big four-poster. We, her children, to whom she had given birth in this room, now stood on either side of Papa, each clutching a hand. The bed was high, only just high enough for me to look down upon my mother's corpse, while Maria could scarcely make out the shape under the sheet. Papa turned the sheet back. In that warm room the face was already yellow and waxen although tear furrows still marked the cheeks. Her hands had been folded upon her bosom so as to clasp her silver crucifix. The flickering candles played a game of shadows with the corpse.

We wept a little at the thought of never seeing Mama again and at the thought of those black clothes. Then we all stood in silence. Our minds were numb. When Papa recited a prayer for the dead, in the Latin of the Roman Breviary, we merely gaped at him. Then he commanded us.

'Cross yourselves . . . now kiss your mother for the last time in this world.'

We could not reach the centre of that enormous feather-bed. The body seemed quite lost in it. Papa had to hold up his children, one by one, so that they could kiss the cold forehead. I touched her hands around the crucifix; they were quite rigid but it was only years later that I learnt the meaning of *rigor mortis.* Mama had been dead many hours.

'Now kneel and say your prayers.'

We did – or pretended to – and he knelt with us. And then, for the second time within the hour, we were made to recite the 'Our Father'.

At last we could go back to the schoolroom. To our amazement

Papa followed us. Not once a year did he enter that room. Miss Grigg turned to him.

'Is there anything else, sir? The children are exhausted.'

'Yes, Miss Grigg, there is something else, something distressing and distasteful. I would let it pass if I could, but even on this day of tribulation a priest and a father must do his duty.'

'Indeed, sir.'

'Yes. This afternoon, crushed and bowed with grief though I was, I accompanied a poor and lonely lady to the church – a widow. She desperately needed my ministrations. Incredible though it may seem, we were spied upon. I heard unseemly noises in the vestry. You, Augustine, and you, Maria Pia, were playing in the garden. I want the truth – did either of you enter the church?'

The silence was complete. Our heads were bowed.

'Very well, I ask you again. Augustine Xavier, did you enter the church today?'

'No, Papa.'

'Maria Pia, did you enter the church today?'

'No, Papa.'

'One of you is lying to me. Augustine, have you told me a falsehood?'

'No, Papa.'

'Maria Pia, have you told me a falsehood?'

'Yes, Papa.'

'So, at last. You have not only incurred my displeasure, Maria Pia – that is nothing – but by prying and intruding upon those at the altar you have committed the sin of blasphemy . . . and with the shadow of death upon the house. And now, to crown all, you have lied to me in the hour of my sorrow. Miss Grigg, this child must be chastised.'

'No, sir.'

'I beg your pardon, Madam.'

'I said "no, sir". With the little girl's mother lying dead in the next room I could not possibly do as you ask. I must refuse.'

'Very well. If physical means are barred to us, we must resort to spiritual. Oh, Almighty God, I am crushed with grief; my child is a blasphemer and a liar. My servants defy me. Tonight I shall read the Book of Job.'

Not a word was spoken. We could hear each other breathing.

'Maria Pia.'

'Yes, Papa.'

'Stand here in front of me. This is my last word. Every day of my life, Maria Pia, almost every hour, I think of "the lake of fire and brimstone that burneth forever". It is only the fear of the terrible torments of Hell that sustains me in my work and in my sorrows. Think of that, Maria Pia, when you place your head upon the pillow tonight. Think of the torments which God has in store for little girls who tell lies. Now, that is all I have to say to you. Augustine, good-night. Miss Grigg, good-night.'

And Archdeacon Barbellion closed the schoolroom door firmly behind him.

'Maria, dear, get out the chequer-board and the draughtsmen. It is too late to go out again now. We will have a quiet game and then you may have supper by the fire in your dressing-gowns. After that, Maria, I will sit by your bed . . . until you fall asleep. And you may have the door open into my room.'

'Darling Griggy!'

For a time we played our game quietly, then I spoke.

'Griggy, was Mama very ill?'

'Of course, Augustine, very ill. That is why she died, dear.'

'But old Doctor Potts? Couldn't he have given her medicine to make her better? He made Maria better when she was sick.'

'No, Augustine, no medicine would have been any good. Poor Mama was too ill.'

'But Papa always says that Doctor Potts is so clever.'

'Maybe, but he is very old . . .'

Doctor Potts at that time – as I still recall – was eighty-six. He had learnt his medicine under George the Third, and had been known to bleed his patients and to use leeches.

'Yes, Augustine, he is very old . . .' and then the next words came from Miss Grigg like a thunder clap, '. . . he's very old. He's a senile old fool. Anyone could twist *him* round their little finger.'

Ye Gods! What had she said? She could have bitten her tongue off. And then she told herself that it didn't matter. She was going away, and her words would soon be forgotten. Children, she said to herself, soon forget. But, you know, she was quite wrong. Maria Pia and I would remember what she had said . . . we would remember it every day of our lives – 'senile old fool. Anyone could twist *him* round their little finger.' We remembered – that and the forget-me-not bowl with the minced goose, and the smell of violets on the landing.

The horses' hooves rang out on the frosty road. Phillippa had ordered the carriage to be left open but she drew her furs more closely around her as she and Eirlys drove back to Windrush through the dusk. They were silent to start with – Phillippa grimly silent, Eirlys now and again looking at her mother in an inquiring way, as if waiting for her to speak. They had left the Rectory behind, where, as Phillippa knew, Papa would now be telling us that Mama was dead. This is the story of their drive as Eirlys told it to me.

It was somewhere near Upper Swell that the two carriages met – Phillippa Gatsby's and Mrs Falkner's. The lane was so narrow that the coachmen had to rein in their horses.

'Ah, dear Mrs Gatsby . . . and little Eirlys, how are you, my love? Really, Mrs Gatsby, your niece gets more like you every day. And so you are coming, I take it, from Nether Molding. Do, do tell me – I am so anxious that I hardly slept last night – how is poor Mrs Barbellion, poor darling?'

Phillippa looked up at Tomkins and Bowlby on the box seat. Their backs were liveried, rigid and correct. But they had ears. How much did they know? Dare she lie?

'Very, very ill indeed, I fear. Sinking fast – very little hope, dear Mrs Falkner . . . but the Rector, needless to say, so brave, a tower of strength, so secure in his faith.'

'Ah, yes, of course. I only stopped the carriage – please forgive me – because you are always so *au fait* with what is going on at the Rectory. But just now, whatever do you think, we met Captain Rowlands on one of his energetic walks. What do you think he told me – I could hardly believe my ears. Believe it or not, he said that he had seen the undertaker at the Rectory. Now, what do you say to that?'

Phillippa never hesitated a moment.

'Ah, yes. I understand that the cook is terribly ill – that would be it.'

'Oh, is that all? But what a pity; the Rector always gave such good dinners. I hope the woman didn't die of cholera, there are three cases, I hear, in Cheltenham. Well, well, we shall miss her cooking. And now I must be on my way. Good-bye, dear Mrs Gatsby, good-bye. And you, dear Eirlys, you've had a lovely Christmas, I expect . . . good-bye, dear.'

On the steep hill out of Upper Swell, as the wheels skidded, the horses slowed to a walking pace, and Bowlby took their heads.

'"Aunt" Phillippa?'

'What is it, dear . . . I'm very tired. Don't talk.'

'Now that "Uncle" Barnabas is a widower shall you marry him?'

'Really, Eirlys, what an impertinent question! You have no right to ask such a thing . . . and with poor dear "Aunt" Emily not even buried. You should be ashamed of yourself.'

'Well, I should like to know.'

'Be silent, and mind your own business.'

'It is my business, you know . . . more than that of anyone in the world. After all, I'm his bastard, and if he marries my mother . . . well!'

'Hush! For shame! How dare you say such wicked things! You are far too young to understand. I can't think what's come over you.'

'Well, I suppose I've grown up all of a sudden. Anyway, I'm not too young to know that I really am his bastard and I know that you had a great scene with him in the study this afternoon.'

'What rubbish!'

'Well, you did have a scene. It must have been terrible. You thought that you would just get married, once "Aunt" Emily was dead – just like that! And he told you that after all he had changed his mind. My God! It must have been terrible. You know, "Aunt" Phillippa, I am almost sorry for you. It must have been ghastly for you. But you did have a terrible scene with him, didn't you? Didn't you? Shouting at each other like lunatics.'

'That will do, Eirlys. We talked things over – naturally –

and I suppose, you little wretch, you were eavesdropping. How like you. You're a wicked deceitful child. I shall consider your punishment later.'

'Pooh! I didn't eavesdrop – didn't have to. You were both so angry and excited that you didn't even close the door properly. I could hear you from the schoolroom landing. So there! You can't punish me for that, you know.'

'We had a talk certainly. It was most necessary. I have already told you that we are all Roman Catholics now – all of us belong, at last, to the true Church of the Lord Jesus. "Uncle" Barnabas is a priest, and a priest forever in the eyes of God. Roman Catholic priests do not marry. You would know that if you were not such an ignorant and irreligious child.'

'And you never thought of it, either of you, in all your plotting and planning. The one thing you never thought of. So now you will have to put up with the second best, still have to be his mistress.'

'Eirlys, how dare you! Not another word. It is a very good thing you are going to school. High time.'

'To school? Oh, so that's it, is it? Just like Augustine and Maria Pia.'

'Yes. Next term your "Uncle" will be sending Maria Pia to a wonderful Convent school near Derby. It is run by some very pious nuns, of the Order of St Charles Borromeo. You will join Maria Pia. The food is simple, the discipline strict, the clothes black. It is just what you need. You have become a very heartless and sinful child. You have wallowed far too long in the luxuries and frivolities of Windrush Court. You should be thankful to think that the nuns will root out your faults. I was surprised indeed that they would even accept a child of – er – your kind.'

'And you – all alone at Windrush. You won't like that, will you?'

'I shall close Windrush. Your "Uncle" and I will of course remain friends. After all he is my Confessor and so I shall always have to live near him, wherever the work of God may take him. I must be near my Confessor for the sake of my soul and my eternal salvation . . . not for the horrible sort of reasons that you seem to think about, Eirlys. You have a nasty mind; I can't think where you got it from.'

'I see. I see. I see it all. The unwanted child got rid of, but always a house somewhere for the "kept woman". Well, God help the nuns when I get to Derby.'

The horses were trotting briskly now, the wheels crunching through the snow where it had drifted a little between the hedges. To start with, Phillippa and Eirlys had talked very quietly, but as their emotions had risen so had their voices. More than once the eyes of the coachman had slid sideways to meet those of the footman . . . such was the understanding between Tomkins and Bowlby that once was enough. Phillippa now closed her eyes as if in agony. Eirlys sat bolt upright; her little heart-shaped face, framed by its ermine bonnet, had never seemed more innocent or more demure. The big grey eyes looked straight ahead; the long lashes, as always, lay so placidly on the soft damask cheeks. The cold air had given a little colour – a faint bloom of peach – to her pale skin. Around her mouth, usually so solemn, there played the suspicion of a smile . . . a rather wicked little smile.

The carriage swung into the drive of the big house. The light from the front door flooded out on to the snow. Already standing there, on the gravel, with a groom at the horse's head, was a heavy black carriage, a species of brougham, hooded and closed. Featherston awaited them on the doorstep.

'Excuse me, ma'am, but there is a lady and two – er – gentlemen to see you. I have put them in the morning-room . . . the – er – drawing-room seemed unsuitable, ma'am.'

'Thank you, Featherston, but what an extraordinary time to call, and the day after Christmas too.'

'Yes, ma'am, that's what I thought, but they were most insistent, ma'am. They said it was an urgent matter of business – quite prepared to wait. In the morning-room, ma'am.'

'Very well, Featherston. Eirlys, go upstairs; I will deal with you later. Now, Featherston . . .'

On the hall-table she noticed one black topper – beaver, not silk – one 'deer-stalker' and one gamp with a parrot handle. In the morning-room she found a large man with a red face and a ferrety man with a pale face. There was a woman, stout and plain and yellow, with a heavy pince-nez, all in grey alpaca touched with jet and a black bonnet. It was the large man who spoke.

'Mrs Gatsby, I believe.'

'Yes . . .'

'Phillippa Thérèse Gatsby – born Cole-Hatt.'

'Certainly, but what is your business at this hour, sir?'

'I am Inspector Hilton, Madam, of the Gloucestershire Constabulary. Here is my card. This is Mr Dunn, my assistant. This is Mrs Doughty – a wardress.'

'Indeed. And in what manner, pray, can your business possibly concern me? The hour is late – it is almost time to dress for dinner.'

Phillippa, so big with child, had drawn herself up, drawn her furs even more closely around her face. She was as white as paper. Her eyes were green as a cat's. More than ever, at this moment, was she one of Rossetti's models – the Monna Vanna, the alluring Siren. Inspector Hilton flinched. He would do his duty to the end but never before had he found himself face to face with a Siren, a Medusa, a Gorgon, the Blessed Damozel, Cleopatra, La Princesse Lointain, Helen of Troy, a *femme fatale* and a tigress – all rolled into one. He was unnerved but held his ground.

'Phillippa Thérèse Gatsby, I have to arrest you in the name of the Law. The charge against you is that on the tenth of August last, at this house, Windrush Court, in the County of Gloucester, you did wilfully murder your husband, the late Colonel Harold Garlick Gatsby, by the administration of strychnine. I warn you that anything you may say will be taken down and may be used in evidence against you.'

He stood with his notebook poised.

'How too utterly absurd. There can be no possible evidence. My husband had had heart trouble for many years. When he was taken ill – he collapsed in the garden on a very hot afternoon – it was I who insisted that his doctor be summoned immediately. I adored him. The whole idea is too ridiculous – there can be no evidence.'

'The full evidence, Madam, will be laid before your legal advisers and also, of course, before a Grand Jury who may or may not return a True Bill. I may tell you, however, that a few nights ago, by order of the Home Secretary, your husband's body was exhumed . . .'

'Oh, no!'

'... was exhumed, Madam, from the churchyard at Nether Molding in this parish. Certain organs were removed, placed in jars and sent to the Chief Pathologist at St Bartholomew's Hospital, London.'

'The whole thing is quite outrageous. I suppose, however, since you insist upon taking it seriously, that I had better send my butler into the town for a solicitor.'

'Not now, Madam. I have the Public Prosecutor's Warrant. For tonight I have made arrangements for your comfort and accommodation at Stow-on-the-Wold Police Station. Tomorrow you will be conducted to the County Gaol at Gloucester where you will be lodged pending your trial. I must now ask you to accompany us.'

Phillippa Gatsby then made the greatest mistake of her life.

'I suppose,' she said, 'that you have been talking to Featherston.'

Eirlys had not gone upstairs as her mother had told her. She had been listening intently from the hall. But now, as demure, innocent and angelic as ever, she was at an upper window looking on to the drive. The light still streamed from the front door, while the rising moon was shining on the snow. She waited. Phillippa came first. Mrs Doughty had a hand on her shoulder. They got into the carriage and the two men followed them. And then, down the winding drive, under the shadow of the trees, Eirlys saw the carriage lamps vanishing into the night. The smile that had been playing for so long around the corners of her mouth became a laugh. She ran downstairs and pirouetted across the hall into the drawing-room. She rang the bell.

'Featherston.'

'Yes, Miss Eirlys.'

'Your mistress has gone out and will not be returning tonight.'

'Indeed, Miss.'

'Yes, Featherston. Dinner for one at half past eight.'

'Yes, Miss. Thank you, Miss.'

'Oh, and Featherston – champagne – the 1833 Veuve Clicquot.'

5 Gatsby *against* the Queen

And all that beauty, all that wealth e'er gave,
  Awaits alike th' inevitable hour.
The paths of glory lead but to the grave

THOMAS GRAY

'Unforgettable' – an over-used word but the only one I can find to conjure up those hectic days that followed upon the great débâcle.

Maria Pia and I were told nothing – absolutely nothing – of Phillippa's arrest and, except for a few walks in the lane with Miss Grigg, were confined to the darkened house until after Mama's funeral – winter days in the schoolroom, blinds drawn, the undertaker's men on the landing, and always those carriages in the drive, coming and going. During those days we never saw Papa, not until we walked behind him as the coffin was borne through the garden – a little snow falling upon the choir-boys' vestments – to lay it before the altar while yellow clouds of incense moved slowly through the draughty old church. And then there was the funeral itself – first a bonfire in the churchyard for the gravediggers, and then Papa's long funeral sermon, preached to a packed but dry-eyed church . . . how could it be otherwise when for so many years so few had seen her? He published that sermon – *Thoughts for Those Who Mourn* – bound in purple vellum, stamped in gilt with the Agnus Dei and crown of thorns . . . that book made money, a bedside book for the bereaved.

The next morning, without even seeing Papa, we were driven into Cheltenham in the dark dawn and taken to London on an early train. In view of Cecil Praz's excessive behaviour towards me, while Maria Pia sat frozen on the opposite seat of the railway carriage, it was as well that Aunt Caroline should meet us at Paddington . . . with her tight-lipped rectitude she at least made an excellent chaperone. After a night at Grillons – and never before had either of us even heard of such a thing as a hotel – we were taken to the vast and gloomy rooms of York House, and there, in Cardinal Wiseman's private chapel, we were baptized afresh into the Roman Church; the fat old man, remembering us at the croquet party, tried to explain to us the meaning of his guttural Irish-Latin, but it all remained, and still does, utterly incomprehensible. In any case our thoughts were far away with our dear Jane Grigg; she too had left the Rectory that morning but, by Papa's orders, on a different train. Somehow or other she and Eirlys plotted to have a few days together at the Trial, but it was many years before Maria Pia and I saw our dear Griggy again.

And then – why then came Derby, Aunt Caroline's large suburban house; the Convent of St Charles Borromeo and a black cloak for little Maria, and for me . . . Stonyhurst. But that – as I was determined as soon as I saw the place – was not for long. The poor Jesuits, who probably mistrusted my good looks and my merry laugh, threw me out before the end of my first term, on charges of infidelity, blasphemy, insubordination and immorality. My back still bears the scars of the tawse, but I had won my battle . . . I got away. The disciples of St Ignatius, however, as I was to discover half a century later, do not relish defeat. The Irish, bless them, loved me because I was the Pope's son, but between the Jesuits and the Roman Curia, you know, there was never much love lost . . . Stonyhurst had its revenge.

Immured in the Convent, and at Stonyhurst, Maria Pia and I were told nothing and knew nothing. No newspaper was ever seen within the walls of either place. It seems incredible that we two children were, very nearly, *dramatis personae* in one of the most sensational murder trials of the century – there was, I believe, some discussion as to whether or not I was too young to give evidence – and that we knew absolutely nothing about it . . . not until years after. But so it was. We were denied dear Eirlys's address and she was denied ours. We were denied Jane Grigg's address and she was denied ours. Griggy, however, managed to smuggle a note over to Windrush and this, probably through Featherston, eventually reached Eirlys . . . the very first missive in a long and very fateful correspondence. But for this smuggled note we might all have been lost to each other for years, if not forever . . . as indeed we almost were.

To start with, at the Convent and at Stonyhurst, Maria Pia was allowed to write one letter each week to me, and I was allowed to write one letter each week to her – censored of course. Alas, I have an engaging gift both for mimicry and for caricature. My marginal sketches of the Stonyhurst masters were as recognizable as they were cruel. All further letter writing, except to Aunt Caroline, was immediately forbidden. This veto, as I discovered later, was applied to both sides, so the priests must have written to the nuns about me.

As for the fate of Eirlys – I don't know whether it was Featherston or the police, it certainly wasn't Eirlys herself, who telegraphed to her Hampshire aunts – those aunts who had once upon a time been known simply as 'the beautiful Cole-Hatt girls'. One was now crippled, but the other two were as beautiful as Phillippa and both, like Phillippa, fashionable hostesses. They were not prepared to be seen dead within a hundred miles of any bastard niece. They were quite frantic when the Prosecution, out of the blue, decided to call Eirlys as a witness. It was a subpoena and the aunts could do nothing about it and so, for ten indescribable and emotional days, Eirlys and Jane Grigg sat together, clung to each other, in the gallery of the little Assize Court at Gloucester.

And then for Eirlys it was back to Hampshire where the aunts, in record time and with two ministers of the Crown to pull wires for them, had the child made into a Ward of Chancery. They shipped her off, with the Lord Chancellor's consent, to a very expensive finishing school in Switzerland – a school at Gstaad for such as her. There, naughtily but not unhappily, with other rich but unwanted girls, she awaited her inheritance.

That inheritance was vast. Harold Gatsby had left the Windrush Estate, with its big rent roll from farms and villages, the house in Montpelier Square and his entire fortune to Phillippa . . . really very decent of him in the circumstances. Phillippa, in her turn, had made a Will ignoring Eirlys and leaving everything to the Holy Catholic Church. Now although nobody ever suggested that she had murdered Harold for his money – she had plenty of Cole-Hatt money anyway – it was legally clear that she could not benefit from her crime. After her death in Holloway it was ruled that she had, in those few months between the croquet party and her death, quite wrongfully enjoyed the Windrush fortune. She had never had any right to it and could not therefore leave it to the Church. There were no legitimate Gatsby children and so – after the lawyers had had a gloriously profitable time playing with it – our Eirlys, our own dear Barbellion half-sister, got the lot . . . held in Trust by the Lord Chancellor. Two years after the Trial, when she emerged from the school at Gstaad, trained to sing and valse and ski, as well as to choose hats and lovers, she was the mistress of Windrush Court.

During the years Eirlys has seldom lived at Windrush . . . too many memories I suspect, although only yesterday she telephoned me from there to give me her annual tip for the Curragh. But she has, for some reason, always kept the place in perfect order, the ancient dream-like gardens more dream-like than ever. Only the fretted and gilded Pugin Chapel – Phillippa's pride – now looks like some neglected relic of an earlier day, which, of course, it is. Now and again, in the summer, in a great straw hat, with trailing scarves, a basket and scissors, Eirlys may occasionally be found wandering a little vaguely among the delphiniums and hollyhocks. She says she hates Windrush but every now and again there is something – something – that makes her go back. I remember a wonderful evening at Windrush. It was at the turn of the century. It was just after Papa's death and we were all back from Rome, and there, in the Lavender Court, Eirlys, Maria Pia, Jane Grigg and I talked and talked until the sun was low. And then, in the evening light, we drove over to Nether Molding to see once again, after forty-five years, the old Rectory, to stroll once again among the gravestones . . . but that is something I am keeping for the end of my story.

Clearly – and I myself speak as a happy carefree Irish rake – we were all Barbellions. As we grew up, all three of us, we found ourselves possessed of our full share, if not of Barbellion wickedness, at least of Barbellion exhibitionism – if I had had no money I might well have gone on the stage – and Barbellion defiance of what the world thinks. In addition to all this Eirlys had her mother's exotic beauty and, like Maria Pia, had remained into her beautiful old age an eternally restless, vivacious creature, with a strange predilection for expensive hotels, ruinous casinos, smart race meetings, caviar and Ming pots. Once, a fateful occasion, I was her escort in Rome, but more often I have visited her in her cool, white apartment – with the Corots on the wall – at the Negresco at Nice, or even more often at the little house in Montpelier Square. It was there, out of the kindness of her heart, that she kept on Featherston as her butler until one afternoon, at the age of a hundred, he faded away, just when he should have been serving tea. Eirlys was shopping in Bond Street when I was called to his room. He had been asking for me – for 'Master Augustine' – and then just as he died he told me something very peculiar about the croquet party and the medicine bottle ... very peculiar but perhaps, you know, he was a trifle delirious and I had better not repeat it ... it was so different from what came out at the Trial.

So much for Eirlys in the lifetime that has passed since the débâcle. Papa – her papa as well as ours – seems to have ignored her completely after his Conversion. He knew, I suppose, that those Cole-Hatt aunts would care for her somehow or other and, his own money being destined for the Church and for Christ, he was doubtless inspired by the Holy Ghost to let his three children have as little as possible. Eirlys, his bastard, I suppose he might ignore but Maria Pia and I were another matter. His London solicitors always paid my school and university fees, also – presumably – made some sort of payment to Aunt Caroline. We, his two legitimate children, also had a beggarly sum of 'pocket money', and then, when I was twenty-one, I had a small allowance. That didn't last long; the day I came into my Irish estates, from my Leapingwell uncle, it stopped dead. I had already been told, however, that when I was eighteen the little Palazzo Barbellion alla Chiaja in Naples – those pretty painted rooms and orange groves – would be mine for life, as also the house in the Via Tritone – with its tiled floors and tinkling fountain – the house where Papa and Monsignor Talbot had once hatched plots ... 'come over to us, dear Archdeacon, we will look after you'. With these two Italian houses, together with those coming to me from my uncle in County Meath – Derravaragh, Merrion Square in Dublin and the mansion in Belgravia – it will be seen that I was not homeless.

Papa did nothing for Maria Pia; after all she was only a girl and he may have assumed that she would take the veil. However, I always said that what was mine was hers, to use as she pleased. As a young woman she preferred her independence; it was therefore from her own home in the Faubourg St Germain that she planned her crazy journeys – camels through Arabia, horses through Persia and yaks through Tibet. But now and again, of course, she found the peace of Derravaragh irresistible, until finally – when travel days were done – she made it her home, working on her memoirs here in this room, the Palladian Library, where I am writing now. Sometimes she would work but more often, I think, she would look out of the window, towards the rushy lakes and beyond that to the distant line of Slieve Bloom – until her death a year ago.

And now, this morning, waiting for me on her window table, are the six little red morocco books, her girlhood 'journal', packed with such careful notes about . . . well, about all kinds of things – eavesdropping at Confession or at the Study door, about old Doctor Potts and how Papa bullied him, about minced goose and strychnine and about 'Bug Specific' – Papa's patent arsenical flea killer – and an awful lot, you know, about Mama's dreadful sufferings and Eirlys's visits to her bedroom . . . and about carriage lamps under the trees.

I am writing all this down not only because it is the story of what happened after the débâcle, but because it is also the story of what happened through those winter days when Phillippa was waiting – waiting and waiting – in her cell at Gloucester, an endless monotony broken only by visits from her solicitor and from a strange priest. What I am writing now may also help to explain why Papa was left untouched to pursue his glamorous journey from a rural parsonage to Divine Infallibility. After all, for the first twenty years after his Conversion, whether as priest, bishop or cardinal, he was still in England. That he was left alone by the Public Prosecutor is almost inexplicable. It shows either great cunning on Papa's part, or else it was scandalous . . . almost certainly it was scandalous.

At Phillippa's Trial he should, at the very least, have been arraigned in the Dock alongside his mistress – adulterer and accessory after the fact. Actually he was called only by the Defence and he testified only to Phillippa's piety. The whole Court in fact – for some mysterious reason – seemed intent upon minimizing the link between Windrush Court and the Rectory at Nether Molding.

Papa was in the Box for only five minutes, and only in the rôle of the Prisoner's priest . . . and then he left for his Aegean cruise.

But then Phillippa's Trial was in any case a farce. Technically, according to the evidence, justice was done. Oh yes, the Jury – although as always a pack of morons – really did 'a true and honest verdict give between the Prisoner at the Bar and Our Sovereign Lady the Queen'. Oh yes, there was no doubt about that. But thereafter, throughout England, the shock was so tremendous – after all, people who go to church just aren't expected to commit murder, that is reserved for thugs – that Phillippa's guilt was used, rather subtly, I think, to screen Papa. For one thing, it was felt that enough was enough. It was taken for granted, with Phillippa's disappearance behind bars, that the curtain had been rung down. Everyone, of course, had enjoyed it enormously but, of course, everyone had to pretend otherwise, had to pretend that they were glad it was over . . . 'all so distasteful'.

If there were any lingering doubts about Papa – and here and there, there may have been – it was probably being said that he had suffered enough or that adultery, after all, although a terrible sin, was not a crime. One must also remember that, although Eirlys, Maria Pia, Jane Grigg and I might tell each other, again and again, that Papa must have been a wife-poisoner, at the time of Phillippa's Trial in February 1855 the cause of Emily Barbellion's death had never been questioned . . . by anyone. For years she had been an invalid, almost bed-ridden, and old Doctor Potts, with Papa at his elbow, had written out the death-certificate with barely a glance at the body – 'heart failure arising from acute diarrhoea and gastritis'. And that, strictly speaking, was quite true – it was the cause of the gastritis that old Potts never questioned . . . why should he? Papa, moreover, gave the world a marvellous display of grief. In the few days that remained to him at Nether Molding he could be seen each morning on his knees at the graveside; there was that funeral sermon bound in vellum, and after that came the pink marble angel eternally hovering over the well-kept turf. Such suspicions as there might be were, after all, only half-formed ideas in the minds of us children, unspoken fears in the mind of a governess who had been dismissed, and in the mind of a discreditable and discredited curate.

And then, I suppose, as we grew older and as the years passed, although Jane Grigg must have hugged her secret thoughts almost every day of her life, Eirlys, Maria Pia and I were just happy Barbellion eccentrics. Our wealth, our lovely houses, our freedom, our rather high-handed and dissolute lives, were a glorious consolation for our macabre childhood. We did not forget Nether Molding, least of all our last Christmas there – that would hardly have been possible – but as we lay in the luxury of our *wagons-lits* between Paris and Rome, and so on to Naples, Venice, Vienna, Petersburg, our wonderful life of ballrooms, race courses and opera . . . well, somehow or other, you know, we let the whole thing fade into the past. We let the dead bury their dead. Anyway, once Papa was inside the Vatican, there was not much we could do; one could hardly expect the Pope to extradite himself at the request of Scotland Yard. So we did nothing, not until now . . . sixty-five years after.

There were other reasons why, to the end of his days, Barnabas Barbellion should go scot free. At the time of Phillippa's arrest it is true that there may have been nothing very tangible to connect the death of Harold Gatsby with the death of Emily Barbellion . . . nothing except gossip and what we children were thinking – in our childish way. But there were other reasons, you know, why the Law left Papa so severely alone. At the Trial itself, after a mere five minutes in the Witness Box he apologized to the Judge, as publicly as possible, for his hurried departure . . . the *Enchantress*, with royalty on board, was awaiting him in the Solent. Papa, of course, had long been moving in such exalted circles . . . weaving a web from his chambers in Albany . . . pulling wires . . . winning golden opinions.

He was also fortunate in that there had already, in one year, been three big scandals – one in Society, one in the Cabinet and one in the Church, all of them very sexy. The Queen was displeased and was against another scandal at all costs. The day after Phillippa was found guilty, the Home Secretary – and Sydney Herbert was a pliant man as well as a Ritualist – took the Trans-European Express. At the Gare de Lyon he told a reporter that he was *en route* for the Crimea. That was plausible; it was the year of Sebastopol and all the world knew that the Home Secretary was the friend of Flo Nightingale. Papa, incidentally, never gave up hope of getting those two into the Roman net. What the world did not know was that in actual fact the Home Secretary changed trains at Belgrade and joined the *Enchantress* at Athens. Thereafter, the Barbellion Case, if there had ever been one, was closed. If the Police had ever had a Barbellion File, it was burnt. And twenty years later when, as Cardinal of England, he was at Buckingham Palace or at Windsor, he was always honoured as a great prince. On the day of his Conversion he had ingeniously divested himself of his whole Anglican life as if it were some outworn garment. So – it has been left to me, in my last years, to prove his guilt.

In the first months of 1855 Maria Pia and I were so totally imprisoned in our schools – the Convent and Stonyhurst – that, as I have said, we knew nothing of either the arrest or the Trial. Eirlys knew. Jane Grigg knew. Eirlys, having been subpoenaed, went to Gloucester. Plotting together, Eirlys and Jane Grigg stayed with Jane's aunt in Cheltenham, driving over to the County Court each morning in the dog-cart, usually through pouring rain. They then hid themselves at the back of the tiny public gallery. I have, of course, all the transcripts of the Trial, REGINA V. GATSBY, but better still I have Jane Grigg, here with me in the Library at Derravaragh, to tell me once again how it all happened.

LENTEN ASSIZE OF THE COUNTY OF GLOUCESTER

WEDNESDAY, 18TH FEBRUARY, 1855

IN REGINA V. GATSBY

JUDGE

Lord John Fitzjohn Grandison, K.C.S.I., K.C.B., a Judge of the Queen's Bench Division of the High Court of Justice

---

COUNSEL FOR THE CROWN

Attorney-General: Sir Travers McKenzie, P.C., Q.C.
Mr Jeremy Whitely, Q.C.
Mr Thomas Graydon, Q.C.
Instructed on Behalf of the Treasury by Messrs Strangeways and Strangeways of Lincolns Inn

---

COUNSEL FOR THE DEFENCE

Sir Frederick Hazlewood Ford-Bryce, Q.C.
Mr Arthur Longville
Instructed on Behalf of the Prisoner by Messrs
Markby and Treloar of Gloucester

INDICTMENT

The Queen
against
Phillippa Thérèse Gatsby
Presentment of the Grand Jury

Phillippa Thérèse Gatsby, aged 37, indicted that she did on 10th August in the Year 1854, at Windrush Court, in the Parish of Nether Molding, in the County of Gloucester, feloniously, wilfully and of her malice aforethought, kill and murder her husband, Harold Garlick Gatsby, Lord Lieutenant of Gloucestershire, by the administration of poison, to wit strychnine.

JURY

Stuart Chamberlain, Alderman	Gloucester (Foreman)
Tom Ball, Farmer	Chipping Sodbury
Adam Brockland, Cordwainer	Cirencester
Isidore Isaacs, Jeweller	Cheltenham
Jacques Le Mesurier, Engraver	Painswick
Patrick O'Donoghue, Innkeeper	Bibury
Keith Platten, Chandler	Gloucester
John Sutton, Miller	Andoversford
Henry Thierens, Tailor	Cheltenham
John Thornbury, Slaughterer	Gloucester
Peter Waddis, Drysalterer	Stroud
Lewis Ramsbottom, Saddler	Stow-on-the-Wold

Every day in the little Assize Court at Gloucester the stench of human bodies mixed itself with the stench of steam pipes, to become more and more foetid as the hours passed. The winter days were dark, the Court was darker still. Through barred windows encrusted with brown dirt, the sky was like night. All day, somewhere up in the roof, the gas jets hissed, but Judge and Counsel needed candles to read their papers. In a Court intended for, perhaps, a hundred people, there were two hundred – their heavy clothes sodden by the February rains. Again and again the Judge, Lord John Fitzjohn Grandison, called for ventilation. Then an usher would open a door, but ventilation was not possible.

Only one person retained any dignity – cool and serene. It was the Prisoner. Phillippa, throughout her Trial, was as white as she had been that Christmas night when they arrested her in the morning-room at Windrush Court. Despite her pregnancy she refused a chair and never once – through all those long hours – did she hold on to the rails of the Dock. Never once did she look towards the Jury or towards the Witness Box. For ten whole days she stood silent and rigid, her eyes fixed upon old Grandison as the sweat, oozing from beneath his wig and his spectacles, ran down his purple face to saturate his Dundreary whiskers. Every day he looked more and more like a drawing by Gillray. In the end he was palpably disconcerted by her presence. He fidgeted. He avoided her gaze. And when the time came to sentence her he stared up into the blaze of gas jets, choking over his words. After that she walked slowly and quietly back to her cell.

Only once, each morning, did she play to the gallery or make a gesture of any kind. Phillippa knew the story of those who had suffered for their Faith . . . from Jesus Christ onwards. She knew, for instance, exactly how Mary of Scotland, three hundred years before her, in front of a great log fire in the Hall of Fotheringhay, came to lay her head upon the block – throwing off an outer robe of black to stand before the executioner all in scarlet – the colour of martyrdom. Every morning Phillippa arrived in Court in a mantle of black Persian lamb; as she let it fall on to the chair behind her she, too, stood before the Court in scarlet. She wore a single locket; nobody knew until she died that it contained a sacramental wafer, blessed for her by Pius the Ninth and kept for her last hour. For the rest, so far as she was concerned, the Court seemed not to exist. She might be guilty, she might be innocent, she might be silent, but she was not prepared to make it an easy trial for anyone.

Jane Grigg had no reason to love Phillippa Gatsby. She not

only knew her wickedness, her heartlessness, but she, more than anyone – except perhaps little Eirlys – had been snubbed again and again . . . as the mere governess. And yet never once throughout the Trial, so she tells me, was she dry-eyed. The Judge and Counsel were disconcerted and embarrassed by Phillippa's sheer presence. Other people wept. Only Eirlys seemed gay.

As Sir Travers McKenzie, leading Counsel for the Crown, rose to address the Court, there was a great hush, curiously heightened by the rumble of wagon wheels on the cobbles outside. On the second day the Judge ordered straw to be laid in the street . . . as if someone was dying. In the gloom of the Court there could hardly be a note of colour – only the white of wigs and papers, only the scarlet of the Judge's robe, made shabby by the more brilliant scarlet of Phillippa's dress.

Sir Travers McKenzie, like all barristers, was an exhibitionist, a frustrated actor just as most actors are frustrated barristers . . . their rôles are similar. He was a heavy man with a heavy humour. He was endowed with a vast yellowish and moon-like face set above a double-chin, or whole series of chins. At this moment he was happy. He would play with this woman. He could see his road clear, all the way to the gallows. He could even pretend to be fair. He took one long look at the Jury . . . yes, that was all right – that Jew in the back row might be too clever, but the other eleven were the usual stupid lot. Yes, he decided that he could be cruel under a heavy disguise of impartiality.

*

SIR TRAVERS MCKENZIE: May it please your Lordship, Gentlemen of the Jury: it is my painful duty, in conjunction with my learned friends, to lay before you the evidence in support of the terrible indictment which you have just heard read – one of the most terrible in the annals of British Justice. You have heard the Prisoner plead Not Guilty. Very well.

You know that the charge against the Prisoner at the Bar is that of her malice aforethought she did murder her husband – the late Colonel Harold Garlick Gatsby, formerly Lord Lieutenant of this County and Master of the Foxhounds, by administering or causing to be administered to him, strychnine.

Strychnine is a most deadly poison of which, as I shall bring evidence to prove, he was made to take a quantity many times in excess of the fatal dose. I can remember no crime, Gentlemen of the Jury, more foul, more malicious, more cunning or more degrading than the one it is now your duty to consider. It is my solemn duty to present to you the evidence for the Prosecution, but so foul is this act that I – yes, even I – must pray to Almighty God that the woman in the Dock may be innocent. That any woman could do this deed must seem to all of us so terrible – nay, so incredible – that we must pray that she is innocent. Well, we shall see.

The Prisoner's maiden name, Gentlemen, was Cole-Hatt. Now, the Cole-Hatts are a family of great substance in the County of Hampshire, landed gentry who, for many centuries, have played a prominent part in the life of their County and their Country, sending sons into Parliament – in the Tory cause, I need hardly say – into Her Majesty's services or even into the Church – two Cole-Hatts in the last century reached the Episcopal Bench and two wielded the Field-Marshal's baton. How tragic, therefore, that any member of such a family could fall so low as has the Prisoner at the Bar. Phillippa Gatsby had every possible advantage in her upbringing and in her education ... delicately nurtured, she was brought up in the paths of piety and gentility. In due course – as an eligible debutante – her parents married her to Colonel Gatsby, a wealthy landowner and the future Lord Lieutenant of this County. A fashionable wedding at St George's, Hanover Square, was inevitable. In short, there seemed to be nothing between Phillippa Gatsby and a life which most young women would consider to be bliss – complete happiness as wife, mother, hostess at the highest level of English Society. Gentlemen, you have before you in the Dock not some wretched creature from the streets but, rather, a great English lady.

I emphasize these points, Gentlemen, because in addressing you on behalf of the Crown, I have, with the greatest impartiality, to show how incredible, indeed how impossible, is the very idea that a woman of such high birth should sink so low. Alas, it is my duty to show how great was the fall. I have to show you how, during the sixteen years when the Prisoner was living as the spouse of Harold Gatsby, she was also leading a life of the grossest hypocrisy – posing as a wife and hostess, as a Churchwoman of deep piety, as a lady-bountiful among her husband's tenants . . . she claims to have given away to the cottagers over a hundred bibles and prayer-books. And yet, Gentlemen of the Jury, I have to tell you that during the whole of those sixteen years – once the honeymoon at Baden was over – Phillippa Gatsby refused ever to share her bed with her lawfully wedded husband. As decent Englishmen I see that you recoil in horror. You may well do so. The Prisoner is charged with a far greater crime than that but, if the Gatsby marriage was childless, then I must ask you – with whom lay the fault?

My only object, Gentlemen, in this terrible situation, is to be scrupulously fair, to give the Prisoner the benefit of any shred of doubt that there may be . . . I only wish that I had been able to find some such shred. Alas, I must tell you that while the Prisoner, through all those years, was posing as a devout Churchwoman, currying favour with the most eminent divines in the land, she was also indulging in the grossest Papistical practices, not excluding fasting, penance and – just think of it – Auricular Confession, intimately and privately with a priest, behind locked doors and at an Anglican altar . . . practices which must be truly revolting to every Englishman, not least to twelve staunch Protestants such as yourselves.

As Sir Travers McKenzie paused to recover his equanimity, to clear his throat, to roll his eyes and to whisper to his Junior, the Jury looked stolidly ahead – only Patrick O'Donoghue from Bibury and Isidore Isaacs from Cheltenham blinked a little at the thought of their own Protestantism. Sir Travers hitched up his gown on his shoulders and glowered around him to command silence.

SIR TRAVERS MCKENZIE: Finally, Gentlemen, as doubtless His Lordship will direct you, I must repeat that unless the guilt of the Prisoner is proved without one scintilla of doubt, she must leave this Court a free woman. In recent weeks you will almost certainly have heard much gossip and innuendo, you may even have read a great deal of nonsense in the newspapers. All this you must dismiss from your minds as if it had never been, basing your verdict solely upon the evidence to be presented to you by my learned friend and by myself. I have said that I shall prove to you that Phillippa Gatsby is a hypocrite, a Papist and an adulteress . . . all things which, under English Law, strange as it may seem, are not crimes; nor, of course, are they evidence of murder. You must dismiss them from your minds as if they had never been. I mention them only to show how loathsome is the character of the Prisoner at the Bar.

It was on the afternoon of August the Tenth last that there occurred the awful tragedy which you now have to consider. At Windrush Court which, as you may know, is the Gloucestershire seat of the Gatsbys, there was a large garden-party, in fact a house-party, although we are concerned only with the events of a single afternoon. It was a fashionable but not a frivolous party. Far from it – among the guests were many clergy, several bishops and several eminent members of the Anglican House of Laity, also – for some reason which I do not pretend to understand – a certain Cardinal Wiseman, the leader of the Papist faction in this country. These Windrush house-parties – annual events – were apparently well-known. They were, in effect, religious gatherings – theological discussion, lectures, devotional exercises and prayer meetings being of their substance. On the afternoon in question, however, some of the guests, having indulged in a game of croquet, were gathered in the shade of the trees to partake of afternoon tea.

Now, I shall be calling Doctor Leonard Clayton, the Gatsbys' family doctor, to tell you that Colonel Gatsby suffered from a chronic but rather mild defect of the heart. From time to time this caused breathlessness and palpitations, but was not in any way serious, certainly not lethal At about five o'clock Mrs Gatsby was deep in conversation with the Cardinal and with her own Rector. Suddenly she was interrupted; her butler, a Mr Bertram Featherston, informed her that his master was not only suffering from his usual palpitations, but had collapsed. Several bystanders – as I shall show – were deeply shocked at the Prisoner's callous indifference to this news. She was reluctant even to send a groom for the doctor and it was left to the loyal

Featherston, with the help of a footman and one of the guests, to carry Colonel Gatsby to the house where, with the aid of his valet, he was laid on his bed.

Now I am not suggesting, Gentlemen of the Jury, that this collapse, in the midst of a croquet party, was the actual moment of murder. Oh no, we are up against something far more cunning than that. The immediate cause of Colonel Gatsby's collapse was almost certainly the heat – it was the hottest day of the year – but, given his heart condition, it was sooner or later inevitable, and it was then, when the poor man was stricken down, that this cruel woman's machinations would be put into operation.

Once Colonel Gatsby was on his bed, Mr Featherston managed to give his master a little brandy and then – and at this point, Gentlemen, please mark my words – and then, in accordance with the Prisoner's instructions, administered a dose of what she called 'his usual medicine' . . . kept in a cupboard in her room . . . separate bedrooms, Gentlemen, and the husband's medicine kept in the wife's bedroom. Make what you like of it – words fail me! In administering the medicine Mr Featherston will tell you that he most carefully followed the directions on the label – 'DOSE: ONE TEASPOONFUL, TO BE TAKEN IN WATER WHEN REQUIRED'. Now remember – for it is the very core of this tragedy – that the medicine was administered upon the Prisoner's instructions and in accordance with the label on the bottle, but – as they will tell you – neither the butler nor the valet had ever seen that bottle before. That is not surprising since it was kept in a cupboard in the Prisoner's room. Moreover, Gentlemen, the label on the bottle was a gross forgery.

THE JUDGE: Do I understand you rightly, Sir Travers – that the label was a forgery!

SIR TRAVERS MCKENZIE: Certainly, Me Lud.

THE JUDGE: I presume, Sir Travers, that you will be bringing evidence to prove that.

SIR TRAVERS MCKENZIE: Certainly, Me Lud, and of the most convincing nature.

THE JUDGE: Pray proceed, Sir Travers.

SIR TRAVERS MCKENZIE: I am much obliged, Me Lud. Now,

Gentlemen, Mr Featherston had some difficulty in getting the medicine glass between his master's teeth. The valet, Mr Beaver, had to hold the Colonel's head while the medicine was poured down his throat. No sooner had this been done than Colonel Harold Gatsby was seized with trembling, cramp, an arched back, a fixed and ghastly grin, bloodshot eyes, paralysis of the limbs, discolouration of the skin, vomiting and diarrhoea. All, as I shall show, classical symptoms. Within ten minutes he had passed from this world, dead from an overdose of strychnine. This is a poison more often used for killing rats; there was an ample supply in the Harness Room.

You and I, Gentlemen of the Jury, have too much worldly wisdom to take too much notice of what may be printed in the daily news sheets. Nevertheless, I cannot completely ignore the fact that both in Gloucester and in London it is being put about – possibly under some malign influence – that this Prosecution is based solely upon gossip and innuendo. A pretty woman, Gentlemen, will always find friends in Grub Street, but also it behoves me to squash this nonsense once and for all. The Crown does not act upon gossip. I shall be calling upon Mr Coleherne, the eminent Home Office Pathologist, to tell you that the body of the late Colonel Gatsby was exhumed from Nether Molding churchyard on the night of 22nd December last, and that various organs were found to be riddled – yes, Gentlemen, positively riddled – with *nux vomica* or strychnine. Colonel Harold Gatsby, the Lord Lieutenant of this County, had been given some thirty times the fatal dose.

With your permission, Me Lud, I will now call my first witness – Miss Eirlys Cole-Hatt.

THE JUDGE: A moment, Sir Travers. I understand that your witness is sixteen years of age – in our legal parlance still an 'infant' and unable, therefore, to take the oath. It will be for me to decide whether or not she is a fit person to give evidence.

SIR TRAVERS MCKENZIE: I am greatly obliged to you, Me Lud. Call Miss Cole-Hatt.

USHER: Cole-Hatt! Cole-Hatt! Cole-Hatt!

Our dear little Eirlys, still in the very deepest mourning for her

'Uncle' Harold, entered the Witness Box. She was, so Jane Grigg assures me, as cool as a cucumber. She cast her big grey eyes upon the Judge.

THE JUDGE: Now, there is nothing to be frightened of, Eirlys.

EIRLYS: Thank you, I'm not frightened.

THE JUDGE: Hm! That's good. You only have to speak up so that we may all hear you, and to speak the truth. First of all, however, pray tell me, Eirlys, do you know the difference between a truth and an untruth?

EIRLYS: Oh, yes, my Lord, of course. The truth is saying what is, an untruth is saying what isn't.

THE JUDGE: An excellent answer, my dear. Sir Travers, you may proceed.

SIR TRAVERS MCKENZIE: I am greatly obliged to you, Me Lud. Now, Miss Cole-Hatt, I have only a few simple questions to ask you, so do not be nervous . . .

EIRLYS: I'm not nervous.

SIR TRAVERS MCKENZIE: Oh, quite, quite. That's good. Now, your full name is Eirlys Magdalen Cole-Hatt.

EIRLYS: Yes, I was named after the Woman taken in Adultery.

SIR TRAVERS MCKENZIE: Really. I don't think, Me Lud, that we need have worried ourselves as to whether this witness was sufficiently mature to give evidence. Now, Miss Cole-Hatt, your home is at Windrush Court, near Stow-on-the-Wold, is it not?

EIRLYS: No, it's not.

SIR TRAVERS MCKENZIE: I beg your pardon.

EIRLYS: I said, no, it's not. After the arrest of – er – Mrs Gatsby, I was immediately removed to the house of my aunt – Miss Elizabeth Cole-Hatt – at Coquet Hall, near Petersfield in Hampshire. I suppose that must be called my home . . . at any rate I'm living there till they decide how to get rid of me.

SIR TRAVERS MCKENZIE: Thank you, but until you were – as you put it – removed to Hampshire, your home was always at Windrush Court, with Colonel and Mrs Gatsby, was it not?

EIRLYS: Yes.

SIR TRAVERS MCKENZIE: And you are sixteen years of age. What was the date of your birth – the year, I mean?

EIRLYS: March 18th, 1838.

SIR TRAVERS MCKENZIE: I see, so you will soon be seventeen. And where were you born?

EIRLYS: How on earth should I know? We once visited Basle and somebody said, 'this is the town where you were born'. It may be true, it may not. I was told so many lies.

SIR TRAVERS MCKENZIE: So you were probably born at Basle in March 1838. Now the Prisoner, Phillippa Gatsby, in whose home you have been brought up, is your aunt?

EIRLYS: No, she is my mother.

SIR TRAVERS MCKENZIE: Hm! Hm! Really! But surely, Miss Cole-Hatt, everyone speaks of you and always has spoken of you as the 'niece' of the Gatsbys – have they not?

EIRLYS: Yes, they have, but it has always been a bloody lie, and I was told just now, by the Judge, to speak the truth. Mrs Gatsby is my mother and Colonel Gatsby was *not* my father. I am therefore a bastard, and in any case 'Uncle' Harold was probably impotent.

SIR TRAVERS MCKENZIE: Really, Me Lud ... the innocent maid!

THE JUDGE: Quite, Sir Travers, quite! Rather overwhelming, but pray proceed.

SIR TRAVERS MCKENZIE: I am much obliged, Me Lud. But Miss Cole-Hatt, if you have always been referred to as the 'niece' of the Gatsbys, and have never in your life been told otherwise, how do you know that you are – er – illegitimate ... if you know what that word means?

EIRLYS: It's in the dictionary. I know, anyway, because when I was about fourteen I was cheeky to a parlourmaid and she said I was only a 'by-blow'. Now, I didn't know what that meant so I asked Micky Slate, one of the stable boys who was in love with me, and when we were alone in the hayloft he said that it meant I was 'born on the wrong side of the blanket'. That sounded pretty silly, too, so I asked Bowlby, the carriage footman, what it meant, and he said it meant I was 'a bloody little bastard'. That was in the dictionary all right, so I had got there at last – a bloody little bastard – that's me!

SIR TRAVERS MCKENZIE: I see. But of course, Miss Cole-Hatt, young though you are, you must know that servants – given half a chance – will say these things.

EIRLYS: Yes, that is why I asked my mother if it was true. At first she denied it and then, in a storm of sobs, she said it was quite true but that her love and my birth had been very wonderful and pure and lovely, and that my real father was one of the greatest men who ever lived. I told her not to be such a fool . . .

SIR TRAVERS MCKENZIE: Did she tell you your father's name, and whether she still loved him?

EIRLYS: No, she simply said he was the greatest man since Jesus Christ. That doesn't sound very likely, does it?

SIR TRAVERS MCKENZIE: But you definitely understood that the late Colonel Gatsby was not your father.

EIRLYS: Oh, no. My mother simply said that 'Uncle' Harold – Colonel Gatsby, I mean – had known of her sin, that he had understood and had forgiven her, and that he had offered me a home forever – as her 'niece'. She said that I ought to be very grateful, that very few 'children like me' were so fortunate.

SIR TRAVERS MCKENZIE: I see. So you, Miss Cole-Hatt, were born in March 1838, probably in Basle – the birth does not appear to have been registered in either Switzerland or England, Me Lud. Your mother, Phillippa Gatsby, and Colonel Harold Gatsby were married at St George's, Hanover Square, the following November. I have the marriage certificate in my hand if your Lordship or the Gentlemen of the Jury should wish to see it . . .

THE JUDGE: That is quite unnecessary, Sir Travers, please get on.

SIR TRAVERS MCKENZIE: I am much obliged, Me Lud. They were married in fact, Miss Cole-Hatt, when you were eight months old – that is so, is it not?

EIRLYS: If you say so. How should I know? I've never worked it out.

SIR TRAVERS MCKENZIE: . . . and had been engaged only six months. I have here, Me Lud, a cutting from *The Times* newspaper, if you or . . .

THE JUDGE: No, no. We will take your word for it, Sir Travers. Do not waste the time of the Court.

SIR TRAVERS MCKENZIE: I am obliged, Me Lud. I think, Me Lud, that the late Colonel Gatsby was an extremely magnanimous man. And now, Miss Cole-Hatt – and here I come to the point – can you tell the Court the name of your father?

EIRLYS: No, of course not . . . at least, that is . . .

But Sir Frederick Hazlewood Ford-Bryce, Counsel for the Defence, was already on his feet – his eyes starting from his sallow face, his hands pushing his wig back on his head.

SIR FREDERICK FORD-BRYCE: Me Lud! I really must object, Me Lud. This is unprecedented. So far, Me Lud, my learned friend has not extracted from this young and innocent girl one iota of evidence bearing upon the indictment. I admit – his case being so weak, so hopelessly weak – that he is within his rights in denigrating Mrs Gatsby's character, that there is in fact little else he can do. Whether, Me Lud, he is doing himself or his case any good by manoeuvring this child into blackening the morals of her own mother, is something that the Jury will have to decide. But to ask this young girl, this sweet and innocent maid, barely acquainted with the facts of life, the name of her putative father, is as insulting as it is obscene. To ask a little girl to discuss her own base birth is wholly deplorable, Me Lud. My learned friend has made his point – seventeen years ago, Mrs Gatsby – Phillippa Cole-Hatt as she then was – committed a youthful indiscretion and paid the price. Very well. It is irrelevant, Me Lud, and enough is enough . . . I object.

THE JUDGE: I think, Sir Travers, that there is some substance in Sir Frederick's objection . . .

SIR TRAVERS MCKENZIE: There is no need, Me Lud, for my learned friend to get so heated. I was only trying, Me Lud, to discover the name of the man with whom the Prisoner – even after many years – might still be in league, or even in love, for whose sake she might have wished to dispose of her lawful husband. However, if your Lordship rules otherwise, the . . .

THE JUDGE: I do, Sir Travers. It was laid down by Lord Justice Ramsbottom, in 1829, in Perkins v. the Battersea Guardians, that nobody, whether on oath or, as in this case, pledged to speak the truth, can possibly name their own father. In the nature of things it must always be hearsay and hearsay is not evidence.

SIR TRAVERS MCKENZIE: Very well, Me Lud, as you please. I bow to your ruling . . . after all there may have been many other men in the life of this deplorable and degraded woman, as anxious as she was to see the late Colonel Gatsby out of the way. Me Lud, I have no further questions to ask the witness.

THE JUDGE: Very well, Sir Travers. Sir Frederick, do you wish to cross-examine?

SIR FREDERICK FORD-BRYCE: Briefly, Me Lud. Miss Cole-Hatt, during the sixteen years of your life at Windrush Court, were you happy?

EIRLYS: I don't remember the first five.

SIR FREDERICK FORD-BRYCE: Oh, quite, quite. But so far as you remember, let us say, the last ten, have you been happy?

EIRLYS: No.

SIR FREDERICK FORD-BRYCE: Indeed. You must, must you not, have been a very demanding young lady. You were, after all, given a home in one of the finest houses in England. I understand that you were surrounded by nursemaids and servants, that you wore the finest clothes a young woman could wish for, that the household dined off the costliest viands, and that you had, first, a nursery full of toys and then, more recently, your own pony in the stables, and always, of course, ample pocket money. True, you might have been lonely but I am instructed that you shared a governess with the two children at the Rectory, thereby securing both companionship and a liberal education. What had you to complain of – you were not beaten, were you?

EIRLYS: No.

SIR FREDERICK FORD-BRYCE: Nor abused?

EIRLYS: No.

SIR FREDERICK FORD-BRYCE: What then? Surely you must have been a very difficult young lady to please. Perhaps Colonel and Mrs Gatsby spoilt you?

EIRLYS: Oh, 'Uncle' Harold – Colonel Gatsby, I mean – gave me all I wanted – money, pretty dresses, ponies . . . all those sort of things, but he hardly ever spoke to me. My mother – over there in the Dock – used to be kind to me years ago, fussing over me, dressing me up and showing me off to her friends . . . until I dragged from her the secret of my birth. Since then, almost every day, she has reproached me with her own sin as if it were my own. I have wept every night.

SIR FREDERICK FORD-BRYCE: Thank you, Miss Cole-Hatt. It seems to me, Me Lud, that this child would naturally be perturbed at the discovery of her own illegitimacy, while her mother would be no less concerned that her own youthful lapse – she was only nineteen at the time – had been unearthed. All that would fully explain a few 'words' on both sides which, no doubt, the child has exaggerated. This witness, Gentlemen of the Jury, may be largely discounted. Mrs Gatsby, quite clearly, was an affectionate, kindly and generous mother, lavishing everything upon this ungrateful girl. It is inconceivable to me, and doubtless to you, that an English lady possessed of such great maternal virtues, could be guilty of such a terrible crime as murder. Thank you, Miss Cole-Hatt.

As Eirlys walked back to the public gallery there were a few who shed tears for her; there were far more who, metaphorically speaking, withdrew the hem of their garments. On Eirlys's pretty face there was a broad grin . . . she had done what she wanted.

SIR TRAVERS MCKENZIE: I call my next witness, Me Lud. Bertram Featherston.

USHER: Featherston! Featherston! Featherston!

Poor Featherston! He was still shaken by the events of last August, and now this awful Trial was bringing it all back – these terrible, bullying, hectoring lawyers. You didn't know whether you were on your head or your heels. He was trembling. Behind his thick steel-rimmed glasses he was bleary-eyed after a sleepless night, but he was immaculate. Once in the Box he held his chin high and, for all his quavering voice, did his best – a gallant little man.

SIR TRAVERS MCKENZIE: Your name is Bertram Featherston; you are fifty-four years of age? Since their marriage you have been employed by the late Colonel and Mrs Gatsby as butler at Windrush Court?

FEATHERSTON: Yes, sir.

SIR TRAVERS MCKENZIE: Are you still living there?

FEATHERSTON: Yes, sir, as a kind of caretaker as it were, on full wages, paid by the solicitors, sir – most kind and considerate – just until – er – er – matters are settled, sir.

SIR TRAVERS MCKENZIE: Yes, yes. Now, Mr Featherston, on the afternoon of 10 August last, Colonel and Mrs Gatsby were entertaining a large number of guests in the garden at Windrush. They had been playing croquet and, since it was an exceedingly hot day . . . Me Lud, I have the meteorological report, Me Lud, if you wish to . . .

THE JUDGE: No, no. Don't waste the time of the Court, Sir Travers.

SIR TRAVERS MCKENZIE: I am much obliged, Me Lud. They had been playing croquet, Mr Featherston, and were glad to relax in the shade of the trees and to partake of afternoon tea. Now, you were present, were you not?

FEATHERSTON: I was in charge of the footmen, the parlourmaids and a couple of pages – about fifteen servants in all, sir. We were very busy as we had to serve strawberries and cream as well as the usual sort of tea.

SIR TRAVERS MCKENZIE: Well, never mind all that. Just tell us, in your own words, what happened . . . round about five o'clock.

FEATHERSTON: Well, sir, it was Father Martin, a nice young clergyman from London – most pleasant and amiable, sir – who first told me that the Colonel was unwell. Now, Colonel Gatsby, sir, had always suffered from a heart defect; from time to time he was subject to palpitations and to attacks of breathlessness. I immediately recognized the customary symptoms. These attacks were not usually serious – half an hour in an armchair or on the bed, a drop of brandy, and all was well again. That afternoon it was different. Perhaps it was the great heat but I realized at once, sir, that the attack was more serious than usual – the Colonel had collapsed.

SIR TRAVERS MCKENZIE: You mean he was unconscious?

FEATHERSTON: His eyes were closed and he was unaware of those around him, but he could still groan. Father Martin summoned a Sister Jessica – a kind of nurse-nun, sir, a friend of that Miss Nightingale – and while she bathed the Colonel's forehead I went over to Mrs Gatsby to tell her what had happened.

SIR TRAVERS MCKENZIE: And how did she take it, Mr Featherston?

FEATHERSTON: Well, sir, she was very deep in conversation with a stout gentleman in red.

THE JUDGE: Do my ears deceive me, Sir Travers, In red? A soldier . . .

FEATHERSTON: Oh, no, my Lord. He was in bright red but I have been told that his name was Cardinal Wiseman, a Roman Catholic I understand. Mrs Gatsby was talking to him and to our own dear Rector, Archdeacon Barbellion.

SIR TRAVERS MCKENZIE: Hm! Highly ecumenical, Me Lud.

THE JUDGE: Ha! Ha! Go on Mr Featherston.

FEATHERSTON: Yes, my Lord. I told the mistress of the Colonel's collapse. I don't wish to be disrespectful, sir, but she was – I would say – very callous like, very indifferent. She was annoyed, I think, at being interrupted and ordered me to get the master to his room and to give him what she called 'his usual medicine'. Father Martin joined us, sir, but she was most unwilling, sir, most unwilling even to let him send for the doctor.

SIR TRAVERS MCKENZIE: I see – a cruel and callous woman. I understand, Mr Featherston, that you and one of the footmen carried Colonel Gatsby into the house and laid him upon his bed?

FEATHERSTON: Yes, sir, and then we did as the mistress had told me. I called Mr Beaver, the valet, and together we managed to get a little brandy between the Colonel's teeth. Then, sir, I went to Mrs Gatsby's bedroom, to the corner cupboard – as she had told me – and found the bottle of white medicine. Apart from some pills it was the only bottle in the cupboard.

SIR TRAVERS MCKENZIE: Was the cupboard locked?

FEATHERSTON: No, sir. There was no key.

SIR TRAVERS MCKENZIE: I see. So Mrs Gatsby could, at any time, have sent anyone she liked to get the medicine and dose the Colonel. Go on, Mr Featherston.

FEATHERSTON: Well, sir, I brought the medicine back to the Colonel's room. The label was quite clear – 'ONE TEASPOONFUL, TO BE TAKEN IN WATER WHEN REQUIRED'. Mr Beaver had to hold the Colonel's jaw while I poured the medicine down the poor man's throat. And then, sir . . .

SIR TRAVERS MCKENZIE: Just a moment, Mr Featherston. Let us go back. Was it *usual* for Mrs Gatsby to keep her husband's medicine in *her* bedroom, in an unlocked cupboard?

FEATHERSTON: I was not aware of it, sir, until that afternoon, when she said that she did so because the Colonel would overdose himself so.

SIR TRAVERS MCKENZIE: Not at all. I mean, he was fussy.

FEATHERSTON: I beg your pardon, sir . . .

SIR TRAVERS MCKENZIE: Not at all. I mean, he was fussy and nervous about his health – much given to pills and medicines.

FEATHERSTON: I wouldn't deny it, sir. Well, sir, within two or three minutes of getting that medicine down him, the death agony began . . . God help me!

SIR TRAVERS MCKENZIE: Quite, Mr Featherston. In my opening speech for the Crown, I have already outlined the symptoms of strychnine poisoning – trembling, paralysis, sweating, arched back, a fixed grin, vomiting, etcetera, etcetera– a most terrible death, but if all this corresponds with what you saw that afternoon we need not go through it again.

FEATHERSTON: Oh, thank you, sir. And all that time, you know, Father Martin was crossing himself and saying what I have since been told were the Prayers for the Dying . . . and in Latin too, sir. It was all a terrible nightmare. And then, sir, worst of all, sir, Father Martin sent me to break the news to the widow. I was in a daze, sir, and I remember still how, as I ran across the lawn, I fell over a croquet hoop.

SIR TRAVERS MCKENZIE: I see, you were clearly much moved by the Colonel's death. Although you have described the Prisoner as callous and heartless, you had found the Colonel a good master.

FEATHERSTON: Oh, yes, sir. Yes, indeed, sir.

SIR TRAVERS MCKENZIE: And Mrs Gatsby, how did she receive your tragic message?

FEATHERSTON: It was uncanny, sir.

SIR TRAVERS MCKENZIE: Uncanny – what do you mean?

FEATHERSTON: Uncanny, sir. So calm, so unmoved, so icy. I thought it terrible. She went into the house with the Rector. I never saw her again until the funeral, but I never once saw her shed a tear. Her maid would say the same, sir – not so much as a tear, sir.

SIR TRAVERS MCKENZIE: I have only one more question, Mr Featherston. You were sixteen years with the Gatsbys – would you describe them as happily married?

FEATHERSTON: I hardly like to say, sir.

SIR TRAVERS MCKENZIE: That is understandable, but I am afraid I must press you. You are on oath, you know. Speak up, my man.

FEATHERSTON: Well, sir, I must say I never heard them quarrel. On the other hand, sir, they never had much to do with each other. The Colonel, sir, was interested only in the estate, the horses and the foxhounds; Mrs Gatsby only in the Church. It was a very silent house, sir. Now, in the dining-room, sir, it quite got on my nerves – an eight-course dinner and not a word spoken from the soup to the dessert. That sort of thing gets a man down, sir.

SIR TRAVERS MCKENZIE: Naturally. Gentlemen of the Jury, in such a house, a house at war with itself, the Prisoner – to put it mildly – can have hardly been expected to grieve very deeply over her husband's demise . . . especially if there was a lover in the background . . . Miss Cole-Hatt's father for instance, a creature whose identity, it would seem, may be denied to us. Thank you, Mr Featherston. No more questions, Me Lud.

Sir Frederick Ford-Bryce, Counsel for the Defence, was on his feet in a flash.

SIR FREDERICK FORD-BRYCE: Mr Featherston, I notice that you wear spectacles.

FEATHERSTON: Oh – er – yes, sir. Why, sir?

SIR FREDERICK FORD-BRYCE: Never mind why. Just answer my questions. It is a rule, is it not, that in the best houses the servants do not wear glasses when on duty. Am I right?

FEATHERSTON: Yes, sir. Most inconvenient for me but Mrs Gatsby was very strict on the point.

SIR FREDERICK FORD-BRYCE: Thank you. Now when you carried the late Colonel Gatsby from the garden into the house, did you don your glasses?

FEATHERSTON: Er – I don't rightly know, sir. I was very agitated and I don't remember, sir, one way or another. No, I don't know, sir.

SIR FREDERICK FORD-BRYCE: You don't know. Well, let me tell you that I know. A few minutes later, running across the lawn to break the tragic news to your mistress, you fell over a croquet hoop, did you not?

FEATHERSTON: That is so, sir. Yes, if I had not put on my spectacles then that would explain my clumsiness, wouldn't it?

SIR FREDERICK FORD-BRYCE: So, you now admit to not wearing your spectacles, and yet, Mr Featherston, although both agitated and myopic, you claim to have read the instructions on, presumably, a small label on a small bottle . . .

SIR TRAVERS MCKENZIE: Me Lud, I shall be producing the medicine bottle as an Exhibit in Court.

SIR FREDERICK FORD-BRYCE: My learned friend, Me Lud, must do as he thinks fit. I hope he won't regret it. Thank you, Mr Featherston, that is all.

FEATHERSTON: One moment if you please, sir. You see, my Lord, I am very short-sighted indeed – most inconvenient. I can only read, sir, if I remove my spectacles and hold the print very close to my eyes. Moreover, sir, the words 'ONE TEASPOONFUL IN WATER' were scrawled in large capitals. Also, sir, Mr Beaver, the valet, read them over my shoulder. Everything we did was quite in order, sir.

SIR FREDERICK FORD-BRYCE: Pah! No further questions, Me Lud.

Sir Frederick, wrapping his gown around him, sat down in a great huff. Father Martin, Vicar of St Monica's, Mount Street, Sister Jessica and Beaver, the valet, were all called in turn to the Witness Box. Their evidence confirmed Featherston's story in every way. Then came an unknown and unexpected witness.

SIR TRAVERS MCKENZIE: Me Lud, I now call Micky Slate, stableboy.

USHER: Slate! Slate! Slate!

In his mustard and green tartan suit, with shining morning face and a cowlick on his moist forehead, Micky Slate, thumbs in his waistband, swaggered down the Court. For just a second – and Jane Grigg swears to this – he turned to the public gallery and gave Eirlys a big wink.

SIR TRAVERS MCKENZIE: Now, Slate, you are on oath and must speak the truth.

SLATE: I know that.

SIR TRAVERS MCKENZIE: Your name is Micky Slate, you are nineteen years of age, and you live with your mother at 4 Mulberry Cottages, Nether Molding.

SLATE: Ay.

SIR TRAVERS MCKENZIE: You are a stableboy at Windrush Court?

SLATE: No, I ain't. I were, but I was sacked when the missis was run in. I'm a road ganger now.

SIR TRAVERS MCKENZIE: But you were a stableboy, for some five years I understand?

SLATE: Oh, ay.

SIR TRAVERS MCKENZIE: Very well. One of your duties was to look after the Harness Room.

SLATE: Oh, ay, I kept the bloody place to rights.

SIR TRAVERS MCKENZIE: And what did you keep in the Harness Room?

SLATE: 'Arness.

SIR TRAVERS MCKENZIE: Of course, but what else?

SLATE: Oh, brushes, curry combs, 'orse-shoes, 'orse rugs, polish, carriage grease, carriage lamps, lamp oil, wicks, whips, cockades, footmen's boots and toppers, anvil, 'ammers,' ammer cloths, pills for sick 'osses, rat poison . . .

SIR TRAVERS MCKENZIE: Ah! Rat poison. Have you any idea how this rat poison is made?

SLATE: Not rightly, but they must put summat in as the rats find tasty – else the little buggers wouldn't eat it, now, would they? And all the rest was this 'ere strychnine, if that's the word.

SIR TRAVERS MCKENZIE: Thank you, Slate. I have no more questions, Me Lud, but I have in Court a Mr Hardy, Manager of the Rat Poison firm, should your Lordship wish him to testify as to the precise quantities . . .

THE JUDGE: No, no, no, Sir Travers. Pray do not waste the time of the Court. Sir Frederick, you wish to cross-examine?

SIR FREDERICK FORD-BRYCE: Just one question, Slate. Did you keep the Harness Room locked?

SLATE: No, there wasn't no key, not as I know of.

SIR FREDERICK FORD-BRYCE: I see. So anyone – I repeat *anyone* – could have walked in at almost any time, and the Harness Room is not, Me Lud, overlooked by the windows of the house. No more questions, Me Lud.

With thumbs in armpits and fingers twiddling, and one eyebrow cocked at the public gallery, Micky Slate swaggered out of Court.

SIR TRAVERS MCKENZIE: I call my next witness, Me Lud. Sir Montague Ridgeon.

USHER: Ridgeon! Ridgeon! Ridgeon!

This was something that Sir Travers had been keeping up his sleeve. Sir Frederick's eyes started out of his head, while the Judge looked curiously at the man with whom, only last week, he had been playing whist at the Athenaeum. The name of the witness was a household word. Very carefully, before taking the oath, he arranged his tall silk hat, his malacca cane and his lavender gloves upon the ledge of the Witness Box. He adjusted the broad ribbon of his pince-nez and thereafter remained fixed in the pose of the well-known Millais portrait, the left hand clasping the silk lapel of his frock-coat, the right resting gently upon the Bible.

SIR TRAVERS MCKENZIE: Your name is Montague Anthony Cotterell Ridgeon. You are fifty years of age. You hold a Doctorate of Medicine from Trinity College, Dublin. You are a Fellow of the Royal College of Physicians. You are, currently, President of the Physicians and Chirurgical Society. You are Senior Physician at the Westminster Hospital, Westminster.

You are Physician in Ordinary to Her Majesty the Queen. You reside and have consultation rooms at No. 46 Harley Street, Marylebone.

SIR MONTAGUE RIDGEON: That is wholly correct.

SIR TRAVERS MCKENZIE: Thank you. Now pray tell his Lordship and the Gentlemen of the Jury, Sir Montague, how you first came to be acquainted with the deceased, the late Colonel Harold Garlick Gatsby.

SIR MONTAGUE RIDGEON: Certainly. I find, My Lord, that it was in May 1853 that Colonel Gatsby first consulted me at my chambers. He was – how shall I put it – somewhat embarrassed. He wished to discuss with me certain extremely intimate matters of a sexual nature such as – rightly or wrongly – he was unwilling to discuss with his family doctor, especially in a small country place.

SIR TRAVERS MCKENZIE: That is abundantly clear, Sir Montague. Pray proceed.

SIR MONTAGUE RIDGEON: Once I had put Colonel Gatsby at his ease, he told me that his private and marital life was highly unsatisfactory. He admitted, with most commendable frankness, that his marriage, from the beginning, had lacked all affection, let alone love. He was, he said, a virile man and, although outwardly reserved, actually passionate. He and his wife were without children. This was not ill-chance, it was not due to any organic defect in him or his wife, nor was it through any fault of his, but simply because Mrs Gatsby – now the Prisoner – had, ever since the honeymoon, been cold and frigid towards him, consistently refusing him her bed. I trust that I make myself plain.

SIR TRAVERS MCKENZIE: Oh, perfectly. So we may conclude that any unhappiness in this marriage was wholly the fault of the wife, not of the husband?

SIR MONTAGUE RIDGEON: That is so.

SIR TRAVERS MCKENZIE: Now, pray tell us, Sir Montague, did Colonel Gatsby ever state, or even hint, that his wife had a lover?

SIR MONTAGUE RIDGEON: No, but he did not say anything to the contrary.

SIR TRAVERS MCKENZIE: And you had no reason, Sir Montague, ever to doubt your patient's veracity.

SIR MONTAGUE RIDGEON: None whatever. What I now have to reveal will show how frank he was with me. He was in very palpable distress. He had in fact, although a pillar of society in Gloucestershire, been compelled to resort to – er – other women when in London – the sad creatures of the streets. In fact he often visited London solely for that purpose. But now, he told me, although his desires were unquenched, so that he could not change his habits, his virility was waning. In brief, he wanted me to prescribe for him an antiperiodic and an aphrodisiac . . . not an unusual request for a man in his later middle life.

SIR TRAVERS MCKENZIE: You did as he asked.

SIR MONTAGUE RIDGEON: Certainly. I prescribed for him a physic containing some aromatic herbs – for the soothing of the mind at night – but also *nux vomica* or strychnine. I told him to get the prescription made up at Bell & Co., of Wigmore Street.

SIR TRAVERS MCKENZIE: And what, Sir Montague, was the dose?

SIR MONTAGUE RIDGEON: Two minims in water, before retiring.

SIR TRAVERS MCKENZIE: A minim is a very small dose, is it not?

SIR MONTAGUE RIDGEON: Certainly – a dose such as could be conveniently dropped into water from the end of a glass rod.

SIR TRAVERS MCKENZIE: And what, Sir Montague, would be the effect of, let us say, a teaspoonful taken in water?

SIR MONTAGUE RIDGEON: Hm! A most extraordinary question, Sir Travers.

SIR TRAVERS MCKENZIE: I fear I must press you, Sir Montague.

SIR MONTAGUE RIDGEON: Very well. I prescribed two minims or one thirtieth of a fluid drachm, with a warning label as to the danger of exceeding this dose. A teaspoonful is usually considered to be the equivalent of one fluid drachm – thirty times the dose prescribed. Its effect, without doubt, would be certain and immediate death . . . even for an elephant.

SIR TRAVERS MCKENZIE: Thank you, Sir Montague. I am deeply obliged. I have no more questions, Me Lud.

THE JUDGE: Sir Frederick – your turn.

SIR FREDERICK FORD-BRYCE: Just one or two questions, Sir Montague. May I take it from what you have said, that if a man resorts to the prostitutes of the London streets, his unhappy marriage must then be blamed upon his wife?

SIR MONTAGUE RIDGEON: In this case, yes. But your question, sir, being taken out of context, is a gross distortion of what I actually said.

SIR FREDERICK FORD-BRYCE: Sir Montague, would you agree that the late Colonel Gatsby was something of a hypochondriac, or at any rate unduly concerned with his own health, with medicines, pills and so on?

SIR MONTAGUE RIDGEON: Yes, there I think I can agree with you.

SIR FREDERICK FORD-BRYCE: So that it would be only reasonable, would it not, for a truly affectionate wife to keep his collection of bottles and pill-boxes under her own care – lest he overdose himself.

SIR MONTAGUE RIDGEON: Since you insist upon putting it like that, Sir Frederick, I suppose I must reply in the affirmative.

SIR FREDERICK FORD-BRYCE: I am glad you agree with me, Sir Montague, that Mrs Gatsby was a truly affectionate wife.

SIR MONTAGUE RIDGEON: Sir, you are now putting words into my mouth. I object . . .

SIR FREDERICK FORD-BRYCE: Very well. Now, Sir Montague, was it not a very serious offence against medical etiquette for you to advise Colonel Gatsby without the knowledge of his own medical practitioner?

SIR MONTAGUE RIDGEON: Your question, sir, is offensively worded. In fact I wrote immediately to Doctor Clayton of Stow-on-the-Wold, enclosing a copy of my prescription and approving of his own treatment of the patient's comparatively minor heart complaint. I hope, sir, that satisfies you.

SIR FREDERICK FORD-BRYCE: Not quite, Sir Montague. Pray tell his Lordship, do you not think that to reveal in public court – quite gratuitously – as you have just done, intimate details not only of a patient's ailments but also of his rather unsavoury private life, is a grave breach of your Hippocratic Oath?

SIR MONTAGUE RIDGEON: No, the patient is dead.

SIR FREDERICK FORD-BRYCE: Pah! No more questions, Me Lud.

SIR MONTAGUE RIDGEON: May I venture to hope, my Lord, that I shall not be further required. I have other patients awaiting me in London.

THE JUDGE: Oh, quite, quite, Sir Montague. We are all very deeply indebted to you for travelling down to Gloucester in this inclement weather. Most kind. Usher, pray escort Sir Montague to his cab. Now, Sir Travers, your next witness if you please.

SIR TRAVERS MCKENZIE: Me Lud, I call Doctor Leonard Clayton.

USHER: Clayton! Clayton! Clayton!

Doctor Clayton was brisk and efficient. Stepping smartly into the Witness Box he rapped out the oath, determined not to be outshone by his great Harley Street colleague. Moreover he knew – although nobody else did – that he was to be Sir Travers's star witness.

SIR TRAVERS MCKENZIE: Your name is Leonard Paul Clayton. You are forty years of age. You hold a Doctorate of Medicine from the University of Cambridge. You are a general practitioner. You reside and have your surgery at No. 8 Sheep Street, Stow-on-the-Wold.

DOCTOR CLAYTON: Yes.

SIR TRAVERS MCKENZIE: I understand that you are – or were – the regular medical attendant to the Windrush Court household.

DOCTOR CLAYTON: Yes. I have been so for ten years – ever since the death of my senior partner in 1845.

SIR TRAVERS MCKENZIE: Have you often had to visit Windrush Court?

DOCTOR CLAYTON: Very little. Miss Eirlys Cole-Hatt has, in her time, suffered from measles and whooping cough. The cook once had pneumonia. The coachman's boy had croup and there have been minor injuries among the outdoor staff. So far as I know Mrs Gatsby has never been ill in her life. On the other hand I called fairly regularly to see Colonel Gatsby. Although a strong man he suffered from a heart complaint – paroxysmal tachycardia. This gave rise, at intervals, to breathlessness and to rather alarming palpitations or paroxysms . . . more alarming than serious. I had no difficulty in keeping this chronic condition under control, although a sudden death, during an exceptionally severe attack, would not have surprised me.

SIR TRAVERS MCKENZIE: That is all quite clear, Doctor. Now, please tell us about the events of 10 August last – the afternoon of the croquet party and of Colonel Gatsby's death.

DOCTOR CLAYTON: Certainly. I had been out hare coursing and on my return home about seven o'clock I found that the Windrush Court groom had left a message for me. I had not unsaddled my horse and was able to ride over to Windrush immediately. When I arrived I found a large house-party in the process of disintegration. I was taken upstairs. Colonel Gatsby was already dead, and had been dead for about two hours. I did not, therefore, witness his last collapse but – as described to me by Mr Featherston, the butler, and by Father Martin, a young priest – it was consistent with sudden heart failure arising from paroxysmal tachycardia *or* from strychnine poisoning. As the former was the disease from which Colonel Gatsby already suffered, the latter, naturally, never occurred to me. I have said that I was always expecting such a death – sooner or later – and I did not hesitate, therefore, about issuing a certificate giving the cause of death as paroxysmal tachycardia. That, my Lord, is why there was never an inquest.

THE JUDGE: I accept your explanation, Doctor Clayton.

DOCTOR CLAYTON: I am much relieved, my Lord. It was only when the loyal and, perhaps, over-zealous Featherston produced the medicine bottle to show me how he had carried out his mistress's instructions that my suspicions were aroused. It had been tampered with.

THE JUDGE: Really, Doctor Clayton, do I understand you aright – the bottle had been tampered with?

DOCTOR CLAYTON: Not actually the bottle, my Lord, but the label, and the bottle's contents. It was not a chemist's label at all, and the stated dose – 'ONE TEASPOONFUL' – was quite ludicrous, assuming that this was Sir Montague Ridgeon's prescription for an aphrodisiac. I slipped the bottle into my pocket and took it home.

SIR TRAVERS MCKENZIE: I intervene, Me Lud, to say that in view of what Doctor Clayton is about to impart, I shall at the close of my case, with your permission, Me Lud, be producing the bottle – with label – as an Exhibit in Court.

THE JUDGE: Certainly, Sir Travers. Pray continue, Doctor Clayton.

SIR TRAVERS MCKENZIE: Just one question, Doctor. To have given Colonel Gatsby a dose, whether the correct dose or otherwise, of Sir Montague's aphrodisiac in order to relieve one of his normal heart attacks, was surely quite wrong?

DOCTOR CLAYTON: Quite wrong, but this was, undoubtedly, the only medicine in the cupboard in Mrs Gatsby's room, to which Mrs Gatsby had directed Featherston.

SIR TRAVERS MCKENZIE: Thank you. Go on with your story, Doctor.

DOCTOR CLAYTON: Well, I took the bottle home. I placed a very small quantity of the medicine upon a glass slide. I carried out a test – it showed an enormous amount of *nux vomica* or strychnine. I then placed an almost microscopic drop upon the tongue of a guinea pig. The poor little beast died immediately in convulsions.

SIR TRAVERS MCKENZIE: Showing all the symptoms, I presume, of strychnine poisoning.

DOCTOR CLAYTON: Yes, indeed. Once again I examined the bottle and the label. The words: 'DOSE: ONE TEASPOONFUL, TO BE TAKEN IN WATER WHEN REQUIRED', had been scrawled in capitals upon an otherwise plain label. It was most curious.

THE JUDGE: It was amazing. You are sure of your facts, Doctor?

SIR TRAVERS MCKENZIE: I have already said, Me Lud, that I shall be producing the bottle. The label is still there.

THE JUDGE: Very well, Sir Travers, we shall await your Exhibit. Go on, Doctor Clayton.

DOCTOR CLAYTON: Thank you, my Lord. I packed up the bottle and sent it, with my report, to the Public Prosecutor. I also wrote to Major Smelley, the Chief Constable of Gloucestershire, telling him what I had done. I heard nothing more until early December. I was then informed by the Home Office that an Exhumation had been arranged for 22 December, in Nether Molding churchyard. I was invited to be present, together with the Home Office Pathologist, Mr Josiah Coleherne, and the Chief Constable. I am told that Mr Coleherne is in Court to give his own testimony. That, my Lord, therefore concludes my evidence.

But Sir Frederick Ford-Bryce was already on his feet, glowering over his spectacles.

SIR FREDERICK FORD-BRYCE: A moment if you please, Doctor. Did you stop the funeral?

DOCTOR CLAYTON: No. That was not my job. I suggested it to the Home Office and, after receiving my report, they still had three days in which to act. They did nothing, but nobody knows more than a lawyer, Sir Frederick, of the delays of officialdom.

SIR FREDERICK FORD-BRYCE: Very well. Now, Doctor Clayton, did you examine the body of the late Colonel Gatsby?

DOCTOR CLAYTON: Yes.

SIR FREDERICK FORD-BRYCE: Carefully?

DOCTOR CLAYTON: No.

SIR FREDERICK FORD-BRYCE: No!

DOCTOR CLAYTON: I had no reason to. I have already told the Court that he appeared to have died exactly as I, his regular medical attendant, would have expected. Only a post-mortem could have shown death as being due to any cause other than paroxysmal tachycardia. Unfortunately the symptoms were very similar to those of strychnine poisoning.

SIR FREDERICK FORD-BRYCE: So, Doctor Clayton, you admit first to having failed to impress upon the Home Office the urgency of stopping the funeral. Secondly, you admit to a purely superficial examination of the body. And then, on top of all that, you actually issued a certificate upon which the cause of death was given quite wrongly as paroxysmal tachycardia – a mild heart complaint – when in actual fact it was due – was it not – to acute gastroenteritis arising from strychnine poisoning. Really, words fail me! This, surely, is a series of blunders reflecting most seriously upon your professional competence and upon your reliability as a witness.

DOCTOR CLAYTON: But I have already explained . . .

SIR FREDERICK FORD-BRYCE: If you have already explained, sir, there is no need to waste the time of the Court doing so again. I have no more questions, Me Lud.

THE JUDGE: Very well. Your next witness, Sir Travers.

SIR TRAVERS MCKENZIE: I call Mr Josiah Coleherne.

USHER: Coleherne! Coleherne! Coleherne!

The brisk youthfulness of Doctor Clayton was now replaced by the elderly melancholy of Mr Josiah Coleherne, emaciated and bowed as if crushed by long years of service to red-tape. He spoke slowly from notes – weighing every word.

SIR TRAVERS MCKENZIE: Your name is Josiah Coleherne. You are sixty-one years of age. You reside at No. 16 Great Russell Street, Holborn. You hold a Doctorate of Medicine in the University of Edinburgh. You are a Fellow of the Royal College of Surgeons. You are a senior pathologist at St Bartholomew's Hospital, London. You are consulting pathologist to the Home Office.

JOSIAH COLEHERNE: That is so.

SIR TRAVERS MCKENZIE: Kindly tell the Court in your own words how you came to be involved in this case.

JOSIAH COLEHERNE: On 15 December last I was summoned by the Public Prosecutor to attend upon him at the Home Office. The Permanent Secretary to the Home Secretary was present. I was informed that a certain Colonel Harold Garlick Gatsby of Windrush Court, in this County, had died suddenly the previous August, and that owing to much local feeling, grave suspicions of foul play had been aroused. He asked me to meet Major Percy Smelley, the Chief Constable of Gloucestershire, and to arrange with him – on the authority, I need hardly say, of the Home Secretary – for an exhumation and a subsequent pathological examination.

SIR TRAVERS MCKENZIE: Thank you, Mr Coleherne. You are most precise. I take it that you were not concerned with the alleged murder, solely with the contents of any organs that you might remove from the cadaver.

JOSIAH COLEHERNE: Exactly so. On the night of 22 December as arranged, Major Smelley, Doctor Clayton, three constables and a gravedigger met me by the Lych Gate of Nether Molding churchyard. There was no moon that night and it was very dark under the yew trees, but each constable carried a lantern.

SIR TRAVERS MCKENZIE: Did anyone observe you, Mr Coleherne?

JOSIAH COLEHERNE: I believe not. There is little night life in these remote villages. There is only one house overlooking the churchyard – the Rectory. The Rector himself, we understood, was visiting Rome. The servants slept at the back of the house and, at that hour, the two children were no doubt sound asleep.

SIR TRAVERS MCKENZIE: Thank you, Mr Coleherne, that is all very clear. Please go on.

JOSIAH COLEHERNE: I was told by Doctor Clayton that the widow had ordered such an elaborately carved tombstone – it was to come from Italy – that even after five months it was still incomplete. There was nothing over the grave except neatly mown turf. The coffin, however, was a costly one and heavy to lift. The gravedigger and the constables carried it to the vestry where it was placed upon a trestle table.

SIR TRAVERS MCKENZIE: Was there any problem of identification?

JOSIAH COLEHERNE: Oh, no. It was a triple coffin – mahogany, lead and cedar. The oolitic limestone of these parts is always favourable to preservation. Moreover, there was an incised silver plate upon the casket and when the lid was removed one of the constables, a local man, exclaimed, 'Ay, that's old Gatsby!'

SIR TRAVERS MCKENZIE: Go on, Mr Coleherne.

JOSIAH COLEHERNE: I opened up the cadaver. I removed the viscera, stomach, liver and spleen. I placed them in jars which I then sealed, the seal being witnessed by the Chief Constable. He then, most kindly, gave me hospitality for the night so that I was able to place my jars in his wine cellar – a cool place. The next morning I put them in a hold-all and conveyed them by railroad to Paddington Station, placing them on the luggage rack where they were under my eye. From the Station I conveyed them by hansom cab to St Bartholomew's Hospital where I there and then carried out exhaustive tests.

SIR TRAVERS MCKENZIE: Yes, and the results of your tests, Mr Coleherne.

JOSIAH COLEHERNE: I found traces of *nux vomica* or strychnine in all the organs. By a simple formula it is possible to calculate the total amount in the body at the time of death. This must have been about thirty times the fatal dose.

SIR TRAVERS MCKENZIE: Thank you, Mr Coleherne, for your very clear evidence. I have no more questions, Me Lud.

THE JUDGE: Very well. In view of the witness's precise statement I should imagine, Sir Frederick, that you have nothing to ask him.

SIR FREDERICK FORD-BRYCE: Just one thing, Me Lud. Mr Coleherne, you said that the coffin was so costly as to be exceptionally heavy. You also said that the tombstone was being carved in Italy and had, in fact, still not been completed. Now, Mr Coleherne, does not this suggest to you that the widow must not only be crushed with grief but must also be a person of the deepest and most tender feeling.

JOSIAH COLEHERNE: I am afraid, sir, that that is altogether outside my province.

SIR FREDERICK FORD-BRYCE: Pah! No more questions, Me Lud.

SIR TRAVERS MCKENZIE: I call my last witness, Me Lud. Inspector Hilton will give evidence of arrest.

USHER: Hilton! Hilton! Hilton!

Inspector Hilton, as stolid and bovine as on the night when he had arrested Phillippa in the morning-room at Windrush Court, now entered the Box.

SIR TRAVERS MCKENZIE: Your name is Clarence Hilton. You are forty-six years of age. You are an Inspector in the Gloucestershire County Constabulary.

INSPECTOR HILTON: Yes, sir.

SIR TRAVERS MCKENZIE: Pray tell his Lordship and the Gentlemen of the Jury about your part in this case.

INSPECTOR HILTON: On 26 December last I was instructed by the Chief Constable, Major Smelley, to proceed to Windrush Court, in the parish of Nether Molding, and there to arrest the woman Gatsby, on the charge of having wilfully murdered her husband the previous August. I was accompanied by my assistant, Sergeant Dunn, and by a wardress from the County Gaol, a Mrs Doughty. Mrs Gatsby was not at home. Her butler told us that she had taken her 'niece' – so-called, my Lord – to a Christmas party at the Rectory, there being other children there. We had to wait some two hours for her return. Holding my warrant in my right hand, I then gave her the usual warning and arrested her. She did not resist. She went very quietly.

SIR TRAVERS MCKENZIE: What did she say?

INSPECTOR HILTON: She said: 'I suppose you have been talking to Featherston.' I presume, sir, that she was referring to the painful nature of her spouse's demise, and all this here 'anky panky over the medicine bottle.

SIR TRAVERS MCKENZIE: Possibly. I have no more questions, Me Lud, but I see that my learned friend is already on his feet.

SIR FREDERICK FORD-BRYCE: Inspector Hilton, was that all the Prisoner said when you charged her?

INSPECTOR HILTON: I think so, sir.

SIR FREDERICK FORD-BRYCE: Hm! You think so. Did she not say whether she was guilty or not?

INSPECTOR HILTON: Oh, yes, sir. She said that the charge was absurd.

SIR FREDERICK FORD-BRYCE: Really, Me Lud. Upon my word! Just now, Inspector Hilton, when being cross-examined by my learned friend, you omitted that from your evidence . . . entirely. Here is this pious lady, a widow crushed with grief, carrying in her womb the only child her husband ever gave her, and on trial for her life . . . and you, Inspector Hilton, are the only man who heard her say that the charge against her was 'absurd' and you deliberately – deliberately – conceal the fact. A case, Me Lud, if ever there was one, of *suppressio veri* leading to *suggestio falsi.*

INSPECTOR HILTON: But when people are arrested, sir, they usually say something like that.

SIR FREDERICK FORD-BRYCE: Inspector Hilton, apart from the Prisoner, how many people have you arrested for murder?

INSPECTOR HILTON: Only one other, sir – a drunken sailor from Bristol.

SIR FREDERICK FORD-BRYCE: I see. And on the strength of one drunken sailor from Bristol you presume to tell the Court what people 'usually' say when charged with murder. I am speechless, but no doubt your superior officers will take note of your conduct. No more questions, Me Lud.

THE JUDGE: Thank you. You said, Sir Travers, that Inspector Hilton would be the last witness for the Prosecution, but you also said, I think, that you had an Exhibit to lay before the Court – this, er, rather sinister medicine bottle. Yes, Sir Frederick, what is it now?

SIR FREDERICK FORD-BRYCE: I have to object, Me Lud. All exhibits, Me Lud, should be on the table when the case opens, available for the Defence.

THE JUDGE: Strictly speaking, Sir Frederick, you may be right. You are relying, I presume, upon the ruling of Lord Justice O'Shea in Gubbins *versus* the Board of Trade in 1784.

SIR FREDERICK FORD-BRYCE: Thank you, Me Lud, that is so. May I, therefore, now open my case, Me Lud?

THE JUDGE: A moment, Sir Frederick. I said 'strictly speaking'. When a life is at stake I am not prepared to prejudice the course of justice by a hairsbreadth . . .

SIR FREDERICK FORD-BRYCE: But Lord Justice O'Shea, Me Lud . . . in 1784.

THE JUDGE: You are forgetting, Sir Frederick, that in this Court *I* am the embodiment of the Law. It is *I* who am now stating a case. Gubbins versus the Board of Trade is therefore dead. Your objection is overruled.

SIR FREDERICK FORD-BRYCE: I am much obliged, Me Lud. I have, however, another more serious objection.

THE JUDGE: Oh dear! Well, Sir Frederick, what is it?

SIR FREDERICK FORD-BRYCE: This controversial bottle, Me Lud, which Sir Travers has been keeping up his sleeve – this bottle, Me Lud, has been handled by the butler, the valet and the doctor. It has been in the doctor's household – the household of a doctor who issues bogus death certificates. It has been in the office of the Public Prosecutor and of the Home Secretary. It has twice been in the hands of the Post Office. I submit, Me Lud, that as an Exhibit, it is now utterly useless.

SIR TRAVERS MCKENZIE: Me Lud, I am not bringing the bottle into Court on account of finger prints or even contents, although the cork still bears the seal of the Home Office, and the label bears my initials.

SIR FREDERICK FORD-BRYCE: My learned friend, Me Lud . . .

SIR TRAVERS MCKENZIE: Me Lud, my learned friend . . .

THE JUDGE: I suggest, Sir Frederick, that Sir Travers shows us his bottle and *I* will then rule whether or not it shall be considered as part of the evidence.

SIR FREDERICK FORD-BRYCE: As you please, Me Lud. I have no more to say.

SIR TRAVERS MCKENZIE: Thank you, Me Lud. I will now ask Mr Bowker, my Senior Clerk, to bring in the bottle.

Mr Bowker, a familiar figure in Lincolns Inn, now gingerly carried a tin tray into Court. It bore a bottle filled with a white medicine, and a steaming spirit kettle.

THE JUDGE: Really, Sir Travers, are you going to treat us to a culinary demonstration?

SIR TRAVERS MCKENZIE: Me Lud, it pleases you to be humorous. I can assure the Court that this is a very grave moment in a very tragic trial. Put the tray upon the table, Bowker. Usher, pray pass the bottle to his Lordship, and then, one by one, to the Gentlemen of the Jury. Please, Gentlemen, take particular note of the label. Meanwhile, Bowker, you may bring your kettle back to the boil.

Bowker and the Usher carried out their instructions while Sir Travers McKenzie turned up his starched cuffs, ready for action.

SIR TRAVERS MCKENZIE: Now, Gentlemen, you have all examined the bottle and the label. Doctor Clayton and the Home Office can certify that the physic inside has not been tampered with since it came into their possession – that what should have been a harmless aphrodisiac now contains a deadly dose of strychnine liable to cause instant death. We are for the moment, however, concerned only with the outside of the bottle. You will have noted that the label bears the words – 'DOSE: ONE TEASPOONFUL, TO BE TAKEN IN WATER WHEN REQUIRED' – this on an otherwise plain piece of paper in crude capitals and in a childish scrawl – possibly intended to evade the handwriting expert. If, however, this was the intention of whoever wrote that label, I shall prove to you in a few moments that it failed. Now, Gentlemen of the Jury – let us see . . .

Sir Travers McKenzie stepped to the table. He took the bottle in a pair of sugar tongs and held it in the steam now hissing from the kettle spout. Then, slowly, gently, with a razor, he peeled off the label.

SIR TRAVERS MCKENZIE: Now, Me Lud, you see that the bogus label is removed. I place it here for future use. Let us see what we have underneath. Behold, Gentlemen of the Jury, a second label. Let me read it to the Court before passing it to you for your inspection. First, at the top of the label, and in print, we have the words: 'BELL & CO. CHEMISTS, WIGMORE STREET, LONDON'. So far, so good. Now below that, in a neat and clerkly hand we have the words: 'THE PHYSIC FOR COLONEL HAROLD GATSBY. DOSE: TWO MINIMS TO BE TAKEN IN WATER', and then again, below that, we have the words: 'IT IS DANGEROUS TO EXCEED THE STATED DOSE', and yet again, at the bottom of the label, the number of the prescription corresponding precisely to the number in Sir Montague Ridgeon's prescription book which he has left with me and which is here in my hand – 'PRESCRIPTION no. 2601.'

THE JUDGE: Thank you, Sir Travers – most illuminating. I rule that your demonstration,the bottle and the label may be considered as forming part of the evidence. Usher, pass them for inspection.

SIR TRAVERS MCKENZIE: I am deeply obliged to you, Me Lud. I had thought that that would conclude my case, Me Lud, but I have one more witness – an important one. He has come post-haste from France and I had feared that he would not be here in time. I now call my last witness, Monsieur Etienne Languet.

USHER: Languet! Languet! Languet!

If the Court expected a 'Moosoo' with an Imperial and a waxed moustache, they were disappointed. Languet was more like a British Sergeant-Major. He stepped smartly into the Box – the hardened professional witness. He spoke English with a slight Cockney twang.

SIR TRAVERS MCKENZIE: Your name is Etienne François Languet. You are forty-six years of age. You were born in Paris but are now a British subject. You reside at No. 64, the Avenue Niel in Paris, and also at No. 22 Fulham Road, London. You are President of The British Calligraphic Society.

M. LANGUET: That is correct.

SIR TRAVERS MCKENZIE: You are an experienced expert in handwriting and have frequently given evidence before the Courts.

M. LANGUET: Yes. In the British Courts, one hundred and six times before the magistrates, and forty-two times before the High Courts – three of which occasions were murder trials.

SIR TRAVERS MCKENZIE: Thank you. Now would you take this label in your hand. It is a little damp as it has only just been steamed off the medicine bottle. Now, Monsieur Languet, have you seen that label before?

M. LANGUET: I have. A week ago in your own office in Lincolns Inn, with Doctor Clayton and an official of the Home Office present as witnesses, I examined it carefully with a magnifying glass.

SIR TRAVERS MCKENZIE: Pray tell the Court what, if anything, it conveys to you.

M. LANGUET: It is full of interest. It is printed in capital letters so that it would be quite impossible to identify it with the handwriting of any particular person ... but otherwise I find it fascinating.

SIR TRAVERS MCKENZIE: How so, pray?

M. LANGUET: The whole device – in so far as it is intended to deceive the Law – is, I need hardly say, quite inept, almost the work of a child. Nevertheless, it is also the work of a sophisticated and educated person deliberately imitating the scrawl of an illiterate. The letters themselves are printed crookedly and are crookedly aligned on the label . . . and yet every letter in itself is perfectly formed and well-proportioned. Admittedly the inscription is short – 'DOSE: ONE TEASPOONFUL, TO BE TAKEN IN WATER WHEN REQUIRED', but there are no spelling mistakes. The usual solecisms of the illiterate – the dotted capital I and the double L at the end of 'teaspoonful' – are both avoided. The only points of punctuation – the colon after 'dose' and the comma after 'teaspoonful' – are correctly inserted.

SIR TRAVERS MCKENZIE: In brief, Monsieur Languet, an educated, if rather immature person, trying to disguise their hand by means of scrawled capitals.

M. LANGUET: Precisely so. Moreover – and this is important – anyone will notice that the thin up-strokes and the thick down-strokes are very marked. In other words, this label is not written with one of these cheap steel pens now in common use, but with a goose-quill of the finest quality such as one would find only in a gentleman's library.

SIR TRAVERS MCKENZIE: Thank you, Monsieur Languet . . .

M. LANGUET: One other point, Sir Travers, if I may – now that the label has been removed from the bottle and I have it in my hand I can examine the paper as I could not do in your office the other day. This label is not a label at all; it is a small piece of paper cut from notepaper of the most expensive brand – hand-woven and with a watermark.

SIR TRAVERS MCKENZIE: Thank you, Monsieur Languet, the Court is deeply indebted to you . . . but I see that my learned friend has a question.

SIR FREDERICK FORD-BRYCE: Mister Languet, can you tell the Court the sex of the person who wrote that label?

M. LANGUET: No. Without any actual handwriting – and there are only capitals here – that is not possible.

SIR FREDERICK FORD-BRYCE: I see. You cannot even tell us whether the writer was a man or a woman. Surely that makes your statement rather useless. I feel sure that the Gentlemen of the Jury will think that this evidence from a foreigner is, to say the least, unreliable. No more questions, Me Lud.

SIR TRAVERS MCKENZIE: I have no more witnesses, Me Lud. That concludes the Case for the Crown.

THE JUDGE: Thank you, Sir Travers – an admirably argued Case. I see, however, that Sir Frederick is quivering with impatience. Yes, it is your turn, Sir Frederick, but as the clock now stands at twenty-two minutes past twelve, I shall adjourn the Court for luncheon. Remove the Prisoner.

Two wardresses quietly escorted Phillippa from the dark Court Room to the even darker cells below.

USHER: Stand for the Queen's Justice! Stand for the Queen's Justice! Stand for the Queen's Justice!

Everybody stumbled to their feet, groping for hats and umbrellas. The Judge's Marshal – sword on high but velvet breeches a little moth-eaten – preceeded him to his carriage – the only one in Gloucester with a powdered footman – hired afresh from a livery stable in Cheltenham for each Assize. Counsel took cabs to The Fleece – the worst luncheon on the Western Circuit – while everyone else shuffled off into the February drizzle. At two o'clock precisely this daily ritual – and this was the sixth day – was put into reverse. Sir John Fitzjohn Grandison, on his return to the Bench, might have been a little flushed by his port, but not so as to make him waste words. Once more he offered Phillippa Gatsby a chair and once more it was refused.

THE JUDGE: Sir Frederick Ford-Bryce, the Court has now heard Sir Travers McKenzie's Case for the Crown. Will you kindly open the Case for the Defence.

Sir Frederick rose from his seat. He adjusted his wig. He adjusted his spectacles upon the tip of his nose – a fine nose. He cleared his throat. He drank from a glass of alleged Perrier Water. He cleared his throat again. He made a gesture of whispering to his Junior. He put his thumbs in his armpits and then, with closed eyes, addressed the hissing gas jets in the roof.

SIR FREDERICK FORD-BRYCE: Me Lud and Gentlemen of the

Jury, now that my learned friend has finished his conjuring tricks and cooking demonstration, perhaps I may be allowed to turn your minds – the minds of everyone in England – to the very beautiful and very tragic figure who stands before us – silent – in the Dock. Gentlemen, I ask you to look upon Phillippa Thérèse Gatsby who is indicted upon the charge of Wilful Murder and has, when arraigned at the Bar, pleaded Not Guilty, before God and her Queen.

It must always be a terrible thing when the fair annals of British Justice are marred by a false verdict, by some miscarriage of the law, such as may send an innocent person to penal servitude or even to the gallows. Even if the victim were, by chance, the most degraded of human beings, a false verdict must always strike at our national pride. When that victim is a beautiful woman of high degree, of deep affection, of devoted piety and carrying a child in her womb, then indeed there is reason for tears. Looking upon Phillippa Thérèse Gatsby, Gentlemen, I might well, without further ado, demand of you, here and now, her life and liberty.

Sir Frederick paused to take a handkerchief from his cuff, to wipe away a tear.

Nevertheless, a charge has been made – the foul charge of Wilful Murder – and that charge must be answered. I shall be brief because I can afford to be brief. Almost, Me Lud, I was on the verge of asking you to dismiss the whole case as frivolous – to rule, in fact, that there was no case to go to the Jury. I decided otherwise only because such a ruling – although legally tantamount to a verdict of 'Innocent' – might nevertheless, like the Scottish verdict of 'Not Proven', leave traces of suspicion, might leave Phillippa Gatsby to be the victim of gossip in years to come. A charge has been made – it must be answered and to the full.

Now never, Me Lud, in all my years at the Bar, have I seen the Prosecution so completely at a loss, never have I seen so dismal a procession of witnesses pass through the Witness Box – all of them either discredited or discreditable.

The Prosecution, Gentlemen of the Jury, so far as I can see, has made only two points to which any reply is needed. It has proved – and indeed it is not disputed – that seventeen years ago – seventeen long years, Gentlemen – Phillippa Cole-Hatt, as she then was, a beautiful young girl whirled away by the delights and temptations of her first London Season, committed an indiscretion. She was seduced and she bore a child. Her penitence and her piety were real. I dare not imagine what agonies of remorse she suffered, but the significance of that child's second name – Eirlys Magdalen – will not have escaped you. In any case, Me Lud, the whole sad episode might have been overruled by you as utterly irrelevant to the present case. I am glad that it was not. Phillippa Cole-Hatt's child, having been born in a clinic at Basle, was given a home forever – and a very luxurious home – by the country gentleman with whom Phillippa Cole-Hatt was to share her life, Colonel Harold Garlick Gatsby. Yes, he gave that poor child a home as if she were his own daughter. Now that, I submit, Gentlemen, is not the basis of an unhappy marriage. And yet it has pleased the Prosecution, rather cruelly, to make great play with the fact that the Gatsby marriage was barren. Maybe it was. It would not be the first happy but childless marriage in the world. We are also told – so poverty-stricken is the Prosecution's case – that Colonel and Mrs Gatsby did not share a bed. Maybe they didn't. One can think of a dozen reasons why two people should not regularly share a bed. Insomnia is merely the first that springs to mind, and insomnia, disturbed nights, was, you may remember, one of the lesser ailments for which Sir Montague Ridgeon prescribed when making up Colonel Gatsby's medicine . . . aromatic herbs mingled with the *nux vomica* or strychnine.

Having, Gentlemen of the Jury, disposed of that piece of nonsense, I come to the one serious matter in the whole of the Prosecution's case, and even that, as I shall show, is without substance. It is – as I fully admit – a fact that the late Colonel Gatsby took an overdose of medicine which, as it happened, contained strychnine, a deadly poison if taken to excess. I must point out that Colonel Gatsby is not the first person in the world to take an overdose of medicine – whether by accident or with a view to self-destruction. It is not part of my case, however, to suggest that he did in fact commit suicide, but I do beg you to remember that he did have the opportunity – a simple overdose – and that there was a more sordid and far less happy side to his existence than was to be seen at Windrush Court. There were some very strange creatures in the late Colonel's life, Gentlemen; it will be my painful duty to bring one of them to that Witness Box. However, as I say, suicide is not part of the Case for the Defence but, Gentlemen, I beg of you to bear it in mind, if only as a remote possibility, when you consider your verdict . . . if it should introduce into the case even one faint scintilla of doubt, then, Gentlemen, the Prisoner at the Bar must go free.

Now, Me Lud, my learned friend has made a great to-do with this hanky-panky – as one witness called it – of the label on the bottle. In fact we have no evidence whatsoever – except that of the half-blind butler and of the young doctor who goes hare coursing when he should be with his patients and then issues false death certificates – that the wrong label *was* actually on the bottle when the fatal dose was taken. All we know is that, at some stage, the real label was covered up by a false one, but that might well be before, during or after the bottle had passed through a dozen hands, whether at the Home Office or elsewhere. As for the suggestion that it was Phillippa Gatsby, of all people, who stuck a bogus label on the bottle, I can only say that there is not one iota of evidence for such a thing. The very idea is inconceivable – inconceivable that an educated and intelligent woman – if fake the label she must – would have done it so crudely – in that crude and childish scrawl. Moreover she was the one and only person in the world who, sooner or later, when Colonel Gatsby had one of his periodic attacks, could herself give him an overdose, without any false label nonsense and without anyone being a penny the wiser. The Prisoner would never have faked the label for the simple reason that she would have had no need to.

No, Gentlemen of the Jury, the whole case for the Prosecution collapses, and collapses utterly, both because no real or tangible evidence exists, but above all because of the obvious absurdity of the charge. To think, for one moment, that Phillippa Gatsby

– of all women – could ever have contemplated the poisoning of her husband, or indeed of anyone in the world, would be ludicrous if it were not tragic. Even if we admit for the sake of argument that the Gatsby marriage was unhappy – and I admit no such thing – then I must remind you that Phillippa Gatsby had her own private fortune, Cole-Hatt money, and could at any moment, *in extremis*, have simply left home . . . it was as simple as that. However, and this is my last word, Mrs Gatsby has herself given you her final and overwhelming answer. After sixteen long years, when so often she must have wept on her husband's shoulder that she could not give him a child, she found at last, some eight months ago, that she was to bear him a baby. That must have seemed to them a miracle. And yet now, today, we have the terrible irony that the father is dead . . . poor little posthumous baby! That child in the womb is the living proof of the love that Phillippa Gatsby bore for the man she is now accused of murdering. The charge is, quite clearly, outrageous and obscene.

Many were weeping. Jane Grigg tells me how strange it was and how tense were her feelings. Eirlys, she said, had gripped her hand until it hurt. How strange that those two – and Phillippa – should be the only ones in the Court to know the true paternity of the child. As Sir Frederick brought his declamation to an end, others wept; Jane and Eirlys were tight-lipped.

That, Me Lud and Gentlemen of the Jury, is Phillippa Gatsby's reply to the calumny brought against her. It is all I need and, I trust, all you will need, to bring in a resounding verdict of Not Guilty.

Me Lud, I will now call my first witness – John Bird Sumner, Archbishop of Canterbury.

USHER: Canterbury! Canterbury! Canterbury!

The sensation in the dark little Court was tremendous. Sir Frederick had kept his secret well. There was a rustle as people turned and craned their necks. One or two stood up as if in church. If, however, anyone expected a cope and mitre, they were disappointed. Old

Sumner was rather fat these days and rather bent. As he moved slowly down the Court the raindrops from his Inverness cape and his gamp dripped on to the bare boards.

THE JUDGE: My dear sir! Your Grace, how very kind of you to come. Usher, pray relieve the Archbishop of his umbrella and provide him with a chair.

CANTERBURY: Oh, thank you, thank you, most kind and considerate . . . lumbago, I fear. But I had to come, you know . . . oh, yes, I had to come . . . this terrible business . . . my dear old friend, Mrs Gatsby . . . got into a fix. Ah, yes, thank you, the Bible . . . the good old book . . . yes, yes, of course, I swear by Almighty God . . .

SIR FREDERICK FORD-BRYCE: Your name is John Bird Sumner. You are eighty years of age. You hold a Master's Degree in Theology from the University of Oxford, also, I think, a Double First in Classics and in Hebrew. You are now Chancellor of the University of Oxford. You reside at Lambeth Palace, London, and, under the Queen, you hold the See of Canterbury.

CANTERBURY: Yes, yes, just so. I don't know where you got it all from.

SIR FREDERICK FORD-BRYCE: Now when did Your Grace first meet the Accused, Phillippa Gatsby?

CANTERBURY: At the font.

SIR FREDERICK FORD-BRYCE: Oh, quite, but she was very young then, was she not?

CANTERBURY: Ten days old . . . dear little thing!

SIR FREDERICK FORD-BRYCE: Quite, quite, I'm sure. But would you be kind enough to tell the Court rather more about your later friendship with Mrs Gatsby.

CANTERBURY: Certainly. At the time of her christening I was Vicar of Petersfield and I have always kept in touch with the Cole-Hatts – staunch and wealthy Anglicans, every one of them. When Phillippa married I assisted at her wedding at Hanover Square – but by then, of course, I held a Canon's Stall at Southwark.

SIR FREDERICK FORD-BRYCE: Yes, yes, Your Grace, but I

think what the Court really wants to hear is your assessment of Mrs Gatsby's character in more recent years.

CANTERBURY: Oh, I was coming to that. Let me see, now, how shall I put it? There is a popular idea, you know, that our dear Church of England is governed by Convocation – by us bishops. Of course we all know that the Privy Council can butt in, but in fact they never do . . . no, they never do – that's all hooey. But there *is* the House of Laity. Now they have a big say – most of them very eminent men indeed, men like . . .

SIR FREDERICK FORD-BRYCE: I don't wish to interrupt Your Grace, but about Mrs Gatsby . . .

CANTERBURY: Now don't hurry me or I shall get muddled. Mrs Gatsby, oh yes, Mrs Gatsby. I'm coming to her but I was just saying about the House of Laity – very eminent men, Lord Halifax, Hope Scott, Wilberforce and, of course, our dear Mr Gladstone . . . all laymen but all immortal souls like the rest of us. And behind them – but discreetly of course as becomes their sex – there are the ladies. No use for all this Rights of Women rubbish but behind the scenes – the hostess and the wife, the teaching at the mother's knee, the hand that rocks the cradle – and all that kind of thing, you know . . . Now, among the most influential, most devout and pious of these great ladies I put first – oh, yes, indubitably first – our beloved Mrs Gatsby. She benefited greatly of course from the spiritual guidance of her Rector, Archdeacon Barbellion. He encouraged her in every way. She became most strict in her religious observances – quite Christlike. And then there were those wonderful gatherings at Windrush Court – outwardly just big house-parties, but in actual fact theological and exegetical meetings dedicated to Almighty God – an inspiration to us all. I attended several although not, I fear, the last one – the one so clouded by the death of Colonel Gatsby. Mrs Gatsby – oh, yes, a great woman.

SIR FREDERICK FORD-BRYCE: In fact, Your Grace, you cannot conceive of Mrs Gatsby as a murderess.

CANTERBURY: A most shocking idea! Utterly absurd! Whoever thought of that, I wonder. Phillippa Gatsby – one of the most upright women in England.

SIR FREDERICK FORD-BRYCE: Thank you, Your Grace. I have no more questions, Me Lud.

The Archbishop was about to leave the Witness Box but Sir Travers McKenzie was on his feet.

SIR TRAVERS MCKENZIE: Your Grace spoke of the Cole-Hatt family as staunch Anglicans, and of the Prisoner as a person who strictly observed her religious duties, mainly in her own parish church and under the guidance of her own Rector, Archdeacon Barbellion.

CANTERBURY: Certainly, that is well put.

SIR TRAVERS MCKENZIE: Is Your Grace aware that four weeks ago, in her cell in Gloucester Gaol, the Prisoner asked for a priest and was received into the Communion of the Roman Catholic Church?

CANTERBURY: I am well aware of it. I am staying here, just for a couple of nights, you know, at the Palace, and my old friend Jimmy Gloucester has told me what happened. It in no way affects my evidence. Not in the least. The history of Christ's Church upon Earth is very complicated. All we can do, each of us, is to seek true Catholicism wherever God may guide us. That is what Phillippa Gatsby and Barnabas Barbellion must have done, together on their knees, through the years . . . as Newman did. An agonizing process but it led them where it did.

SIR TRAVERS MCKENZIE: So you do not, Your Grace, regard Papistical practices, Carnal priests, Jesuitical superstitions, candles, incense and the Confession Box, as casting any doubt upon the Prisoner's integrity.

CANTERBURY: No, sir, I do not. In the face of vulgar opinion, such as you have just expressed, Conversion may be an act of supreme courage.

SIR TRAVERS MCKENZIE: Thank you, Your Grace. Clearly you are a Ritualist or a Puseyite as I think they are called. We shall see whether these twelve honest Englishmen agree with you or not. No more questions, Me Lud.

The Archbishop left the Witness Box, shook hands with the Judge, and then, to everyone's astonishment, shambled over to the Dock and shook hands with Phillippa. Then he vanished into the rain.

SIR FREDERICK FORD-BRYCE: Me Lud, I call my next witness – Father Barnabas Barbellion.

USHER: Barbellion! Barbellion! Barbellion!

There was a little cry from Eirlys as she clung very close to Jane Grigg. They had not known for certain whether he would be called or not. Jane is sure that for the first time in the whole trial Phillippa actually moved her head, to the left, away from the Witness Box. It is certain that not once did she and my father look into each other's eyes. He entered the Box, Jane says, with slow and calculated dignity, still the eternal actor. It was the first time Eirlys and Jane had seen him in his Roman cassock and biretta. He produced his own Douai Bible upon which he took the oath.

SIR FREDERICK FORD-BRYCE: Father Barbellion, you are better known in this part of the world as Archdeacon Barbellion. I trust that I address you correctly.

Barbellion bowed his acquiescence.

SIR FREDERICK FORD-BRYCE: Well then, Father Barbellion: you are thirty-six years of age. In 1839 you qualified as a Master of Arts in the University of Oxford and were ordained as a priest in the Church of England. After serving minor curacies you were inducted into the Living of Nether Molding in this County, a Living in the Gift of the Gatsby family. Two months ago you resigned your Living before a Notary Public and have now given your allegiance to Rome. I understand that you are at present residing with an organization calling itself the Oblates of St Charles, in Bayswater, London.

BARBELLION: Your facts are correct. My present home is quite temporary.

SIR FREDERICK FORD-BRYCE: Now, Father Barbellion, I am somewhat embarrassed in my cross-examination because I gather that your relationship with the Prisoner has been that of Priest and Penitent . . .

BARBELLION: There is no need for embarrassment. It is the least personal relationship upon Earth. The priest is the mere instrument of God.

SIR FREDERICK FORD-BRYCE: Nevertheless it is a fact, is it not, that in your own church at Nether Molding you frequently conducted Auricular Confession, with the doors locked. Now this, as you must be aware, may seem slightly shocking to a staunch Protestant Jury, and may even seem to invalidate your evidence. Will your evidence, they may wonder, really be 'the whole truth' or will parts be withheld under what, I believe, is called 'the Seal of the Confessional'. I must ask you, are you free to speak, Father Barbellion, or are you if necessary – in the true spirit of martyrdom – prepared to defy the Law with your silence? Would you care to say a word on all this so as to clear the air – if I may so put it.

Barbellion smiled the cold smile of pity for such abysmal ignorance, and then chose to address himself to the Judge.

BARBELLION: I am very glad, my Lord, to be able to dispose of these popular errors concerning Christ's Holy Catholic Church. First, as to Confession – it is enjoined upon us both in Holy Writ and in the Anglican Book of Common Prayer that we should confess our sin. In the Anglican Church, in recent centuries, Confession, like Fasting, has fallen into desuetude. It has never been condemned, it has been neglected. Some few of us have tried to remedy this laxity. Confession and Fasting are precious rites which we would restore to their proper place.

As to the so-called 'Seal of the Confessional' there is, my Lord, much nonsense talked. True, once a sin has been confessed and absolved, the matter is closed forever . . . it is God who has forgiven. But – and this I would emphasize – absolution is not automatic . . . real penitence must exist and also, if possible, restitution. The Confessor is usually concerned with Sins rather than Crimes. The Seven Deadly Sins – Anger, Sloth, Envy and so on – are deadly states of mind, conducive to crime, but not in themselves criminal. They may be absolved. If, however, the Penitent should confess to an actual crime then, indeed, absolution must be withheld until restitution has been made and, also, until there is surrender to the Civil Power – to the Police.

THE JUDGE: That is all very clear, Father Barbellion, and to withhold absolution – what does that involve?

BARBELLION: It involves Excommunication, my Lord. There

can be no Sacraments for the unabsolved sinner. And that, my Lord, brings me to the very crux of my evidence . . . may I continue?

THE JUDGE: Please do, Father Barbellion.

BARBELLION: Very well then. Let me say, first, that the Sacraments, the Body and Blood of her Saviour, meant far more to my Penitent, Phillippa Gatsby, than did life itself. That is certain. Had she confessed to me such a terrible crime as murder – as she assuredly would have done – then of necessity she would have been excommunicated until her surrender to the police. And excommunication, the loss of the Sacraments, would have been more terrible to her than the gallows itself. She never did confess such a crime and therefore I know that she did not commit it. I stand here, my Lord and Gentlemen of the Jury, upon my oath, to say that for sixteen years Phillippa Gatsby has been my Penitent. As a young girl she sinned once, grievously. Since then she has committed no sin from which I could not instantly absolve her. The question raised by Sir Frederick Ford-Bryce, the 'Seal of the Confessional', simply does not arise. Phillippa Gatsby stands before you a pure and innocent woman. That is all I have to say.

SIR FREDERICK FORD-BRYCE: Thank you, Father Barbellion. That seems very conclusive. I have no more questions, Me Lud.

THE JUDGE: Yes, Sir Travers?

SIR TRAVERS MCKENZIE: Father Barbellion, tell me, was the late Colonel Harold Gatsby also one of your Penitents?

BARBELLION: No.

SIR TRAVERS MCKENZIE: And we may take it, I suppose, that he was never present at his wife's Confession?

BARBELLION: Certainly not. That was a matter solely between her and Almighty God. I was a mere instrument.

SIR TRAVERS MCKENZIE: Ha! No more questions, Me Lud.

THE JUDGE: Thank you, Father Barbellion.

BARBELLION: Just a word, my Lord, if I may. Can I take it that my presence here will not be further required? I recently suffered a most crushing bereavement and am now in need of rest and recuperation. My dear friends, Lord and Lady Granville, are holding the Admiralty yacht, the *Enchantress*, in the Solent until I can join them. We then sail for the Isles of Greece. His Eminence Cardinal Wiseman and the young Prince of Wales, with his Tutor, are on board. If you need me further, my Lord, I must telegraph them.

THE JUDGE: No, no. No need for that. Dear me, the Prince of Wales – I had no idea. We must not keep you a moment longer. Good afternoon, Father Barbellion, and *Bon Voyage.*

BARBELLION: Thank you, my Lord.

And he was gone . . . to the Isles of Greece.

THE JUDGE: And now, Sir Frederick, your next witness.

SIR FREDERICK FORD-BRYCE: I call Miss Primrose Jones.

USHER: Jones! Jones! Jones!

The sensation in Court caused by the presence of the Archbishop of Canterbury was nothing compared to that caused by Primrose Jones. She was a sonsy bitch and, walking to the Witness Box, with a wonderful swagger, she knew that all eyes were upon her. With flounces and ribbons and muff and earrings, and the embroidered paletot over her phenomenal crinoline, not to mention her dark Celtic skin and black eyes, she came as a gust of fresh air to that stuffy Courtroom . . . and at the end of a long day. She showed good teeth when she smiled, but a marvellous pout when she was cross.

SIR FREDERICK FORD-BRYCE: Your name is Primrose Jones, you are . . .

THE JUDGE: A moment, Sir Frederick. This witness has not washed.

SIR FREDERICK FORD-BRYCE: I beg your pardon, Me Lud.

THE JUDGE: You must know perfectly well, Sir Frederick, that female witnesses may not appear before Her Majesty's Judges with rouge or powder on their faces. For once, as the hour is late, I will let the matter pass, but I cannot have the Court turned into a Music Hall.

SIR FREDERICK FORD-BRYCE: I am obliged, Me Lud. Now, your name is Primrose Jones. You are a spinster. You are nineteen years of age. You reside at No. 4 Dean Street, London. You formerly plied the trade of seamstress to Madame Thierry of Grafton Street.

PRIMROSE JONES: Yes, I suppose so.

SIR FREDERICK FORD-BRYCE: You were dismissed for lack of, punctuality.

PRIMROSE JONES: Well, ye' can call it that. It was an eighteen-hour day, and at five bob a week ye' can't buy a clock, ye' know. I was going half-blind anyway . . . with the stitching.

SIR FREDERICK FORD-BRYCE: Anyway, you were dismissed. How do you earn your living now?

PRIMROSE JONES: What's that to do with you?

SIR FREDERICK FORD-BRYCE: I think, Me Lud, that we may take it that the witness had to choose between the drudgery of domestic service, sewing, *aut id quod dicere nolo*. She chose the latter.

FOREMAN OF THE JURY: We would like to know what that means, my Lord.

THE JUDGE: It may be summarized as meaning that which is unspeakable. In other words this young woman is now a prostitute in the purlieus of Soho.

Every man in Court, unless his wife was with him, craned his neck. Every woman, momentarily, lowered her eyes to show how shocked she was. Then they all had a good look. After all it wasn't every day that one could see a real live prostitute. Could this really be Gloucester?

SIR FREDERICK FORD-BRYCE: Now, Miss Jones, in the course of plying your trade or, er, profession, did you ever meet a Colonel Harold Gatsby?

PRIMROSE JONES: Yes, two years ago, at two o'clock in the morning, on the corner of Carlton Gardens, under the trees. He'd just come out of the Travellers Club.

The people of Gloucester were having the time of their lives. The Master of the Foxhounds and Lord Lieutenant of the County, drunk at two in the morning, and picking up a tart. Well, it just showed, didn't it?

SIR FREDERICK FORD-BRYCE: You accosted him?

PRIMROSE JONES: No, he accosted me.

SIR FREDERICK FORD-BRYCE: But still you were there to be

accosted, weren't you? A respectable young woman at that hour . . .

PRIMROSE JONES: I'm not respectable. The Judge has just told everybody that . . . thank ye' for nothing, my Lord.

SIR FREDERICK FORD-BRYCE: Well, never mind that. Tell us what happened next.

PRIMROSE JONES: Well, what d'ye think? He went home with me of course . . . I had a very cosy place in Dean Street – warm, ye' know, and very pretty, all potted plants and bead curtains and all that. He came back a week later, and after that he was my bloke . . . again and again. He was keeping me.

Phillippa, rigid in the Dock, never moved a muscle.

SIR FREDERICK FORD-BRYCE: Yes, and then?

PRIMROSE JONES: Well, I went up in the world – not half! Old Gatsby set me up in a little cottage – honeysuckle round the porch, ye know – in Park Village West, out Regent's Park way. Everything as pretty as paint. I gave up all my other blokes. And then, after a few months, the mean old bastard vanished – never saw him again. The old, old story. He'd left me with a lease in my name, a dose of clap *and* something to remember him by. Christ, they're all the same!

THE JUDGE: Moderate your language, young woman.

SIR FREDERICK FORD-BRYCE: And so you never saw Colonel Gatsby again?

PRIMROSE JONES: No, but I damned nearly did. I got his address – some old Army List – and then I came down here, leastways I came to Windrush Court.

SIR FREDERICK FORD-BRYCE: But you never actually saw him?

PRIMROSE JONES: No, I did not. I was sent round to the back door. I was given a glass of water – I ask you, a glass of water! – and half a sovereign for my fare home, and told to bugger off – clear out, they said, or they'd put the dog on me.

SIR FREDERICK FORD-BRYCE: So you went back to London?

PRIMROSE JONES: No, I didn't. It was too late. I rummaged around the stable yard. I found a nice kind of lad there – his name was Micky Slate. My God, he was surprised to see me. He beamed all over as if I'd just come down from Heaven. We made a night of it in the hayloft. The next morning he gave me a cocoa in the harness room, and then I was off. Well, that's my story but I don't know why I'm here. You paid me a hundred quid to come to Gloucester but you haven't told me a bloody thing. If that lady over there poisoned old Gatsby, well, all I can say is Good Luck to her!

THE JUDGE: Now, you mustn't talk like that. Behave yourself. A tragic tale, Sir Frederick, but I admit that I haven't quite grasped its significance, from the point of view of the Defence, that is.

SIR FREDERICK FORD-BRYCE: I'm sorry, Me Lud. I thought the story would make its own point. This young woman has shown us two things. First, that under cover of darkness it was quite easy for any stranger to hide in the stables overnight – including the harness room with all that rat poison lying around – and then, with some simple tool perhaps, to enter the house. A most extraordinary situation, Me Lud.

THE JUDGE: I imagine, Sir Frederick, that most country houses are rather like that. The plate is the only thing that is ever really locked up.

SIR FREDERICK FORD-BRYCE: Possibly, Me Lud. Anyway, the second thing that Miss Jones has shown us is that there were dark places – very dark places indeed – in the life of Colonel Gatsby. I cast no aspersions upon this deplorable female – I certainly don't accuse her of murder – but an unhappy marriage, Me Lud, is not the only motive for poisoning. The woman scorned may be a harlot or a wife . . . in fact, anyone with access to the harness room. I hope, Me Lud, that the point of Miss Jones's evidence is now clear. If so, I have no more questions.

THE JUDGE: Abundantly clear. Now, Sir Travers.

SIR TRAVERS MCKENZIE: Miss Primrose Jones, did you murder Colonel Gatsby?

PRIMROSE JONES: WOT! Don't be so bloody silly . . . me!

SIR TRAVERS MCKENZIE: Thank you. So, when you came down to Gloucestershire, I take it that your only object was to get money – the Danegeld of the betrayed woman.

PRIMROSE JONES: I suppose so – whatever that means.

SIR TRAVERS MCKENZIE: And you never even entered the actual house at Windrush Court.

PRIMROSE JONES: I've said I didn't, haven't I? They slammed the front door in my face – I've told you.

SIR TRAVERS MCKENZIE: Quite. And, of course, leading the – er – rackety life that you do, you wouldn't know the date of your visit.

PRIMROSE JONES: Yes, I would. It was Derby Day.

SIR TRAVERS MCKENZIE: Indeed! About two and half months before the death of Colonel Gatsby. In that case, Me Lud, any further questions would be pointless.

*

The 'revelations' about Harold Gatsby did, I think, rather shock Jane Grigg – so worldly-wise in some ways, so very much the little English governess in other ways. They did not shock our little Eirlys. That innocent grey-eyed child, as the days passed in that winter of '54 and '55, seemed more and more to become the sharp and sophisticated woman of the world who, in her eighty-second year, can still charm us all. When she had lain in the hayloft with Micky Slate, his big arms round her little white body, he must, you know, have told her quite a lot about Primrose Jones . . . and about other things, including rat poison. By the time he'd finished there was certainly nothing much left about Colonel Gatsby and his tarts that would have surprised her.

Although Jane Grigg went on making notes, the evidence of Primrose Jones virtually ended the Trial. It seemed to leave Phillippa as the only person in the world with a motive. In fact, of course, the Trial went on for two more days. There was Sir Travers's final speech for the Prosecution – really very damning indeed until you had heard Sir Frederick for the Defence. But, by and large, with that strange mixture of malice and pomposity that is the stock-in-trade of the Bar, they both did no more than summarize the evidence of their own witnesses, and discredit the others.

I have said that half a century later I discussed the whole thing – the death of Harold Gatsby and of my own mother – with that great Counsel, Sir Edward Marshall Hall. He reminded me that Gatsby *versus* Regina was in the year 1855, and at that date

Phillippa, as the Prisoner at the Bar, could not give evidence in her own defence, submitting herself to cross-examination. It was not, Sir Edward reminded me, until the Criminal Defence Act of 1898 that this concession was made to Justice. It had in fact, he added, proved a two-edged sword, and it may well be that had Phillippa chosen to enter the Witness Box, Sir Travers McKenzie would have torn her to shreds. Her one speech, in reply to the Judge, when it did come, took precisely one minute.

Lord John Fitzjohn Grandison was a just judge, according to his lights, but a garrulous one. He too summed up the evidence all over again . . . 'on the one hand, Gentlemen of the Jury, but on the other hand . . .' all through the last and tenth day his fine voice droned on. There was the usual warning that the Prisoner must be given the benefit of even 'a scintilla of doubt' and then, only at the end, did the Judge make his three points – all damning. The first was that the Colonel had beyond doubt – as the exhumation showed – been given an overdose of strychnine. The second point was that Colonel Gatsby's life in London – while commonplace enough to men of the world – must suggest that his marriage was not, and never had been, what the good people of Nether Molding had imagined. The Judge's third point was in answer to Sir Frederick's, that Phillippa Gatsby of all people was the one who had no need to forge the label, since the bottle was in any case under her control, in her room. If, however, as the Judge pointed out, her object had been to get the overdose administered to her husband by a third person – as it happened, the innocent Featherston – then the forged label would indeed be necessary to the crime. And with that, he left the whole case to the Jury.

They filed out at five minutes to six. Lord Justice Grandison announced that if they were out all night he would not adjourn the Court. They returned to the Jury Box at twenty minutes to nine.

*

CLERK OF ARRAIGNS: Have you agreed upon your verdict, Gentlemen of the Jury?

FOREMAN: We have.

CLERK OF ARRAIGNS: And how say you, do you find the

Prisoner Guilty of the murder of Harold Garlick Gatsby, or Not Guilty?

FOREMAN: Guilty.

CLERK OF ARRAIGNS: Phillippa Thérèse Gatsby, you have been found Guilty of wilful murder, have you anything to say why the Court should not proceed to sentence?

PHILLIPPA GATSBY: Sixteen years ago I was guilty of intimacy with a man who has now passed out of my life. I bore him a child. Of all other charges I am – before Christ my Saviour – completely innocent.

THE JUDGE: Phillippa Thérèse Gatsby, after a long and fair trial wherein everything possible was said in your favour, and after a prolonged consideration by the Jury, you have been found Guilty of a most hideous and heinous crime. Have you anything to say why sentence of death should not now be passed upon you?

PHILLIPPA GATSBY: My Lord, I am with child.

This had been blazingly obvious for days, and was indeed known to all England. Nevertheless, the ritual had to be carried out.

THE JUDGE: Very well. Clerk of the Court, I instruct you to empanel without delay a Panel of Twelve Matrons to examine the Prisoner's plea that she is pregnant.

The Clerk of the Court was no fool. Twelve Gloucester mothers – all wives of his friends – were already waiting in the Jury Room.

CLERK OF THE COURT: The Panel of Matrons sits, Me Lud.

THE JUDGE: Let the Prisoner be taken to them.

Through a silent Court she walked in scarlet. She walked slowly with her hands folded upon her pregnancy, like a medieval statue. Within ten minutes she came back to the Dock. There was now a great rustling and shuffling. Into the already crowded and stinking room there were injected twelve women . . . the bombasine, the satins and the crêpe of crinolines all crushed together. As if by some tribal instinct every woman had put on black for the day – a black regiment of British matronhood. One stepped forward.

THE JUDGE: You speak for this Panel of Matrons.

FOREWOMAN: I do, my Lord.

THE JUDGE: Then you have examined the Prisoner as to her Plea that she is pregnant.

THE FOREWOMAN: We have, my Lord. We find that the Plea is justified. The Prisoner is eight months gone.

THE JUDGE: Phillippa Thérèse Gatsby, I will not prolong your agony. It is against the Laws of God and of Man that in condemning you to death I should also condemn the child in your womb. The sentence of this Court is that you shall be imprisoned and put to hard labour for the term of your natural life. Remove the Prisoner.

*

Three weeks later in the hospital at Holloway Prison she died very quietly. The priest whom they allowed her told both the Home Secretary and Cardinal Wiseman that he knew, before God, that she was innocent. She had given birth to a stillborn baby, a little brother for Eirlys.

Nearly two thousand miles away, under magic skies, the stewards of the *Enchantress* were setting out a picnic upon the warm and honey-coloured marbles of the Acropolis. In the shadow of the Parthenon the Prince of Wales's Tutor was lecturing him upon the Glories that were Greece. In the sun the ladies twirled their parasols, and laughed. Over there, at a corner of the Erectheion, Cardinal Nicholas Wiseman was talking to Father Barbellion of the theological niceties of the Byzantine Creed; Barbellion, as a dutiful son of Rome, listened . . . planning, meanwhile, in his own mind, his next step up the ladder . . . and the next and the next. The Aegean, out beyond the Piraeus, was amethyst, but then it was an early spring that year, all through Europe. Even in the churchyard at Nether Molding the crocuses were out on the graves.

6 To Stroll among the Graves

E'en from the tomb the voice of Nature cries.
E'en in our ashes live their wonted fires

THOMAS GRAY

In the years that followed – the fifty years that followed – there were meetings between us. They were few but, when they did happen, they were joyful. Those were times to remember and to talk, and to talk again. I have already said that Eirlys and Jane Grigg, in a rather special way, wrote to each other – so assiduously – and I have said that those were the letters I have never been allowed to see. All through the years they flew to and fro across Europe, all in Italian.

So much for Eirlys and Jane. Not more than half a dozen times did Maria Pia and I see our old governess. She had, we believed, a pleasant room in a Home for Gentlewomen at Tunbridge Wells – where eventually she was to die – and from there she would travel a little – Brittany or the Lake District, doing pale water-colours – or the occasional delirious week with Eirlys in Nice. Jane always seemed the very epitome of the retired English governess and yet, you know, I shall always wonder what those two talked about. Was it about that last Christmas at the Rectory, or those ten days when they sat together at the Gloucester Assize? They must have found something to talk about.

Maria Pia and I, of course, never lost sight of each other for long. She had her own home in Paris. She would use the house in the Via Tritone and the little Palazzo in Nice, *en route* to the East, but there were times when, for all I knew, my little sister was sleeping under desert stars or among the fallen columns of Palmyra . . . she would vanish for months and then, without so much as a postcard, would turn up again at Derravaragh at any time of the day or night.

No, after the débâcle, or, at any rate, after Eirlys had left that school at Gstaad, to become such an elegant woman of the world, it was she and I who were together most often and so happily – half-brother and half-sister but also, I am sure, half in love. And yet, over our happy meetings there lay a strange and curious inhibition, strange and curious silences, something – for all our love for each other – we could never talk about. It lay like a barrier between us – the silences of Eirlys.

I have never used my mansion in Belgravia, a great gloomy place, heavily upholstered, fully staffed but with the blinds eternally drawn. In London, wherever else in the world Eirlys might be, I knew that I could always use her pretty little house in Montpelier Square where the sun always seemed to shine upon the window boxes and the white front door. Whenever I turned up there, out of the blue, old Featherston would be there to look after me ... until the day he died, muttering peculiar things about the medicine bottle.

More often, however, I would call on Eirlys in Nice on my way to Rome, to talk yet again to those old cardinals. I used her London house for myself but preferred to visit her in that cool, white apartment in the Negresco. It was there, after dining late on her balcony, that I would escort her to the Casino. She would be wearing some creation from Worth – I remember one that shimmered with a thousand tiny diamonds, like a city seen at night – and so often round her neck would be Phillippa's fabulous choker – the Cole-Hatt sapphires. And then, over supper, she would drink Veuve Clicquot – a glass too many and with an air as if she was proposing a toast to something or to somebody.

For all these occasional happy meetings it was more than a generation before I could bring together at one time and in one place all the survivors of what, I suppose, I may call the Barbellion Mystery. True, every now and again, one might find Maria Pia turning up at Derravaragh, Eirlys entertaining me at Nice, or Jane Grigg at Montpelier Square ... just for shopping and a matinée. And then, once in a while, Jane might have a gorgeous week with Maria Pia in Paris ... but all four of us together – never. To the world these were just meetings of old friends recalling old days – no sign that we were chained to each other by our knowledge of those two unnatural deaths at Nether Molding, in the summer and winter of 1854 – chained together by a secret we shared but never discussed.

So, we led our lives – offspring of a murderer and a pope – only now and then arranging that our paths should cross. But whenever even two of us were together – in the Casino at Nice, at the ballet in Petersburg, as Wagnerians at Bayreuth, enjoying the daffodils on St Stephen's Green or – far more often – just sitting quietly by the lake at Derravaragh, we might be quite gay and carefree, as if we were still children in the Rectory garden, until suddenly there would descend upon us that uncanny silence. Then we would become aware of ghosts – the ghost of an old jam pot on the study shelf, a jam pot full of flea killer, the ghost of a white bowl with the remains of minced goose and a silver spoon, while upstairs would be Mama's quilted coffin . . . all ghosts that would not be exorcized but must not be mentioned.

It must seem odd that never in that whole half century were we all four together – never all at once. There were chances enough but somehow it never happened. Then one day it dawned on me that through the years it had always been Eirlys who had prevented it. As I looked back I realized that all the difficulties and excuses, all the 'prior engagements', had been of her making. Was it perhaps that she knew something that we others did not know, that she had wormed some secret out of her mother? Perhaps. But it was all rather inexplicable. After all, I loved my sister Eirlys and would swear that she loved me likewise . . . her 'darling Gussy'. And yet never would she do this one thing for me – gather us all together.

Not at any rate for over fifty years. And then, rather suddenly, with a new century, a new reign and a new Pope – Papa five years dead – something happened. An entirely new light was about to be thrown upon the death of Mama. The Gatsby Case had been closed – legally closed in that little dark Court at Gloucester, and closed forever three weeks later when Phillippa's baby boy was laid beside her in the coffin. The Barbellion Case, on the other hand, had never been closed. Indeed, after Papa's cruise in the *Enchantress* it had never existed – not officially.

But now everything was altered – overnight as it were. I had been waiting for it so long that I had almost forgotten it until one morning it dropped through the letter-box – a long blue envelope from the Home Office – their consent to the exhumation of Emily Barbellion.

Then indeed I acted. Without a word to anyone about the Home Office I positively ordered Eirlys – yes, 'ordered' is the only word for it – ordered her to open Windrush Court for a week and to invite us all. It had, I told her, become both necessary and urgent that we should all be together at Nether Molding before the end of May. To my astonishment she surrendered – by return of post. And so it was arranged.

Of course I had been working for this all my life, or so it seemed to me. Both in London and in Rome I had always kept the Barbellion story alive. I had made a nuisance of myself. I had talked every ten years or so to the Commissioner of Police, only to be told that there was not even a Barbellion File . . . of course not, that was the point. I talked to every Home Secretary, as one succeeded another, only to find that each one – briefed by his officials – rejected me each in the same words – exhumation was an extreme measure, Mrs Barbellion had been a confirmed invalid, there were no grounds.

I tried to get the support of the Roman Church, on the score that they might like to see an ugly myth disposed of forever. I talked to Cardinal Newman – a 'great hater' Papa had called him – but all he really wanted was to avoid unpleasantness. I talked to Father Faber at the Oratory only to be told that my whole idea was 'impossible' – Popes were not only Infallible, they were infallible from the hour that their mothers had conceived them – at no time upon Earth could they err. An extraordinary conversation with a young acolyte who, years later, became Ronnie Knox's valet, was more promising – a mixture of gossip, spite, scandal and malice that was utterly fascinating but, alas, utterly unreliable.

Cardinal Vaughan always disliked my visits to York Place. He probably resented my existence since there should, after all, be no such person as a Pope's son. He certainly never let me so much as glance at the Wiseman papers. The Earl of Shrewsbury, kinsman of that Monsignor Talbot who, until his brain cracked, had been Papa's *éminence grise* at the Vatican, sat tight-lipped in his great hall at Alton – the Pope's character was something – he made it quite clear – that a gentleman did not discuss; one would as soon think of gossiping about Jesus Christ.

In Rome itself as long as Papa lived I met with a wall of silence. This was inevitable. And then, with Papa dead, the old cardinals who had known him also began to die, one by one. Except, of course, that there was always old Cardinal Cavalle. He had, I am sure, a soft place in his heart for Maria Pia and for me. As a boy he had been a server, or something of the kind, in the huge church of St John Lateran. This is the church, of course, where the Pope as Bishop of Rome has his throne . . . it is *his* church and cathedral whereas St Peter's belongs to all the world. The Lateran clergy, therefore, pride themselves upon knowing all the Papal sins and scandals – they collect them in a big book. Cavalle – beautiful youth and devious diplomat that he was – had got his red hat from Pius the Ninth at a very early age, so that when his master died he was there, still a young man, in the Conclave of 1878 to vote – God knows why – for the Cardinal of Westminster, former Rector of Nether Molding. Cavalle was there again, nineteen years later, to lead Maria Pia to her father's deathbed. And, almost incredibly, he was still there when I visited Rome a couple of years ago – vain and talkative in senility but still amusing and malicious. Moreover he had been a very good friend of Brother Justin. In fact he was the Confessor of the Pope's Confessor . . . one could not get much nearer the throne than that.

It is not for me to pass judgement upon any intimacy between Justin and Cavalle. Strange things happen in a celibate priesthood and I am not at liberty to exploit those things for my own ends. Cavalle must have known a lot. All he ever told me, however, was that when Pope Paschal the Fourth died in Rome on that pale winter morning of 1897, the new Pope, Leo the Thirteenth, granted a dispensation to Brother Justin, Paschal's Confessor, to 'break the seal' – something almost unprecedented in the long history of the Church. Whatever this dubious monk may or may not have revealed to Leo, and presumably to him alone, the dispensation itself was a Pontifical Act of extraordinary significance, a *colpo di stato Domineddo*. Leo the Thirteenth, like Justin and Cavalle, must have known a lot.

I had to assume that Leo would never reveal Papa's Confession to any living soul. That was something between him and Christ his Judge, who was also Paschal's Judge. If these secrets were written down – and in the Vatican everything is written down – then in all probability they were now in Leo the Thirteenth's sepulchre in the Sistine Chapel, clutched to his breast. He would take them with him to the grave. That was certain.

As for Brother Justin, that is another story. Armed with a Papal Dispensation, did he talk in his cups? Did he talk in bed? Did he talk too much to his own Confessor, the garrulous Cavalle? When I last saw Cavalle – over ninety – he was as talkative as ever but so evasive. For an hour in the Vatican Gardens, as we sat over our coffee and cognac in the Oval Court, I plied him with questions. I induced in him the garrulous stage of intoxication – but he told me nothing. He treated me, for the tenth time, to the spiciest scandals, except the one that mattered. Perhaps, after all, he knew nothing but was too vain to admit it.

The fact must be faced – if the one really irrefutable proof of my mother's murder – my father's last Confession – was indeed upon a parchment within a golden casket, within a coffin of lead, within a coffin of cedar, within the alabaster tomb, beneath the marble paving of the Sistine Chapel, then with what did that leave us? If the exhumation of an English clergyman's wife – fifty years dead – was, as I well knew, a very troublesome business, then the exhumation of a Pope from under the floor of the Sistine must be a thousand times less likely – a pity, because one would find that – unlike Mama – he had been embalmed.

In my rather inebriated chat with Cavalle we had reached this sort of deadlock when I saw that the old boy was giving me a distinctly curious look.

'You know, my dear Augustine, you are kicking against the pricks. Can't you see that? If you really want to know how your mother died – and I can't imagine why you should – then go back to England, to the police and to your own bureaucrats. We Romans, you know, we cardinals and aristos, can never be of the slightest use to you – to help you would be mortal sin.'

'How so? I don't understand.'

'Of course you don't. You damned Englishmen are so sure of yourselves that you never even think. When His Holiness Paschal the Fourth died, you and your sister were waiting for the news, waiting in your house in the Via Tritone. She was sent for to kiss his forehead and to join in the Prayers for the Dead. She was sent for, you were not.'

'I know. I have often wondered why. But Your Eminence, what are you trying to tell me?'

A huge grin spread over his wrinkled face.

'My dear Augustine, have you forgotten that at Stonyhurst you were really a very naughty little boy?'

'Fifty years ago!'

'What's that got to do with it? Once the Jesuits have put their black mark upon a man, then that is that. We clergy, especially the Curia, were long ago notified of your dreadful sins – and in the Junior School too! Dear me! Dear me! You were naughty!'

'No worse than a thousand boys . . .'

'Oh, the dirty words and the goings-on in the cubicles – all that could be forgiven . . . but your gift for caricature! No, no. The black mark is upon you, dear Augustine, until the Day of Judgement – sinful son of a sinful Pope. Dear me! I can only hope that your Latin exercises and French verbs were better than your conduct. No, my boy, if you really want to arrange an exhumation – and you seem determined – then go back to England . . . Whitehall, not the Vatican, is the place for your intrigues.'

That was the last time I saw the old man. So, the Jesuits had had their revenge. I had always been told they would and they, I suppose, were satisfied. On the other hand, if the tawse had scarred my back, Stonyhurst had taught me a little of the pleasures of life. It had been a good bargain.

I went back to London, and to Ireland. I had to start all over again. I made Montpelier Square my base. I danced at Lancaster House with the Home Secretary's wife, exercising all my notorious Irish charm upon a notoriously susceptible woman. I took her to luncheon at the Carlton. I escorted her to Ascot. I slept with her at Mentmore. The Home Secretary really took it very well so that in the end I was able to ask them to Derravaragh, just after the Punchestown Races. It was at Derravaragh, in bed with her husband, that she worked upon him to achieve *my* ends. Over the port and my excellent brandy I had already persuaded him – or almost – that he needed a new Permanent Secretary. She did the rest. I had just the man – ready up my sleeve. Billy O'Grady was the best law student ever to come out of Trinity College. He was also – praise be to God – one of the boyos from Mullingar. The thing was as good as done. I had discovered that you can do in Ireland what you cannot do in Rome, and that an Irishman will do anything for the Pope's son – a blessed thing, surely, in the eyes of Almighty God. Yes, the thing was as good as done. Billy O'Grady had pledged himself to dig up Mama. And so at last the long blue envelope has arrived. And Eirlys has surrendered. In the spring we shall all four of us stroll among the graves . . . and then we shall see.

It was the last week of May, as hot as any day in June. Eirlys was a superb hostess. If there was something in our meeting that she dreaded – and Heaven knows what it could be – she hid her feelings well. She was buoyant and had never been more glamorous. She had welcomed us that morning with kisses and hugs, and then with food and wine that were not of this world. We all drank the Windrush 1833 Veuve Clicquot. It was almost the last in the cellar, she said, but it must always be her celebration drink!

After luncheon we had coffee on the terrace, in the shade of all that dark topiary, with the goldfish flashing in the little square lily pond . . . nothing had changed, except that there were no croquet hoops on the lawn. The afternoon passed in a warm, indolent, sleepy and delicious silence . . . all of us so glad to be together, so unwilling to talk. It was hot. I had put on a boater with the Old Stonyhurst ribbon! Eirlys, although still so lovely in her seventies, had shaded her face with the most enormous picture hat imaginable, all wreathed in tiny flowers. Maria Pia and Jane had their parasols, one lined with pale pink, the other with pale green, to match the leg-of-mutton sleeves and the big bustles. The footman and the maid, I thought, as they put out the wicker tables and served the tea, were far too young ever to have known anything about us.

It was not till evening, when the scented logs were burning, that we began to talk, and then, with the ice broken, we almost talked the night away. It was little Maria Pia who, in her firm way, decided that that was what must happen. The Barbellion Mystery must be dragged back into the light of day, and disposed of forever . . . we had not all come to Windrush for nothing.

'Let us talk about Papa . . . but, there, I see already that Eirlys disapproves of that.'

'No, no, no, not if you want to, but it's all so very long ago, isn't it. Let the dead bury their dead. Can't we leave it alone? You agree with me, Griggy?'

'It might be wiser, I suppose. I don't know.'

'Wiser. It might be boring to talk about it, or useless or painful, but not, surely, unwise. I can't see that. What a curious remark, Griggy. Anyway, there are still gaps to be filled in – gaps in the old story. For instance, you know, Eirlys, don't you, that in those first years after he broke up the home, and after your mother was – er – taken away, Gussy and I never even saw Papa. Of course none of us ever actually met him or spoke to him again, but I mean we never even saw him as a priest, as a public figure . . . we were in Derby, you see – Aunt Caroline and all that. Did you see him, Eirlys?'

'Of course. You know, we all know, that Jane and I saw him for five minutes at Gloucester Assize – my mother in the dock, my father in the witness box; and then for me, after that, it was the school at Gstaad, and the Hampshire aunts. But Jane, you saw him, didn't you – quite soon after the débâcle.'

'You saw him – oh, I didn't know. Where, Griggy?'

'Well, you see at first they could only make him quite an ordinary priest – Father Barbellion. But at least they gave him a very fashionable church where he could bring in shoals of fashionable converts. They gave him the Church of the Holy Rood, Upper Brook Street – just off Park Lane.'

'He must have loved it!'

'Yes, Gussy, and I went there one Sunday to hear Mass. You know, it was just like Eucharist at Nether Molding, only more so. There was a kind of gallery above the West Door and when your Papa led in the Procession – censers swinging, candles aloft – there were boys up there to shower down rose petals.'

'Ye Gods!'

'As you say, Gussy. And the old ladies next to the aisle – they kissed his ring as he passed or even the hem of his vestment. Somehow it all made me feel a little sick – knowing him as I did – but of course there was still the fine voice, the flashing eye, the actor's hands – the same as ever except that the orotund Latin seemed to suit him so much better than our old Anglican Prayer Book . . . it certainly made Nether Molding seem a long way off. And so, you and Maria Pia have never even spoken to him again?'

'No, Griggy, but there was once a time when I might have done – it was in Rome – you remember, Eirlys?'

'Of course. It must have been in the winter of '78. Pius the Ninth was dying and the Cardinals were all gathering for Conclave . . . carrion crows over the corpse. Oh, yes, I remember. I remember so well, Gussy, how you were my escort in Rome; very smart you were, a *café-au-lait* suit and a dark brown topper . . .'

'My dear, that was nothing . . . your hat, I can see it now, after thirty years. It was part of the scene, like the fountains in the Piazza, except that the fountains were baroque and the hat was pure rococo . . . rather like you, you know, so bizarre but so irresistible. I suppose we were just a little in love, weren't we? I was certainly being rather gallant and fashionable towards you. It was all very marvellous.'

'Yes, dear boy. I remember how we had been drinking our morning *chocolat* at the Caffé Greco. Out in the street the puddles were all frozen so that we were able to walk dry-shod, between the carriages, all the way from the Corso, across the bridges, to St Peter's.'

'Puddles frozen – yes, it was Christmas. Christmas in Rome. In those days that was very chic, was it not?'

'Hence our hats perhaps.'

'Yes, and I remember that I was still admiring yours when it all happened. We were standing together, you were on my arm, just at the foot of the Scala Regia, where the marble steps flow out past the Swiss Guard on to the Piazza. And then suddenly – I can almost feel it now – you gripped my elbow. "Look, Gussy," you said, "look, there is Papa!"'

'It's as if it were yesterday. It was a strange feeling, after all we had been through, after that last Christmas at the Rectory, after all those years. He was in one of his more grandiose moods, a mood of swaggering dignity. There were two of them, and with terrific poise and – one must admit it – terrific splendour, they were coming down the great stair, and so out into the shadow of Bernini's Colonnade – the Cardinals Norfolk and Barbellion.'

'Yes, Eirlys, they were a tremendous pair. Norfolk, you know, had resigned a commission in the Guards, for the priesthood, and was the finest figure in Rome. I remember you saying that he would strip well! Oh, yes, you did. But Papa – well, he had aged a little so that his face was a death-mask . . . but still very austere and forbidding of course . . . somehow more distinctive than ever a mere Norfolk could be.'

The young footman came in to put logs on the fire. The day had been hot, the evening was cool. He brought us fresh coffee. As Eirlys dismissed him for the night I turned to Maria Pia, wondering why I had never told her this story of our Christmas in Rome – she had probably been on the other side of the world.

'It was unforgettable, Maria – the sanguinary splash those two men made against the honey-coloured travertine of the Colonnade. Other cardinals, I suppose, had some sort of red silk for their cassocks, rochets and so on; these two, Norfolk and Barbellion, had watered silk from Japan, sent by Jesuit missionaries to be tailored by Poole of Savile Row . . . Gamarelli was good enough for the Pope but not for them. After all, in their own eyes, they were splendid symbols of the Eternal Church, and beneath those huge Tuscan columns they looked it. One must at least grant them that. And then, Eirlys, what happened then?'

'Why, you remember, I gripped your elbow again. "Whatever would he think, dear boy –" that's what I said to you, "– whatever in the world would he think if he knew who was watching him?"'

'Yes, that's what you said, but I was wondering even more what would happen if I dared to walk up to him – he was only ten paces away – "Your Eminence," I would have said, "Your Eminence, I am your son, Augustus Xavier Barbellion, and this lady, Eirlys Magdalen Cole-Hatt, is your natural daughter." But I knew that it just wouldn't do. Of course not. He might have called the Guard, or simply turned his back. I struggled with myself but my courage failed me. But then, to be fair, what man on earth would have dared?'

'Nobody. And then, Gussy, you remember how you had looked forward to being my cicerone in St Peter's, pointing out all the *monumenti* with your gold-knobbed cane. But instead we walked back to Tiber and there, looking down into its muddy waters, we talked of how we might stop him becoming Pope . . .'

It was Maria Pia who interrupted.

'But why on earth, Eirlys, when Pius died did they ever make him Pope? I have never understood. There were better cardinals than Papa.'

'Yes, my dear, in your philosophy, but the Vatican, you know, works in a mysterious way. You must remember that great Vatican Congress of 1871 – the Infallibility Congress. There were over four hundred bishops in St Peter's – they ran out of mitres and had to make them of cardboard – and that was the Congress, you know, that gave old Pius his Infallibility . . . but only by a cat's whisker, and only in matters of Faith and Morals. Pius was rather annoyed but he always remembered that it had been Papa, Cardinal Barbellion of Westminster, who, sobbing with emotion, had gone down on his knees to Pius, begging him not only to declare himself Infallible, but to declare that no Pope personally had ever sinned or ever could sin upon this Earth – in short, to identify himself with Christ. And so, you see, Maria Pia, Papa was rewarded – he too became Infallible.'

'Yes, that's how he became Pope. And yet that day, as Eirlys and I stood by the river – with Pius already on his deathbed – we were foolish enough to wonder how we could stop it. Papa, we said to each other, must never be Pope.'

'Yes, Gussy, and you said that the Norfolks or Cavalle should be told what a wicked creature he was, so that they could pass it on to Conclave. You even thought that they should be told he was a murderer, although they would never have believed that nonsense . . . nor shall I.'

'It's not nonsense, Eirlys. I shall prove it before I die, perhaps even tomorrow.'

'Tomorrow indeed! Don't talk rubbish, Gussy. Murder! You know, dear boy, that such things don't happen to people like us.'

'But you can't make a man Pope if there's so much as a suspicion of murder.'

'Well, there was, and they did. And why not, pray? In the last eighteen hundred years at least a dozen popes have committed murder. I admit it was usually only concubines, but still . . . When will you learn, Gussy? After all, you were brought up a Catholic after a fashion. You should know that mortal sin is one thing, that crime is another. If you despoil the Sacrament, or something of that kind, then you are anathema. But murder, rapine, loot, bastardy, adultery, fornication, incest, sodomy – Mother Church has dealt with these things for so long and in such high places that she can take them all in her stride. If we had told Conclave itself that Papa was a murderer, with the blood dripping from his hands, it would have made no difference. He would still have become Paschal the Fourth.'

A log flared up and spluttered on the hearth. In the shadows at the far end of the Library the Louis Quinze clock chimed and struck three. Three o'clock in the morning and nobody had really noticed, least of all little Jane Grigg who had been holding her breath.

'And tell me, did any of you ever see him after he was Pope? Yes, of course, you did, Gussy.'

'Twice. I saw him once on his white mule – looking more like a warrior on a battle horse – and then, before he washed the beggars' feet, they carried him through St Peter's on the Gestatorial, a huge crowd cheering and clapping. It was marvellous, and he wallowed in it, but perhaps the second time I saw him was even more marvellous. It was pure chance. I was walking out on the Appian Way when His Holiness Pope Paschal the Fourth drove past on his way to Castel Gondolfo – six coaches, each with six horses. He was alone in the first, on a kind of throne. The other five were stuffed with chamberlains and cardinals, and of course there were Zouaves and outriders. As I stood by the side of the road I thought of Mama deep in her grave at Nether Molding, and here, in golden coaches, was the apotheosis of a wife-poisoner. But there, I see that once again Eirlys does not agree.'

'No, I do not. You have an absolute obsession, Gussy. He was vain, hypocritical, immoral, ruthless, cruel, possibly even mad – but not, not, a wife-poisoner. It is too absurd. I refuse to discuss it further. It is very late but we are all here at Windrush – and at your request, Gussy – so let us get down to business and divide up the swag.'

'Really, Eirlys, what on earth are you talking about?'

'I may have used rather a low expression, but it is clear. There can be only one possible reason for this gathering. Paschal the Fourth has been dead for some years, but then the Vatican works slowly. I presume, Gussy, that you are here to tell us that the Holy Catholic Church is about to do the right thing by the Pope's children . . . well then, tell us – how many million lira?'

So, that was why she had agreed to our meeting!

'Eirlys, you are being perfectly ridiculous!'

'Not at all. You have been to Rome. I have my spies. You have seen the Cardinal-Deacon. You have seen the Camerlingo and, needless to say, that old fool, Cavalle. Well then, tell us.'

'There is nothing to tell. Papa didn't leave us any money in his Will. Not a penny. It was not to be expected; he had done with us forever in 1854. He knew that you, whom he had never acknowledged anyway, would have the Gatsby and the Cole-Hatt fortunes. He knew that I would sooner or later have the vast Leapingwell estates in Ireland and in London, and that I would always care for Maria Pia, unless of course she went into a Convent – the correct thing for a Pope's daughter. As for poor Griggy, I don't suppose, my dear, that he ever gave you a thought.'

'Why should he? I was only a servant. I only got the job for my Italian.'

'So you see, Eirlys, you are talking great nonsense . . . no money from the Vatican for any of us, and never will be. Cavalle made that quite plain.'

'How?'

'Well, at Stonyhurst I was a rather naughty boy . . .'

'. . . and ever since.'

'Don't be such a fool, Eirlys. I offended the Jesuits and they "blacked" me, to Eternity. So, dear Eirlys, you may as well disillusion yourself. Not even the Curia will offend the Society of Jesus . . . nothing for the Barbellion children in this world.'

'Then what, may I ask, are we all here for! Gussy, you have got us here under false pretences, just to ride your old hobby-horse – the murder. Really!'

'I think, dear girl, that you have been mixing too many brandies with the Veuve Clicquot. Anyway, it is time we all went to bed. I shall have more to tell you tomorrow.'

The big Lanchester was waiting in the drive. The day was still as hot as if it were June but, under veils and dustcoats, the ladies were cool in organdie and muslin. It was a nostalgic drive through the lanes, the banks yellow with primroses. How many scores of times had Eirlys, perched alongside her mother in the carriage – so smart and so pretty – driven between those hedges, Bowlby and Tomkins on the box seat, erect, liveried and cockaded . . . and now we had the goggled chauffeur. But it must have been that last Christmas ride with Phillippa that was uppermost in Eirlys's mind – snow on the roads, and then, when they got back to Windrush, carriage lamps under the trees and policemen in the morning-room.

As for Nether Molding it seemed much the same as it did fifty years ago. It was still buried in its wooded valley. The blue smoke still rose from the dozing cottages. The hens still scratched in the lane. The Rectory still seemed too big for the church. Its paint, however, had been smartened up a little, its patches of damp and decay had gone and, in general, the days of the flea killer seemed to be over.

We were received on the doorstep by an old Rector, the Reverend Richard Pertwee, a widower I think, and so feeble that I suspected that his bishop had given him the house as a place in which to die. He knew of course that one of the rectors of Nether Molding had become Pope, but he told us that in the village there were no legends or memories of the Barbellion era. His congregation, he explained, was seldom more than a dozen; he could just manage the services and the occasional weddings and funerals. I asked him if anyone remained from Papa's day.

'Only old Simmonds – he was your father's coachman, I think. We got him into the Gatsby Almshouses but, alas, the Trustees had to get rid of him; he would dig his garden, you see, on the Sabbath . . . so he's in the Workhouse now – quite senile. At least I've never actually heard that he's dead.'

I asked if we could see the house as well as the church and garden.

'Of course. Go wherever you like, anywhere. I'm all alone here. Enjoy your memories, all of you, and then perhaps you will come back here and take a little refreshment in the study . . . then, Sir Augustine, we can transact our business . . . oh, yes, I have the letter for you.'

At this remark Eirlys's eyebrows shot up to the top of her head, and she gave me a very sharp look. We all went upstairs and now, as if by right, Maria Pia seemed determined to take charge. She never hesitated. There were the eight heavy mahogany doors with their brass knobs. She went straight to the big bedroom. The serge curtains were half-pulled, as they had always been, and it was dark in there, as it had always been.

'It hasn't changed,' she murmured to herself, 'it hasn't changed.'

And then she turned to me.

'Yes, Gussy, still a four-poster with the huge pillows – the pillows where Mama always seemed so lost. The *prie-dieu* was there, and the Spanish Madonna with the red light was over there, where that wardrobe is now. And it was just there, at the foot of the bed, that they put the coffin, with its pretty mauve quilting, until the next morning when they lifted in Mama and screwed down the lid . . . you remember.'

We remembered all right, although she had been speaking as if to herself. I saw the tears in her eyes. After all, this was the room where she had been conceived and born and where her mother had for so long been an invalid, only to die in pain.

'Yes, Gussy, and you remember that when we kissed her – although there was a fire in the grate – she was quite cold and stiff. It was teatime, so I think she must have died in the morning – the morning of St Stephen's Day. I wonder why they never told us. Even now I sometimes dream about the coffin – quite clearly, you know.'

It was Eirlys who put her arm round her.

'Don't distress yourself, darling. It's all so long ago. This probing of old wounds, Gussy, is no use. I can't imagine why you've brought us all here. I don't understand you at all.'

'You will, Eirlys, you will.'

Then we went into the old night-nursery. It was now a mere lumber room – clearly the house was far too big for the old Rector

– but Maria Pia, the tears streaming down her face, explained how all the furniture had been arranged . . . fifty years ago.

'Yes, and sometimes, Gussy, you remember how we would have terrible dreams – dreams about death and Hell. Papa never allowed us to forget the lake of fire and brimstone that burneth forever. I think the dreams were worse when we had fleas. I would wake screaming and Griggy would come in to comfort us and hold my hand until I was asleep again.'

Then Maria Pia went to the bedroom window. Holding back the curtains and raising a half-lowered blind, she pointed across the garden to the short, broad Norman tower, almost hidden among the dark yews and the elms.

'And that,' she said, 'is the church – the church where Papa preached those sermons of his, and where he did such strange things – I know what he did in there . . . with "Aunt" Phillippa. I know. And you remember, Gussy, that night when there were lamps under the trees, over there in the churchyard.'

I remembered all right. But in the schoolroom it was Jane Grigg's turn – the toy cupboard, the bookshelves, the place where Papa had hung Holman Hunt's *Massacre of the Innocents*. And, oddest of all, there was still the kettle ring where Griggy used to make our gruel at bedtime.

And then we all went downstairs. I saw Maria Pia hesitate a moment outside the study door. I saw a little shudder run right through her, and then she went out into the garden. The daffodils were dying and the lawn was only roughly scythed, but it was still the garden where we had played together as children, and the rooks were still as busy as ever in the elms.

And so through the little gate into the churchyard. We thought we would have to hunt for Mama's grave in the long grass, but Maria Pia walked unerringly to the spot, as if the funeral had been only yesterday. We knew that Papa had erected a huge angel there, holding a lily, all in pink marble set upon a pedestal. But now there was nothing – nothing but a square of neatly mown turf. All around us the graves were old and lichen-covered, leaning at all angles, grey and green and damp. But now, in the midst of them and quite new to us, was a gorgeous and obtrusive affair of polished granite with inlaid slabs of white Carrara with gilded lettering. This tomb was enclosed by an ornate railing. We stood in silence while Maria Pia, almost in a whisper, read the inscriptions.

OBIIT

To the Everlasting Memory of Harold Garlick Gatsby,
G.C.B., K.C.V.O.
Beloved Husband of Phillippa Thérèse Gatsby
BORN: Anno Domini MDCCCVII
DIED: Anno Domini MDCCCLIV
Colonel of the Queen's Own Rifle Brigade
Justice of the Peace
High Sheriff of Gloucester
Lord Lieutenant of the County of Gloucestershire
Church Warden of the Parish
Master of Foxhounds

*

WITH CHRIST WHICH IS FAR BETTER
R.I.P.

Also to the Everlasting Memory of Phillippa Thérèse Gatsby
Widow of the above and Daughter of Sir Claud Cole-Hatt
of Piddlington Park in the County of Hampshire
BORN: Anno Domini MDCCCXVIII
DIED: Anno Domini MDCCCV
She died tragically in North London and is there interred
with her infant child

*

SAY NOT THE STRUGGLE NAUGHT AVAILETH
R.I.P.

We had walked slowly back to the house in absolute silence. Old Pertwee was waiting for us in the hall.

'Come in, come in. Dear me, how fascinating for you all after so many years – old scenes, old memories! Come in, come in to the study – a glass of Marsala perhaps and a slice of seed cake. What perfect weather for your visit. Now here we are; I suppose this was the study in your father's time.'

It suddenly dawned upon me why things had changed so little.

Here, in the study, the books were different – fewer of them and the big brown folios all gone – but yes, surely, that was Papa's desk and that was his chair – I should know, I had bent over it often enough to be thrashed. But, of course, as a celibate priest Papa would have no use for all this domestic furniture; he must have sold it to his successor or to the diocese. When we had sat down with our Marsala and cake, it was Maria Pia who forestalled the old man in anything he might have said.

'Mr Pertwee, we found that our mother's grave was just grass. Where is the marble angel?'

'Ah, yes, Miss Barbellion, you may well ask. A very strange story, somewhat before my time. It was my predecessor, Mr Grainger – out in the mission field now – who had to deal with it. You see, the grave had fallen into disrepair and so the churchwardens wrote to – er – His Eminence – he was at Westminster by then – to ask for instructions. They had an astonishing reply. I have seen the letter. "So be it," he wrote, "so be it. Obliterate the grave. Time effaceth all things." Astonishing and a little ruthless, I think.'

'I see, Mr Pertwee. Ruthless, yes, but quite in character.'

'Yes. And so Mr Grainger put down plain turf – there are some crocuses underneath – and sold the angel to a mason's yard. He put up a simple plaque in the Chancel – just the name and dates. I think he did right.'

'Oh, perfectly right. But there is another matter. One can see that the turf has been disturbed quite recently. Why?'

'Ah, yes, of course – only three weeks ago. But that is a matter for your brother. Most reverently done, I can assure you, most reverently done. But your brother must tell you about that. This is Mr Stansbury's letter, sir. It has been waiting for you here for some ten days.'

So, by a kind of ironic justice, like the last act of a Greek tragedy, it was in Papa's own study that I told my sister, Maria Pia, my half-sister, Eirlys Magdalen, and our old governess, Jane Grigg, of the exhumation.

'It had become necessary,' I said, 'that the whole story of the Barbellion Mystery should be wound up once and for all – necessary for us and, whether they like it or not, necessary for the

Vatican. Three weeks ago Mama's coffin was lifted from the ground. Mr Pertwee, here, was present, also the Chief Constable and a brilliant young pathologist, a Mr Stansbury. The operation was a simple one. It was done in daylight with a constable on guard at the Lych Gate, and the coffin just laid on the grass. After fifty years we cannot, I suppose, expect very much – it is only popes who are embalmed – but Stansbury was curiously optimistic. Officially he reports to the Home Office but this is his letter to me – I had it sent under cover to Mr Pertwee to await us here. Now, shall I break the seal?'

Maria Pia had given a little cry, as if in pain, but thereafter hardly spoke again that day. Jane Grigg, half-stunned, went on muttering time and time again, 'It was unwise, Gussy, it was unwise.' The behaviour of Eirlys was more curious. We were all seated with Mr Pertwee around the big desk, except Eirlys. She had deliberately set herself apart on the sofa, and was now playing the rôle of *grande dame*. This suited her well enough sometimes but in the circumstances was ridiculous. Her outstretched arm had one finger on top of the parasol handle and, for the seed cake, there was a great to-do with unbuttoning and buttoning of her long gloves, and the rolling up of her little veil . . . an affected fuss.

'Gussy,' she said, 'you are a perfect fool. After fifty years there can be only dry bones, and even if the body was stuffed with arsenic it would prove nothing . . .'

'I was not aware, Eirlys, that anyone had mentioned arsenic . . .'

'Oh, well, arsenic, strychnine or whatever it is. You still won't know that Papa put it there. It is much more likely to have been my mother. She was always in and out of that bedroom, and, after all, Gussy, two poisoners in one parish is unlikely – a million to one against. However, have it your own way, break the seal.'

And so I did, and here is Mr Stansbury's letter, or the more essential parts of it.

St George's Hospital,
Hyde Park Corner, London.
20th May, 1905

Dear Sir,

On May 5th last, with the help of two gravediggers, and with the Reverend Richard Pertwee and the Chief Constable of the County as witnesses, the body of the late Emily Barbellion was exhumed from the churchyard at Nether Molding. There was no problem of identification, the silver plate on the coffin, although tarnished, being still legible.

The coffin was ostentatious but cheap – there was no inner shell and the outer carvings were simply glued on to deal boards. It had therefore rotted considerably and of the inner quilting only a few shreds remained. After fifty years I did not of course expect a cadaver from which I could actually remove any organs. That there was any flesh on the bones at all was indeed what first aroused my suspicions – arsenic being such a powerful preservative. Such flesh as there was, however, disintegrated within a few minutes of exposure to the air so that the crucifix upon your mother's bosom dropped through the skeleton on to the floor of the coffin, with a rattle.

The most surprising characteristic of arsenic is its extraordinary power of spreading and penetrating the whole body and even the body's surroundings. I had read but had not personally had experience of it – that it could even permeate the surrounding soil. Accordingly I took samples of the deceased's hair – two tresses from the skull, which appeared to have grown somewhat after death, and a little pubic hair, as being nearer the intestine. I also took a chunk of the coffin lid, three samples of soil from the bottom of the grave, and the crucifix.

My analysis, carried out in the laboratories at St George's, by Marsh's Test and other means, showed approximately a total of 1 grain in the ends of the hairs, ½ grain in the fragment of the coffin lid, 1½ to 2 grains in the soil, and a positively visible coating of metallic arsenic all over the silver Christ on the crucifix. These quantities are rather negligible although death has been known to occur from a dose of only 5 grains. They are, however, taken from tiny samples and would suggest, by their mere existence, that your mother died from a dose of not less than, say, 100 grains. This may have been administered in small but increasing doses over many weeks.

Your own memory of your mother's last days, since you were only thirteen at the time, must be taken with great reserve. You do tell me, however, that you most clearly recollect the jaundiced skin, the red inflammation around the eyes, the bloody vomit, and the excessive thirst. Classical symptoms.

Taking everything into account I have no doubt whatever that Emily Barbellion (1805–1854) died from arsenical poisoning feloniously administered, and I have reported in those terms to His Majesty's Secretary of State for Home Affairs.

I am, sir, yours most truly,
JEREMY STANSBURY

So, it was over. In the intervals of enjoyment and self-indulgence it had been the occupation of a life time. I had achieved, at last, what I had set out to achieve. I had proved that my father, Barnabas Barbellion, His Holiness Pope Paschal the Fourth, formerly Cardinal Archbishop of Westminster, Anglican Rector of Nether Molding, had in the year 1854 poisoned his wife with arsenic. Nothing could be plainer. It remained only for a statement or edict to be issued by the High Courts of England and by the Curia in Rome – overruling all previous statements as to the cause of death.

In the Rectory study there was silence, not a word was said – not until we were out in the drive. Eirlys then had the grace to ask old Pertwee to dine with us that evening – she would send the Lanchester for him. He had the tact to refuse.

That afternoon we rather ostentatiously avoided each other. I dressed early for dinner and then, while the ladies were completing their toilettes, I paced the lawn alone, the great wide and velvet lawn of Windrush. There was the fresh green of spring on the trees, but in my mind it was the dark and heavy foliage of August. I was alone, but in my mind there were half-a-hundred guests. I was an old man, but in my mind I was wearing my cream-coloured Fauntleroy suit. There was the silence of a windless garden, but in my mind I could hear the click of mallets upon croquet balls. There was not a servant in sight, but in my mind I could see them bearing strawberries and cream towards the shade of the deodars.

And then, thinking of the servants – all those grand Windrush footmen and parlourmaids – I naturally thought of Featherston. I could see him running across the lawn, with Colonel Gatsby already dead upstairs – running across the lawn without his spectacles – poor old man – only to stumble over a croquet hoop. And then, you know, just as a speck of dust may lodge in your eye, or a tooth may occasionally nag, so I realized that for months that was what the memory of Featherston had been to me. I had tried to forget him, to push him from my consciousness, and always he came back . . . to nag.

Always, whatever else I might be doing, I seemed to be back in his little attic at Montpelier Square – while Eirlys was out shopping in Bond Street. He was a hundred and he was dying. He could only speak between little gasps of breathlessness. I had to kneel by the bed to hear him.

'Master Augustine,' he said, 'Master Augustine – is that you? I must tell you something. You must listen. It was in the Library, you know. Yes, I had gone there to put something on the table – I think it must have been *Blackwoods* – yes, that would be it, *Blackwoods*, it always came on Wednesdays. And she never heard me, never heard me – she wouldn't, of course, not on that thick carpet.'

'But who, Featherston? Who never heard you?'

'Why, Miss Eirlys, of course. It was Miss Eirlys who was there, in the Library. She was at the bureau, with her back to the room. You know, Master Augustine, she was writing with the master's goose quill, and then – I'm sure of it – and then she was pasting a label on the medicine bottle ... yes, yes, the master's medicine bottle ... that was it ... the bottle ...'

He struggled to breathe a little longer, and then he died. He must have been delirious, I suppose. All nonsense, what he was saying, of course. He was a hundred and he was dying. So he would not really know what he was talking about, would he? No, no, of course not. Surely, he must have been delirious.

7 Testimony of Eirlys

Implores the passing tribute of a sigh
THOMAS GRAY

Hotel Negresco, Nice.
Alpes Maritimes, France,
19 September 1932

My half-brother, Augustine Xavier Barbellion, has told the story of the Nether Molding deaths – the deaths of Harold Gatsby, of Phillippa Gatsby and of Emily Barbellion – at enormous length and with much circumstantial detail. Sitting there, in his Library at Derravaragh, the boy has always had too much time on his hands. He has now proved, at least to his own satisfaction, that his poor mother, Emily Barbellion, died from arsenical poisoning, but seems to have taken it for granted that it was 'Papa' who administered the arsenic on the eve of his Conversion to Roman Catholicism and for the sake of the celibate priesthood. In fact, Gussy, in my opinion, has written a great deal of nonsense, devoting years of his life to chasing a mare's nest. However, a careful study of his testimony will show how unwittingly he has given all the clues to the real truth, and how utterly wrong he was in his conclusions. It is well, therefore, that everyone who reads his testimony should also read mine . . . herewith.

Gussy instructed his executors to withhold his testimony from the world until after his death. He died last year, in his sleep, in that little house in the Via Tritone in Rome. I immediately issued an injunction against his executors to stop publication until after my own death and that, even then, my testimony must be included with his – a most necessary corrective. As I was myself one of Gussy's executors and the other was a drunken solicitor in Mullingar, it is not surprising that the injunction succeeded.

I am now the only survivor of the affair. All dead and gone – Phillippa in the little graveyard of Holloway Prison, Barnabas under his gilded and marble slab in the floor of St Peter's, old Cardinal Cavalle high on his catafalque in the Church of St

John Lateran, Cardinal Wiseman, so oily and amiable, down in that dusty crypt off Victoria Street, Harold Gatsby beneath his polished granite monstrosity in Nether Molding churchyard, poor little Emily sleeping undisturbed at last beneath the turf and the crocuses, the dubious Cecil Praz in the cemetery at Père Lachaise, almost next to Oscar Wilde, the ashes of Maria Pia scattered on the yellow waters of Lough Derg, Gussy in the Protestant Cemetery in Rome, alongside Shelley and Keats, my most beloved Jane Grigg down among the worms in the Municipal Burial Ground at Tunbridge Wells, old Featherston at Kensal Green . . . all dead and gone, all except me.

My full name is Eirlys Magdalen Cole-Hatt. I was named after the tiny flowers on the river bank where I was conceived, and also – as I told the Judge – after the Woman taken in Adultery. How charming! I am ninety-four years of age but of sound mind as well as of sound body. I reside variously at this Hotel Negresco, at the Palazzo Barbellion alla Chiaja in Naples, and at my house in Montpelier Square in London. I was the illegitimate daughter of Phillippa Cole-Hatt, later Mrs Harold Gatsby, and of Barnabas Barbellion, later His Holiness Pope Paschal the Fourth.

I was brought up at Windrush Court, the seat of the Gatsbys, two miles from Nether Molding where the Living was in their Gift. I was presented to the world, under the name of Cole-Hatt, as Phillippa Gatsby's 'niece' and was told always to speak of her and Colonel Gatsby as 'Aunt' Phillippa and 'Uncle' Harold. I had to speak of the Rector as 'Uncle' Barny and of his invalid wife as 'Aunt' Emily. This, even at a very early age, I found confusing, nonsensical, hypocritical and extremely silly, but then, you see, I was a very precocious child.

When I was fourteen I lost my virginity to Micky Slate, the stableboy, lying with him in the hayloft. I enjoyed it. He was a bonny fresh-faced lad and when, some two years later, he had that girl from London, Primrose Jones – well, I admit I was jealous. However, Micky at least taught me the facts of life. He told me all about rat poison, and set me on the path to unearthing the secret of my own birth. I was then able to tax my mother with having allowed herself to be seduced by 'Uncle' Barny when she was nineteen; she was furious . . . just as if I had been the sinner rather than her.

As I also said at the Trial, I had a most miserable childhood, weeping every night until I had cried myself to sleep. Materially I lacked nothing – toys, nursemaids, clothes, ribbons, ponies – those sort of things were mine. My mother fussed over me and dressed me up and curled my hair – I was a beautiful child – and then showed me off at all the 'at homes', tea-parties, garden-parties and church fêtes to which I had to accompany her in the carriage. In private she was quite horrible to me, inventing nasty punishments and continually throwing my bastardy in my face. 'Uncle' Harold, on the other hand, never spoke to me at all . . . I can remember many a long dinner, once grace had been said, being eaten in complete silence, a footman behind each chair. If I complained I was told that I was a most ungrateful and wicked little girl – for which I might go to Hell – and that 'Uncle' Harold had given me a wonderful home – and so he had, one of the loveliest houses in England – and that I should be eternally thankful, especially 'someone like me'.

I shared the schoolroom lessons of my so-called cousins, actually my half-brother and my half-sister, Gussy and Maria Pia. Every time my mother and I drove over to Nether Molding in the carriage I knew that she was visiting her lover and that when not taking wine with him in his study she would be on her knees to him at the altar . . . she must have had much to confess. Gussy and I, throughout our lives, have enjoyed a curiously incestuous love-hate; oh, I loved him all right but, instinctively I suppose, resented all his delving and prying into my secrets. As for little Maria Pia – I was fond of her but, somehow or other, I think she always suspected me of great and unmentionable sins – she is the only person I have ever known who really had what is called 'a woman's intuition' . . . and I was frightened of it. No, it was just a little from Gussy but, above all, from my beloved Jane Grigg that I had all the affection that has ever been mine in this world. Those hours in the Rectory schoolroom were Heaven; then, and ever after, in our letters, Jane Grigg and I told each other everything . . . yes, everything. Griggy knew what others didn't.

Not only were my 'Aunt' Phillippa and my 'Uncle' Harold

altogether beastly to me, but so also was my real father, my 'Uncle' Barny . . . but then of course he was a beastly man. Once he and Phillippa had realized that my own bastardy was known to me – was no longer a secret – then they had to tell me, again and again, how their own love, years ago on the river at Bablock Hythe, had been pure, mystical and blessed – blessed in the eyes of the Lord. They went on about it so that really I sometimes began to wonder whether, like Jesus Christ, I had not been born of a virgin. They made it equally clear, however, that while they, in the eyes of God, were absolved, pure and undefiled, I was probably damned. I was told that I must never expect to mix with 'nice' children and that, if ever I went to school, it would have to be abroad where there were schools for such as me. Ultimately, they said, the place for me would be a convent.

Then, you know, one afternoon, when Gussy and Maria were playing in the garden, out in the sunshine, I was taken to the study where the blinds were half drawn. 'Uncle' Barny and my mother told me to kneel down and pray – that this was a solemn occasion. 'Uncle' Barny had been studying my 'case' in his big brown books. They had glorious news for me. I was told that, in spite of my inherently sinful and defiled nature, they had decided that I might yet escape the torments of Hell . . .

'Thank you,' I said.

. . . but that I could not of course, like other children, ever hope to inherit Eternal Life – no Heaven for me.

'Thank you,' I said.

. . . no Heaven for me, but so long as I never told lies, never forgot my prayers and was always grateful to my elders and betters, then I might just possibly go to a place called Limbo. This, I gathered, was a sort of twilight world where all the millions of unbaptized infants, as well as a few good people – like Noah, who had lived too soon to know about Christ – would float about for ever and ever, neither in bliss nor in torment.

'Thank you,' I said, 'I shall be able to talk to Noah about his animals.'

I was told not to be flippant, that flippancy in such solemn matters was almost as sinful as blasphemy – and that I should be grateful for the good news.

I went away and hid myself in a corner of the churchyard. I howled. I howled and sobbed all night. I wept very bitterly as I thought of an Eternity in Limbo. Hell would be better. Then, as it grew light and I looked out on the sunlit lawn, I knew that there could be no such place, that it was all a piece of cruel and very wicked nonsense invented to frighten little girls. After a night of weeping I no longer believed a word of it. I had suddenly grown up. I had become the sophisticated and hardened woman of the world that I have been ever since . . . and still am. Moreover, my mother and father were not only unkind, they were fools. Did they really expect me to believe their nonsense? Anyway, from now on I need have no scruples. My way was clear. Somehow or other I would make them destroy themselves. I would send them both to their own Hell. And if 'Uncle' Harold or 'Aunt' Emily had also to be destroyed in the process, well and good. I was, perhaps, just a little sorry for 'Aunt' Emily but, after all, lying day and night in that darkened Rectory bedroom, what had she to live for? . . . far better dead. Standing there beside my bed that morning, naked and my eyes red with weeping, I held my arms above my head in exultation. I might be mad, but I was wonderfully happy in my madness.

I have said that I was beautiful and sophisticated and precocious. I was also clever, and since I was alone so much I had read a great deal. Nobody ever stopped me from using the big Windrush Library. I read, for instance, every word of every volume of *The Newgate Trials*. It was taken for granted in those days that a really nice child would not look at a newspaper. Much I cared! I buried myself in one of the big armchairs and, during the Trial of William Palmer and of Madeleine Smith, I devoured every word of *The Times* Law Reports. When 'Uncle' Harold came back from London I went into his dressing-room – I was always prying in those days – and read the prescription lying open on the dressing-table. I saw the words '*nux vomica*'. I already knew from Micky that was just another name for strychnine. Like a thunderbolt it came to me – I remembered everything Micky had ever told me about the rat poison in the harness room. You see, I had asked him about it simply because I loved the pictures of dead and dying rats on the tins. Strychnine! Glorious strychnine!

And then, almost the next week, came another gift from

Heaven – arsenic at the Rectory. It was in the middle of our Italian lesson that Gussy, with his merry laugh, announced that his fleas had kept him awake all night. He began to show us his bites until Jane Grigg told him to shut up. Even then he chattered on about the old jar in which Papa kept the powder, 'Hartley's Bug Specific', the famous arsenical flea killer. Gussy laughed and laughed. Of course I realize now, nearly eighty years after, that today it would be impossible to buy such deadly poisons. Things were different then; you just told the chemist what you wanted the stuff for – rats or fleas – and walked out of the shop with it.

So, my course was set – strychnine at Windrush, arsenic at the Rectory. The whole idea was immature, adolescent if you like, but it was not unintelligent. On the contrary it was fiendishly clever, planned in innocence, in hatred and in joy. It was quite inconceivable to the adult mind that a child could do such a thing. It was, in a way, almost too naïve . . . like Constance Kent, or like Lizzie Borden who axed her parents . . . nobody could believe it.

First, then, I realized that there had to be an overdose of strychnine for 'Uncle' Harold. I did not risk actually using the rat poison. I did not know its strength or whether it might discolour the medicine. Micky had given me my information and that was enough. I wasn't going to be caught out stealing one of his tins – he might have missed it. So I worked on the idea of the bogus label. It was a crude dodge – and might have been spotted – but as it happened it worked. I was lucky. 'Uncle' Harold collapsed on that hot afternoon in the garden and a few minutes later died in paroxysmic agonies. Doctor Clayton sequestered the bottle, sent it to the Home Office, and in due course gave such damning evidence that Phillippa would certainly have been hanged by the neck until she was dead, had she not, for the second time in her life, been carrying 'Uncle' Barny's child in her womb. My good luck was that when 'Uncle' Harold collapsed everyone was so busy with the croquet party that it was left to Featherston – loyal but myopic and not very bright – to measure out the dose.

Luck, because it threw a delicious cloak of mystery over everything. Phillippa was, as it were, guilty in more ways than one. She had the opportunity – control of the bottle – and she had the motive – a lover and an unfaithful husband. In addition, when the

Defence pointed out that Featherston, not Phillippa, had poured out the medicine – the Judge suggested to the Jury that Phillippa might well have intended that the medicine should be given to Harold by a third party – so, you see, she was caught both ways.

I suffered only one moment of qualm, when that handwriting witness said that the label was 'childish'. I need not have worried. 'Childish' does not mean that the thing is done by a child, it may mean no more than that it is crude or very simple. That the murder might have been committed by a child never entered anyone's head . . . why should it?

Jane Grigg and I, watching and listening, clinging to each other, heard the Judge pass sentence. The commuting of the death sentence to penal servitude was, for me, a terrible anticlimax. I wanted Phillippa to die. My real moment of triumph had been that winter night when they arrested her and I saw the black carriage drive away under the trees. It was then that I had pulled off my first trick. That was the night when, all alone in the great dining-room – to Featherston's amazement – I drank the 1833 Veuve Clicquot. It became an anniversary that I have celebrated ever since, on St Stephen's Day . . . 'Vengeance is mine, saith the Lord'.

The Rectory affair had to be planned rather differently. After reading the Madeleine Smith Trial, and other cases, I realized that 'Aunt' Emily must be given her arsenic in small but steadily increasing doses, and that it must be well disguised in highly flavoured food.

The whole situation was wide open to me – another gift from Heaven. We were all in and out of that bedroom – 'Uncle' Barny every day, Phillippa and I three or four times a week. We were always bringing Emily flowers and fruit from the Windrush conservatories, and delicacies from the kitchens. Such things as beef-tea, arrowroot, potage, gruel, savouries, curries, fricassees and goulash were always being carried upstairs – with such kind inquiries – to disappear through that heavy mahogany door. Everything was done to tempt poor Emily's appetite.

'Uncle' Barny – the future 'Servant of the Servants of God' – in those days served his own wife's meals . . . but then so did I. I would tempt dear 'Aunt' Emily with such delicious kickshaws, kissing her and begging her to eat just a little, for my sake . . . and I did it, you know, when the others were at Confession. It was not surprising that when Barnabas Barbellion visited Rome and Phillippa would not take me near the Rectory in his absence – no Sacraments from Cecil Praz for her – not surprising that Emily felt so much better.

My chance to administer the last and most deadly dose came on Christmas night. Augustine in his testimony – often so unreliable – has told the story of how Phillippa came to the schoolroom after tea, telling me that I must look after 'Aunt' Emily that evening, while the rest of them went to Vespers. I did. Possibly Emily was already dying. I made sure of it. The remains of the minced goose in its little white bowl was on the desk in the study – God knows how it got there – and so I heated it up on the schoolroom kettle-ring. Then I stirred in five grains of 'Bug Specific'. The poor woman must have died in the night . . . it was about three o'clock in the morning when Gussy heard the doctor's carriage wheels in the drive.

Of course, like Phillippa, 'Uncle' Barny had the opportunity and the motive. His opportunity lay in regular visits to the bedroom with invalid food, and in his control of the store of flea killer. His motive lay, quite simply, in his adoration of his mistress and his fatherhood of her unborn child. I felt sure, therefore, that in the end he would go to the gallows.

There was just one thing, unfortunately, that never occurred to me. Whatever his conduct towards Phillippa might be, nobody for one moment would ever suspect the Archdeacon of Gloucester and Rector of Nether Molding of being a murderer. It was clearly impossible. To his children and to their governess, living in the same house, he was what he was – a monster of iniquity. To the world he had always presented himself as the most upright, venerable, devout and scholarly of churchmen. The world took him at his own valuation. Why not? And yet, you know, I was very inexperienced; it never occurred to me that if Emily was poisoned he would not be arrested, convicted and hanged. In fact, he was never even suspected.

So, it came to this – I had destroyed Harold Gatsby – to whom I could hardly have been more indifferent – while Phillippa Gatsby had died in childbirth as she might have done anyway. I had destroyed Emily Barbellion – for whom I was a little sorry – while Barnabas Barbellion, whether cruising in the Aegean or as a fashionable Mayfair priest, had become one of the great ones of the earth. Perhaps I was not quite so clever as I had thought.

There is one thing I find it difficult to write about even now, with everyone dead and gone – my relationship with Jane Grigg. It is all so redolent with emotion. We loved each other passionately. We told each other everything until the day she died. In that world of Nether Molding and Windrush, and ever afterwards, we were both of us really quite alone, and each of us was all the other had. Gussy loved me a little in his frivolous way, but Griggy was the only person who was ever kind to me . . . and I needed kindness.

It was therefore a very terrible moment when she discovered the sort of person I had become – so delinquent and depraved. It was a November morning; Phillippa and Barnabas were in the study, Gussy and Maria Pia were in the garden. I thought Griggy was with them. In fact she was in her room; coming out on to the landing she took me unawares. I was by 'Aunt' Emily's door. I had put her tray on the floor and was kneeling by it sprinkling 'Bug Specific' from the jar and stirring it into the soup.

The scene that followed, the tears we both shed as she took me in her arms, her profound pity for me, are just things I cannot write about. She had what in these days, I suppose, would be called a nervous breakdown. She went away for three weeks. I wanted to kill myself; I walked in the lanes wondering how to do it, always lacking the courage to swallow either rat poison or flea killer. I did not mind being wicked – I exulted in my wickedness – but I had hurt my Griggy and therefore could not live. She never betrayed me and she never would; she had, I think, terrible visions of Phillippa and Barnabas sending me to some awful Reformatory – thus solving one of their own problems, how to get rid of me. Of course I had to promise Griggy very solemnly that there would be no more playing with flea killer. And, of course, I broke my promise. Nevertheless, when 'Aunt' Emily died, with every symptom of arsenical poisoning, Jane Grigg never reproached me or questioned me or, indeed, said a word of any kind. On the whole subject of Emily Barbellion's death she was completely silent. It was to be a lifetime before I knew why.

It was after the exhumation in 1905 – when Gussy had his little moment of triumph, all cock-a-hoop over Emily's dry bones – that I went back to London, taking Jane Grigg with me for a week of shops and theatres. In Berkeley Square the spring green was on the trees and the sunlight was on the grass. We sat in silent contentment, sipping our tea in Gunter's window. At last I had to say what was on my mind.

'It's strange, isn't it, Griggy, that Gussy should be so sure of himself.'

'Why? At least a hundred grains of arsenic – twenty times the fatal dose.'

'Oh, I don't mean that, but so sure that his Papa put them there.'

'But didn't he, Eirlys, didn't he?'

'What on earth do you mean, Griggy? What on earth do you mean? You don't really think I ever kept my promise to you, that promise made in a storm of tears, that promise never to touch the flea killer again . . . how could I keep such a promise?'

'Of course not, my dear. Once set on a path like that, how could you? I never expected you to keep *that* sort of promise; you hardly knew what you were saying when you made it. No, no, I merely looked the other way. And don't forget that this poor little governess had a few scores of her own to pay off. I was a servant under notice.'

'Well then, you looked the other way, and I broke my promise. So what do you mean about "Uncle" Barny and the arsenic? I just don't understand you. Can't you realize that it was I who poisoned "Aunt" Emily – me, me, me!'

'You don't understand me, Eirlys, because you never knew or understood "Uncle" Barny's real motive – the real reason why he wished Emily dead. It was never, you know, just a commonplace sex murder, just a murder for Phillippa's sake. It was a murder for ambition.'

'Ambition?'

'Of course. He could always have kept Phillippa as his mistress –

even popes do that, you know – but he could not, he simply could not have a wife.'

'But why, why?'

'Because, my love, His Holiness Pope Pius the Ninth, or at any rate his Chamberlain, Monsignor Talbot, had offered Barnabas Barbellion everything in this world – "come over to us, dear Archdeacon, and we will look after you" – offered him everything in this world as a celibate priest of the Roman Church, but could offer him nothing as a married man . . . there was nothing to offer.'

'But, Griggy, what do you mean? It may, alas, mean that I was a very wicked and depraved child, but it was I, after all, who poisoned Emily Barbellion with "Bug Specific" . . . and you know it.'

'I know nothing of the kind. By the time Christmas was upon us, Emily was already dying, probably from earlier doses, but there must always be a final and fatal dose. If we count Phillippa as an Accessory after the Fact there were four people in the Rectory that winter all plotting to kill poor Emily. At any rate there were three, you and your natural father and, of course, me. One of us must have murdered her . . . but we shall never know who it was, shall we?'

Bibliography

Brown, Latham and Stewart, C. G., *Reports of Trials for Murder by Poisoning* (Stevens & Sons, 1883).

Butler, Samuel, *The Way of All Flesh* (J. M. Dent & Sons, 1903).

Drew, Mary, *Acton, Gladstone and Others* (Nisbet & Co., 1924).

Faber, Geoffrey, *Oxford Apostles* (Faber & Faber, 1933).

Froude, Rev. Richard Hurrell, *Remains*, 4 vols (Rivington, 1838).

Holloway, John, *The Victorian Sage* (Macmillan & Co., 1953).

Holy Bible, 'Epistle of Paul the Apostle to the Hebrews', Chapter 7.

Irving, H. B., *Trial of Mrs Maybrick* (William Hodge, 1912).

Mozley, Rev. Thomas, *Letters from Rome on the Occasion of the Oecumenical Council, 1869–1870* (Longmans, Green & Co., 1891).

Newman, Cardinal, *Apologia Pro Vita Sua* (Longmans, Green & Co., 1914).

Purcell, Edmund Sheridan, *Life of Cardinal Manning*, 2 vols (Macmillan & Co., 1896).

Rolfe, Frederick (Baron Corvo), *Hadrian the Seventh* (Chatto & Windus, 1904).

Strachey, Lytton, *Eminent Victorians* (Chatto & Windus, 1918).

Trevor, Meriol, *Newman*, Vol. 1; *The Pillar of Cloud*, Vol. 2; *Light in Winter* (Macmillan & Co., 1962).

Woodforde, Rev. James, *Diary of a Country Parson*, 5 vols (Oxford University Press, 1926).

More about Penguins and Pelicans

Penguinews, which appears every month, contains details of all the new books issued by Penguins as they are published. From time to time it is supplemented by *Penguins in Print*, which is our complete list of almost 5,000 titles.

A specimen copy of *Penguinews* will be sent to you free on request. Please write to Dept EP, Penguin Books Ltd, Harmondsworth, Middlesex, for your copy.

In the U.S.A.: For a complete list of books available from Penguins in the United States write to Dept CS, Penguin Books, 625 Madison Avenue, New York, New York 10022.

In Canada: For a complete list of books available from Penguins in Canada write to Penguin Books Canada Ltd, 2801 John Street, Markham, Ontario L3R 1B4.